BEAUTY AND THE BAYOU

BOYS OF THE BAYOU BOOK 3

ERIN NICHOLAS

ISBN: 978-1-7338901-3-7

Editor: Lindsey Faber

Cover design: Angela Waters

Cover photography: Lindee Robinson

Models: Michael Scanlon and Kandace Gauthier

1

"NAILED. POUNDED. DRILLED."

Sawyer Landry stopped with his hand on the doorknob to his office and turned at the sound of a male voice. He didn't see anyone and it sounded like the voice was coming from around the corner of the building.

"Don't forget hammered and banged."

He also didn't recognize that female voice. It wasn't Kennedy, Maddie, or Tori. There weren't many other females who'd be down here at this time of day. Sawyer scowled and headed around to the dock. Who the hell was here at seven in the morning? Was someone here early for their boat tour? Or were there some teenagers making out down here on the dock where they didn't think they'd be caught?

"Of course, there are also terms like *pole* and *shaft* and good old *tool* if you want to go with nouns versus verbs," the guy said.

The woman laughed. "Why are there so many sexual terms that are also construction terms?"

"Well, building *is* hot and dirty."

Sawyer's scowl deepened. He didn't see anyone on the benches outside their main building where the tourists gathered to wait for their airboat and swamp boat tours, but the voices were coming from over here for sure.

"Come on, you have to stretch," the guy said a moment later.

"I'm trying. It's too long."

"Use your other hand."

"I can't. I need that one right there."

"How bad do you want it?" the guy asked her.

"Bad," she said. "But I might need to get someone else to do it."

"Hey, there's only so much I can do from here."

"I know."

Sawyer stepped around the last row of benches and saw... not what he'd been expecting to see.

A woman was lying on her stomach, hanging off the edge of the dock, reaching under the boards with one hand, while gripping the railing with the other to keep from pitching over the edge.

She was dressed in dark green hip waders—tall rubber boots that covered not just the feet and lower leg but went all the way up to the hips—and a bright orange life jacket. There was also a bright yellow hard hat beside her on the dock.

"A little more," the man's voice said. From underneath the dock.

Sawyer had no idea what was going on.

He was, however, aware that this was the first time he'd stopped to admire a woman's ass in about nine months. The space between the top of the woman's boots and the lower edge of the life jacket framed the magnificent curve of a denim-covered ass that stopped him in his tracks. Literally.

Not a bad way to start a Monday morning.

But fine ass or not, there was a stranger lying on his dock, dangling over the edge, doing...he had no idea what. He didn't know what to think of her outfit and the hard hat, either. Was she here to go fly fishing? Boating? Build something? She seemed dressed for all three. Her conversation about pounding and nailing came back to him, and Sawyer was proud of the fact that his gaze only lingered on her ass for another millisecond.

"What the *hell* is going on?"

"Eeep!" The woman gave a startled little scream and jerked.

The motion started her body sliding forward, headfirst off the edge of the dock, her hand slipping on the railing where she was holding on. Or trying to.

Well, shit.

Sawyer instinctively took a huge step forward and grabbed for the first thing he could get a hold of—the back waistband of her shorts.

He pulled her up, sliding her until she was completely on the dock. There was a moment where they both just paused. Then suddenly she rolled to her side and pushed up onto her knees. The move, with his hand still tucked in the back of her shorts, brought Sawyer down onto one knee. The perfect level for her to throw her arms around his neck. Apparently.

She squeezed him tightly as she gushed in his ear, "Oh my God, thank you!"

Sawyer simply couldn't move. He hadn't been expecting anything about her reaction. Hell, he hadn't been expecting anything about *her*. He found himself frozen with her pressed against him, gripping his neck tightly. And his fingers against the bare skin of her lower back below her life jacket. Her silky, warm bare skin.

"Juliet!" the male voice called from down below them. "Are you all right? What the hell happened?"

The woman pulled back and looked up at Sawyer for a moment. Then she blew out a breath and gave him a half smile. "Thank you for saving me." She unwound her arms from around his neck and started to sit back on her heels.

But his hand was *still* tucked into the back of her shorts and that kept her pressed against him. Surprise and awareness flickered in her huge, brown eyes and Sawyer realized he hadn't been hugged by a woman other than his mother and grandmother in months. It had a lot to do with the fact that he bit the heads off of most of the women—okay, most of the *people*—around him on a regular basis.

Suddenly he pulled his hand from the shorts and sat back. The woman did the same, taking a deep breath.

Was her heart pounding because she'd nearly pitched over the edge of the dock and gone headfirst into the mud below? Or was it because being pressed up against him had done something to her libido like it had his?

Did it matter?

He didn't even know who the hell she was, and she was trespassing.

"You shouldn't just go around hugging strange men." He pushed to his feet.

She scrambled to stand as well and took a big step back. "Oh, wow, you're totally right. I just...reacted. Sorry about that."

For a second, Sawyer lost track of what they'd been talking about.

This woman had more than a gorgeous ass. She was stunningly beautiful from the front, too. Even in a bright orange life jacket.

She also smelled like lilacs.

He realized that he'd gotten a huge whiff of her scent when she'd been in his arms. It had to have only been a few seconds, and he'd been a lot more focused on the skin against his fingers. But yeah, she smelled like lilacs.

That didn't seem to fit now that he took her all in. She had long dark hair streaked with red and gold, skin that was a warm beige, and the biggest brown eyes he'd ever seen. She also had curves. Really, really nice curves. Even in her goofy outfit, it was impossible to miss the generous breasts, flared hips, and gorgeous ass. Okay, he couldn't see that ass now, but he remembered it. Well.

The hip waders didn't fit her. She was short and the tall boots were loose on her, causing a gap at the top that gave him more than a glimpse of the smooth, fawn-colored skin of her thighs.

Cinnamon. If she smelled like cinnamon, that would fit. No, cardamom. And yes, he knew what cardamom smelled like. His grandmother and her best friend cooked and baked constantly, for family and for a living. This girl definitely should have smelled spicy rather than flowery.

And that might have been the stupidest thing he'd ever thought in his life.

But she was checking him out, too. Her eyes ran over him from head to toe. There was six feet and four inches of him to go over, and it took her a little longer than it had taken him to scan her five-foot-five or so. Or maybe she was just taking her time.

He let her. He was a stranger. They were alone. In a new-to-her place. She *should be* sizing him up.

Or maybe he just liked her eyes on him.

He noted that she didn't study the scar that ran from the corner of his mouth, up over his cheek, to his hairline. She didn't avoid looking at it, either. She'd taken it in like she'd looked over his shoulders and hair and boots. Like it was just a detail to catalog.

He hadn't even thought of being with a woman since the accident that had caused that scar, and he was shocked by the urge to flirt—or step close and catch this woman's mouth in a kiss—that shot through him now. Hell, did he even remember *how* to flirt?

Finally, after the silent perusal had stretched a little beyond two people just meeting for the first time and nothing more, he pushed all of those thoughts away and propped his hands on his hips. "I was talking about *you*," he told her.

Yeah, he wasn't upset about the way she threw herself into his arms after he'd saved her. He could use a little more appreciation for the things he did to keep people safe around here, as a matter of fact. Sawyer shook his head. That was a whole other, ongoing issue that had nothing to do with this here and now.

"Getting up close and personal with a guy who just walks up on you suddenly when no one else is around could be damned dangerous." As he spelled it out for her, he realized just what a great point that really was. He frowned. "Seriously, you shouldn't be down here alone. What the hell are you doing? What if you'd fallen off the dock and no one was here?"

She glanced at the railing. "I knew I should have tied myself to the post."

Sawyer blinked at her. "What?"

"I thought about tying a rope around my waist and around that post." She pointed to the upright that supported the corner of the roof that extended over the dock on this side to provide shade. "That way if I slipped, that would have kept me from going over."

"Or it could have ended up wrapped around your neck with you still hanging over the edge," Sawyer said with a scowl. "Or it could have slipped down and ended up around your ankle and you could have gone over the side and then swung back and whacked yourself against the dock underneath." He could see those scenarios plain as day in his mind and his scowl deepened. It took him a second to focus on her again and realize that she'd gone a little pale. "Hey, you okay?" he asked. Was she going to pass out? Shit, what would he do then? He supposed he'd carry her over to Ellie's, his grandmother's place. Everyone would be there having breakfast.

He stepped forward. He needed to keep her from crumpling to the floor and whacking her head that way first, he supposed.

She took a step back.

Sawyer frowned and stepped forward again.

She held up a hand to stop him. "What are you doing?"

"Making sure I'm close enough to catch you if you faint."

She swallowed. "I'm not going to faint. I don't think," she added.

Sawyer sighed. "I really need to you not to faint."

Her eyes widened. "*You* need me not to faint?"

He nodded. "I really don't want to explain you and"—he looked around—"this. And if I have to carry you, unconscious, into my grandma's bar, I'm going to have to explain. And I don't even know who you are or what you're doing here."

"Well, if you don't want me to get woozy, you have to stop talking about how I could have strangled myself or given myself a serious concussion."

"But you could have," he said simply. It was a fact.

She nodded. "Yeah."

Sawyer cocked an eyebrow. He wasn't used to people agreeing with him when he did his worst-case-scenario thing. Mostly people rolled their eyes. Sometimes they argued with him. Sometimes they tried to reassure him. The only thing he wanted and liked, however, was when people said, "You're right. I'll be careful." That was all he wanted in life. Well, and for people to actually *be* careful.

The bayou wasn't a place to fuck around. There were a lot of things that could be dangerous here. From the insects, snakes, and animals to the sun, weather, and the bayou itself. Drowning was a possibility out here just like it was around any body of water. His brother, sister, and cousins had all grown up down here. They should know what they were doing. They should know what precautions to take and what to do if something happened. But he'd lost a friend who'd known the bayou

7

like the back of his hand, and Sawyer had since become obsessed with keeping everyone else safe.

He knew others used the word obsessed. He owned it. He didn't care what they thought. As long as everyone stayed safe, they could think he was an asshole or a kook.

That included this woman.

"So how do I get down there?" she asked, moving toward the railing and looking over.

"Down there? Under the dock?" he asked. "You don't. You keep your sweet ass right up here."

She glanced at him quickly. Probably because of the "sweet ass" comment. Oh, well, she could think he was a sexist pig or that he was hitting on her. Again, he didn't care. As long as she really did keep her sweet ass up here.

"I dropped my phone down there," she said after a second.

"Too bad." He shrugged.

She frowned. "Too bad? I can't just leave my phone down there."

"Well, there's no way to get it."

"I can't climb down there somehow?" she asked, looking around. "I could climb down the bank there." She pointed to the rise behind the muddy, grassy bank.

"No, you can't."

"Why not?"

"You might slip and fall in."

She swallowed hard but said, "I have hip waders and a life jacket on."

He looked her up and down, this time not trying to hide it. She'd practically invited him to. "Why *do* you have hip waders and a life jacket on? And a hard hat?"

"Because I thought I might need to wade into the water or walk through mud."

"You don't know how to swim?"

"Isn't it always safer to have a life jacket on around water?"

Sawyer opened his mouth. Then snapped it shut. Having a life jacket on around water was, of course, safer than not having one on. That was just common sense.

He supposed he was used to a lack of common sense around here.

He and his brother, Josh, and cousin, Owen, owned and operated one of the most popular tourist attractions outside of New Orleans. Boys of the Bayou Swamp Boat and Fishing Tours offered airboat tours as well as fishing and hunting expeditions. They took hundreds of strangers out on the bayou every week. The majority of those people had never been to the bayou before and had very little practical knowledge of things like alligators and snakes, and many had a surprising lack of knowledge of boat and water safety. At least in Sawyer's estimation. Added to that, the fact that many of the groups were bachelor and bachelorette parties, fraternity and sorority groups, spring break revelers, and other similar gatherings, who had decided to step out of New Orleans for a little more unique experience, there was also a general party air—and often blood alcohol levels above "totally sober"—that contributed to people not taking his safety talks as seriously as they should.

His family and other people in Autre, Louisiana didn't take things as seriously as Sawyer would like, either. They'd grown up here and thought they knew everything. But familiarity led to complacency and a feeling of invincibility that could be damned dangerous.

That's what had happened to Tommy.

A shaft of pain went through him, as it often did when he thought of Tommy, his business partner and best friend. He and Tommy Allain had been inseparable since they'd been born. Their grandfathers and fathers had been best friends, too. They hadn't really had a choice but to like one another, but it had worked out that they'd had everything in common and disagreed on nothing that a bottle of whiskey and some fishing couldn't fix.

Most days, he still couldn't believe Tommy was gone. It had been nine months but it hadn't gotten less painful. The only thing that felt better was the gash on his face and even that still twinged sometimes.

So yeah, Sawyer overreacted when it came to safety.

He didn't give a fuck how everyone else felt about that.

"And the hard hat?" he asked when he couldn't come up with anything else to say about her life jacket.

She lifted her chin. "I think head protection is incredibly important at all times."

Okay, that was a weird answer. Who thought about head protection "at all times"?

But damned if he didn't like it.

He was the last guy to fault someone for being prepared. Even overly prepared.

He realized that he really liked that this gorgeous creature was also cautious.

Was he developing a little fetish for protective wear? Well, that was fucking weird. But he supposed there were worse things.

"So why can't I go down there with all of this on?" she asked, waving her hand down her body to indicate everything she was wearing.

"There are cotton mouths down there." It was true. He'd burned one nest, but there was a good chance there were more. One thing they were never short on down here was critters.

Her brown eyes widened. "Those are snakes, right?"

"Yep. Nasty ones. Very poisonous."

"Damn," she breathed. "I didn't look up snakes." She squinted up at him. "Can they bite through rubber boots like these?"

He eyed her footwear. No, they probably couldn't. But he didn't like the idea of her tromping around where those fuckers might be. "What if you slip and fall on one and it bites your arm?" he asked.

Her arms were bare. She was clearly wearing a tank under the life jacket. There was a lot of exposed skin.

Smooth, silky, tan skin...

"Ugh." She looked like she was going to be sick. "Yeah, okay, I'm not going down there."

A really strange, surprisingly strong surge of satisfaction went through him. Someone was listening to him. Someone was believing him when he said something wasn't safe. Damn, that felt good. He didn't have to argue, or get firm, or glare. She just said, "Yeah, okay."

He could get used to that.

"Who was the guy on the phone?" Why did he care? Did it matter? Not even a little.

He just liked her. Yeah, the brown eyes and curves were part of it. Of course they were. But he also liked her because she was wearing a hard hat. And listening to him. That second thing for sure. But the hard hat was something. It was overkill. Who needed a hard hat on when walking around on a dock? Even if you were leaning over the edge of it? But overkill with safety was okay with him.

God help him if she ever put safety goggles on.

"Brandon." Then she lunged for the railing as if just remembering about her phone and the guy on it. "Brandon! Oh my God, he's probably so worried."

Sawyer leaned to look over the edge, too. Her phone was upright, lodged in the mud, the screen now dark. "You'll have to call him back on my phone or something."

"I don't know his number!" she exclaimed.

"You don't?"

"I just tap on his name and it dials."

"You don't know your boyfriend's number?" He was absolutely fishing for information with that question.

She looked up at him with an eyebrow arched.

Ah, she knew he was fishing.

He didn't care.

"He's my client, actually," she said when he just met her gaze and waited. "And my friend."

"Client?"

"I'm an attorney," she told him. "I helped him with a couple of things. Now he's helping me."

"Helping you what?" Suddenly Sawyer remembered that he had no idea what she was doing here. On *his* dock. Before business hours. Acting startled that he'd shown up. "What are you doing here anyway?"

"I was showing Brandon the dock. The underside of it, actually, when you snuck up on me and scared me and made me drop my phone."

Oh, he was on to her already. Even if she hadn't told him she was an attorney, he was used to people turning arguments around on him and saw right through it. His sister was great at it. And she'd learned from his grandmother. Ellie Landry was good at a lot of things—guilt trips for one—but admitting she was wrong was not one of them.

"Why did Brandon need to see the underside of my dock?"

"Because he—" She paused and frowned. "Wait, *your* dock?"

"Yes. My dock," he said. "So not only did I save your pretty neck from going over the edge and possibly ending up paralyzed, but you're also trespassing, and I haven't called the cops. You owe me twice."

"Paralyzed?" she repeated.

He nodded. "If you'd gone headfirst, you could have suffered a serious spinal injury. Your hard hat, which you weren't even wearing, might not have protected you. Just the right angle and—"

"Okay," she broke in. "Okay. You're right."

Yep, he *really* liked those last two words she'd said. The chances of her becoming paralyzed were probably slim, but it *was* a possibility.

"Why did Brandon need to see under the dock?" Sawyer repeated. He was very familiar with Kennedy redirecting conversations she didn't want to have.

"Just to confirm the design and materials. I've looked most of it up, but he's done construction before—not docks, but he's done a couple of decks and other stuff. Decks and docks are very similar in construction."

Well, yeah. Okay. But... Sawyer stared at her. What the hell was she talking about? "Design and materials for what?"

Instead of answering, she dropped to her knees. "Hold my feet." She got down on her stomach and scooted to the edge of the dock, ducking her head under the bottom rail.

Sawyer looked down at her. And blinked.

There was a long pause, then she looked back at him. "Hold. My. Feet," she said again. Slowly. As if he was stupid.

Frankly, he was feeling kind of stupid. "What for?" he asked, definitely sounding stupid, too.

She looked over the edge of the dock. "If you hold my feet and lower me over the edge, then I won't fall in the water or step on snakes or strangle myself or whack my head or paralyze myself. Then you can pull me back up."

She thought she was going to hang from the dock with him holding her ankles and actually reach her phone? Even if that was possible, which it was *not,* he was a complete stranger. She was just going to trust him to hold her ankles and pull her back up?

"No way," he said simply.

She looked back. "Why not?"

"That will never work."

"You are really big." She winced. "I mean you look really strong. I think you could do it."

Sawyer felt something happening that hadn't happened in a while. At least not on a regular basis. He felt the urge to laugh.

"What if your boots slip off?" he asked. "I'll be up here holding empty boots and you'll be down there with the snakes. Hopefully not paralyzed."

"Dammit," she muttered. She sat up and started to push one boot down.

It took Sawyer a second to stop her. She was baring more of that smooth tan skin after all. He didn't dwell on the fact that women came down here in shorts every single day, and he hadn't felt distracted like this in a long time.

Still, he wasn't going to hold her by her bare ankles off the edge of the dock, either.

"Even if I could pull you back up"—she was petite. He was sure he could pull her back up if she was hanging off the edge of the dock—"you still wouldn't be able to reach that far down. The phone's gone, darlin'. Let it go."

She stopped with the boot, looked back down at the mud below, and sighed. She put her forehead on her bent knee. "Of course it is," she muttered.

"Tell me about Brandon's need for design and materials for *my* dock."

She tipped her head back, staring up at the exposed wooden beams overhead. "We're going to rebuild the dock." Then she frowned at him. "And how is this *your* dock?"

He moved closer so he could look down at her directly. "I own it."

"No. Wait." She glanced over his left shoulder at the sign that hung on the side of the building. "The Landrys own Boys of the Bayou, right? Well, and Bennett. And Maddie is kind of like a Landry. Am I on the wrong dock?"

Sawyer felt trepidation trickle down his spine. She knew his partners' names.

Hot on the heels of the suspicion, however, was resignation. Mixed with frustration. What had they done?

He owned thirty-five percent of the Boys of the Bayou. What the fuck was this woman doing here, knowing all four of his partners, without him having a clue about what was going on?

"I'm Sawyer Landry," he said, his tone firm and don't-fuck-with-me. "Josh is my brother. Owen is my cousin. Maddie is a family friend. Bennett is our newest partner."

Juliet's brown eyes grew rounder. "*You're* Sawyer Landry?"

"Yes." The majority partner, thank you very much. The other four each owned about half the amount he did. Bennett and Maddie each had seventeen and a half percent, while Josh and Owen each owned fifteen.

"Wait, you're...working here. You're around?" Juliet asked, breaking into Sawyer's thoughts.

"Clearly," he said. Then he frowned. "Why wouldn't I be around?"

"Well, I read the brochure and everything online, but I guess I assumed you were older and retired or something? I mean...why weren't you at the meeting? And why are you acting like you know nothing about me being here?"

Sawyer lifted a brow. "Because I *don't* know anything about you being here."

"They didn't tell you about me?"

"I think I would have remembered mention of a gorgeous brunette comin' down here to give me a hard time," Sawyer told her.

She looked startled by the "gorgeous" bit—which was ridiculous because this woman's gorgeousness was like the bayou being muddy...it just was. But she quickly recovered.

"So why weren't you at the meeting?"

"What meeting?"

"The meeting in New Orleans last week where we set this all up."

His four partners—two of whom were blood relation and one of whom he liked better than almost all of his blood relation put together—had met with this woman last week and hadn't told him? What the fuck was going on?

"Why don't you tell me what *you* think y'all set up?" Sawyer asked. "And we'll go from there."

"I don't *think* we set it up. We did set it up," she said firmly as she got to her feet. "I'm Juliet Dawson."

Sawyer just looked at her.

"Dawson," she repeated. "I'm Chase Dawson's sister."

Okay, there was a tiny niggle at the back of Sawyer's mind with that name.

"Chase Dawson. The dumbass who did that."

Juliet pointed down the dock to the end that had been busted up when a bunch of stupid frat boys had taken an airboat out for a spin—uninvited and untrained—and realized too late that airboats don't have brakes. Thanks to Owen and Maddie, they'd jumped off the boat at the last minute before the boat had crashed into the dock, but the boat had been totaled and the dock smashed to pieces.

Sawyer frowned at her. "You're the kid's sister?" he asked, disbelief rocking through him. Then anger. "The kid who could have killed his friends? Who could have killed *my* friends? And *himself*?" Sawyer took a step forward. "The kid who decided that because I'd thrown him and his drunk buddies off one of my tours, that they could come down here and *steal* a boat?" He took another step. "And drive it down the bayou? Then take out one of my docks and set me back on the tours that my partners and I need to making a *fucking living*?"

He was definitely shouting by the end of his tirade, and he realized he was now towering over her.

To Juliet's credit, she didn't shrink away. In fact, she stood

---

straighter and faced him squarely. She nodded. "Yeah. That's him. The dumbass."

Sawyer blinked at her again. Not because of those brown eyes—though they went beautifully with her full lips, which were impossible to ignore now that he was nearly on top of her—but because she looked truly sorry. She wasn't sticking up for her brother. She was acknowledging what had happened. And she wasn't scared of Sawyer.

He was a big guy, with a deep, loud voice. He was intimidating when he got pissed. He knew that. He didn't get pissed that often, but— Okay, that wasn't entirely true. Over the past nine months, he got pissed off on a daily basis. Not to mention worried. But he'd been a nice guy before that. Laid-back, even.

"Why are you here?" he asked her, propping his hands on his hips.

He wasn't trying to make her nervous, exactly. But if he could get some answers, and get her off his dock, he'd be happy. Or at least not as pissed off.

Why did he have the sense that he needed to get her off of his dock? And then far, far away? He wasn't sure. There was just something about her that made him think *this is going to complicate my life.*

There was no specific reason for that feeling. Except that his four partners had been conspiring behind his back, and just looking at this woman made him forget what he'd been about to say.

"To make up for what Chase did."

He blinked at Juliet. Again. Fuck. Then he looked down at her feet. "Not sure why you need hip waders to write a check."

"No, I'm—" She blew out a breath and stepped forward as she reached out. "Let's just stop this."

Her tiny hands encircled his wrists and pulled his hands from his hips. It was likely the surprise at her moving into his personal space—something not many people had done in the past few months, for fear of getting bitten probably—or the shock at her touching him that enabled her to move him. He was clearly much stronger than her. But his arms dropped easily to his sides as he stared down at her.

"There. Much better." She tipped her head to look up at him, and *not* stepping back. "You don't need to be all angry and defensive."

Sawyer felt both of his brows arch. "Excuse me?"

"I'm not your enemy and I'm not here to fight with you."

Her breasts brushed his stomach as she took a deep breath, and Sawyer felt his body tighten. What had she just said? Something about fighting with him? He honestly had no idea suddenly. He took a big step back. But his hands stayed at his sides.

"I'm also not here to write a check," Juliet told him. "Chase and I are going to rebuild the dock for you."

That also made no sense, but Sawyer wasn't sure if it was because of what she'd said or because of her breasts.

"*You* are going to rebuild the dock?" he repeated. Was that what she'd said?

The lilacs and brown eyes and breasts...what the hell was going on? He needed to get his shit together.

"I am. With my brother."

"As in, with your own two hands?"

"Yes."

Sawyer's eyes flickered to the hard hat on the dock behind her. "Are you in construction?" What were the chances that the guy who had trashed his dock actually knew something about construction? Not very damned likely. That just wasn't how Sawyer's luck had been working lately.

"No," Juliet confirmed.

Yeah, he'd figured. He sighed. "Then why would *you* rebuild the dock?"

"Because when you mess something up, you should be the one to try to fix it," she said. "Chase needs to do this."

All right, Sawyer could respect that. He agreed with making reparation for the things you did wrong. But he really wanted this dock to be, well, functional. Solid. Usable. "Why would I let you rebuild my dock when you and your brother have no clue how to actually do that?"

"Because you need your dock rebuilt," she said. "And you shouldn't have to use your time and money to do it."

"Yeah, well, that's all true."

"So, we're going to pay for the materials and take care of everything."

"No offense, Ms. Dawson," Sawyer said in a tone that he knew conveyed clearly that he didn't really care if she was offended. "But I'd really like to have a professional rebuild my dock. I'm all for you payin' for it to assuage your guilt though."

She frowned. "Chase won't learn anything from that."

"It's not my job to teach Chase things."

"No, but it's *my* job," she said. "My little brother will *not* turn into an entitled asshole, Mr. Landry. He *will* be getting his hands dirty, developing some blisters, sweating through his favorite designer T-shirt to rebuild the dock that he helped demolish. He doesn't get to steal your boat, endanger everyone around him, and destroy your property without any repercussions."

Damn, this woman was beautiful. Even more so when she was agreeing with him about avoiding snake bites and concussions. But she was downright gorgeous when she was riled up and impassioned about something. And it was clear she was impassioned about this.

It also happened to be something he agreed with.

"I appreciate everything you're saying, Ms. Dawson," Sawyer said, wondering how he'd gone from having his hand tucked in her shorts to Mr. and Ms. He really did appreciate what she was saying. He supported the general idea. Just not when it came to *his* dock. "But I can't let a spoiled frat boy rebuild the dock I need to have fully functional and completely sound for my business."

"I understand that," she said quickly. "I take safety *very* seriously. Brandon is one of the best, and I've done a ton of research and I've got some guys lined up from here to help and—"

"You've got guys from *here* lined up to help?"

"Yes. A Mitch and Leo? I emailed a Kennedy about it and she said she'd find some local guys who could help."

"Okay, that's it," Sawyer said. He needed to yell at someone but even he, who really wasn't picky about who he yelled at these days, knew that he couldn't yell at Juliet. She was here with good intentions. Crazy intentions but good. Seriously, though, how the hell did this little woman, who thought she could video chat with someone to figure out "design and materials," think she was going to rebuild a functional boat dock? That was ridiculous. "Let's go." He turned on his heel and started in the direction of his grandmother's bar.

The main culprits would be there. Owen and Josh, Maddie and Tori, and freaking Kennedy, who had lined up their cousin Mitch—who could actually be helpful—and their grandfather Leo who, while seeming much younger than his seventy years, was a troublemaker and would spend his time telling stories, most of which would be tall tales, drinking sweet tea, and flirting with Juliet rather than actually building anything.

"Wait, go?" Juliet called after him. "Where are we going?"

He turned back. "Well, at least you're asking questions before going off with some strange guy."

She gave him a look. "You had just saved me," she said. "The adrenaline was rushing and I just reacted. I don't go around spontaneously hugging strange men."

"I'm not complainin'," he told her. Having her up against

him had been the best part of his day. The day hadn't been going on for very long, but he knew that wasn't going to change. "But I'm glad you're acting at least slightly skeptical."

"So, are you going to tell me where we're going?"

"We're going to get my *partners* and my *employee*"—oh yeah, he was going to remind his baby sister that she worked for him —"to admit that this was all just a big joke they're pulling on me."

"Wait, *what*?"

He nodded. "Yeah, sorry."

"No." She shook her head. "This is binding. The lawyer did the mediation paperwork and everything. We committed money and two weeks' time and labor to this."

"Two weeks?"

"That's how long Chase has until he has to report to school."

Sawyer sighed. It would be great if *any* of this made sense. "School?"

"He starts med school in two weeks. So, we're here until then. We'll get as much done as possible and then pay for someone to finish it. Maybe Mitch and Leo," she said, perking up.

"No. Mitch and Leo are not going to be finishing it," Sawyer said. Even if he thought Leo could get off his barstool before ten a.m. and not take an afternoon fishing break every day, he needed Leo and Mitch both driving the buses for Boys of the Bayou. They did the hotel pickups and drop-offs in New Orleans for all of the tourists that came down for their tours.

But two weeks was enough time to rebuild a dock. If you knew what you were doing.

"But—"

"Juliet," Sawyer said. Saying her name gave him a little jolt. It wasn't a *bad* jolt. It almost felt like excitement. But it was weird. "I'm sorry that your brother is on the road to becoming an entitled asshole, but that's not really my problem. A functioning, safe, and solid dock for my business *is*."

"You don't think that the entitled assholes in the world are kind of *all* of our problem?" she asked dryly.

He'd give her that. "Still, I can't even keep *myself* from being an asshole, so I don't think I can be worrying about preventing someone else from becoming one."

"You're an asshole?"

"You can't tell?"

She tipped her head, studying him. "I mean, I saw a glimmer here and there, but no, not really."

Yeah, well, she should stick around.

Except she should *not* stick around.

"You kept me from falling off the dock."

"I would have done that for anyone," he said. She didn't need to think that he had a soft spot for her. He didn't. Of course not. That would be ridiculous.

But she laughed lightly—and he felt that jolt again, stronger this time.

"The fact that you would save *anyone* from falling doesn't make you an asshole, Sawyer."

Damn, her saying *his* name was also jolt-inducing.

He cleared his throat. "Maybe you're not a great judge of asshole-ness. Maybe your brother is fine."

"He is fine," she said. "But it's a tenuous situation."

Again, Sawyer had the urge to laugh. He shook his head. "How so?"

"My two older brothers are assholes. The guys he's been living with and hanging out with in his fraternity are definitely assholes. Without some good influences, Chase could easily be won over to their side."

Sawyer was startled to hear a small chuckle actually emerge from his chest. "So what? You're tryin' to save your little brother's soul in two weeks' time?"

"Something like that. But—" she added, looking just a hint shy for a moment.

"But?" he prompted.

"I need a little help."

Sawyer didn't want to know more about all of this. He had plenty of people to help already. Still he said, "What kind of help?" He was a Landry. He couldn't resist getting involved in other people's business. It was a genetic flaw for sure.

"Giving him a good influence," she said. She shrugged. "I know it sounds pathetic and you probably think my brother is a spoiled, rich kid who..." She sighed. "He *is* a spoiled, rich kid. But he's got potential. And I think that some hard work and being around guys who do actual hands-on work for a living could be good for him."

"You don't know anything about us." But Sawyer couldn't deny that her words stirred him. They did all work hard and they were all good guys—well, not him, but the other guys— who could be a good influence on a spoiled kid who'd had a pretty cushy life.

"I know that your family has owned this business for three generations. I know that you guys not only own it but actually do the work. And I know I only met Owen and Josh and Bennett and Maddie for a little bit last week, but I could tell that they really care about each other. I just thought they seemed like guys that could be good influences on Chase."

Sawyer snorted at that. Josh and Owen as a good influence on someone? Right. They were both happier and stayed home more since Tori and Maddie were in their lives, but nothing could take *all* of the mischief out of a Landry boy. "My most common phrase to those two? Quit fucking around."

She tipped her head. "But is that on them...or is that more about *you*?"

Sawyer lifted a brow. She thought she'd already figured him out, huh? "How about a little of both?"

She smiled, and fuck if it didn't hit him in the gut. "But they're hardworking guys, who run a family business in their hometown and who were willing to give my brother a chance to do the right thing. They're about as opposite from the guys my brother hangs out with as you can get. I think it would be good for Chase to be around them. And if they're also laid-back and like to have some fun, that's great, too, actually. I want him to see that you can have fun without it involving platinum credit cards and yachts."

Yeah, well, there sure as hell weren't a lot of yachts on *these* waters.

She pressed her lips together, then added, "I'd love for him to see what it looks like when someone truly has your back. What real family and friends look like. From what I've read and seen, I think that could happen here."

Sawyer opened his mouth to reply, but he wasn't sure with what. She couldn't have said anything better to get on his good side. Well, other than, "You're right" and "I'll do anything you say." Those were both pretty good, too.

"How could you tell that after being around them for only an hour?" he finally asked.

Juliet shrugged. "How they talked to each other maybe? How they just *were*. Maddie and Bennett, too. They gave each other a hard time and didn't hesitate to disagree, but it was clear they were a united front when it came to what was best for the business. I admire that. And I read all about the business, the history with your grandfather and his best friend starting things up, and you and Tommy taking it over and then bringing the other guys on. It's clear there are deep roots here."

She'd done her homework. She'd noticed the bond between Josh, Owen, and Maddie. She respected the history here, and she wanted her brother to be influenced by Josh and Owen and even Bennett—who was a good guy even if he hadn't been raised on the bayou. Bennett had a similar respect and affection for the way they'd built and maintained the family business and kept it in their hometown, for better or worse. Josh and Owen, even Maddie and Kennedy, drove Sawyer crazy. But they did work hard. They also played and laughed and loved hard. He loved them to his bones. He knew they loved him, too, and had his back. Hell, they'd been putting up with his grumpy, grieving ass for months now.

If Juliet Dawson wanted her little brother to spend time with *his* little brother and cousin in an effort to make him a better guy, Sawyer couldn't really find fault with that.

Dammit. He was intrigued by this woman. He hadn't been intrigued by anyone or anything in a very, very long time. Maybe intrigued was a strong word for it, but she was...not irritating. And even that was something.

"Come on. I'll buy you breakfast and we can see what my brilliant partners thought was going to happen here."

"Just remember, I do have the hard hat." She bent to pick it up and plopped it on her head.

She looked adorable in it.

Fuck. Adorable? He hadn't even *thought* that word in months. Even about the cute kids that came for swamp boat tours. Of which there were many. But Josh and Owen kept most of those groups on their tour boats lately. Sawyer, who had once been the best one with the kids, was too fucking grumpy to deal with kids and their tendencies to bounce in their seats, stand up on the boat when they weren't supposed to, and reach out for things they shouldn't. He'd snapped at a few, made two cry, and Owen had taken him off kid tour duty.

It was for the best. He liked the little ones—elementary school ages—but his scar would probably scare them.

But Juliet was a little adorable and didn't seem a bit scared of him. She also seemed like she'd stay in her seat if she was out on a boat tour. He wouldn't have to snap at her even once.

Sawyer nodded. "The hat's a point in your favor, I'll admit."

"Oh, and safety goggles."

She *did* have safety goggles?

He sighed. Dammit. He might be screwed here.

Screwed. There was another building term that could also be sexual.

2

SAWYER LANDRY.

She'd read about him in the brochure and online, but no one had mentioned that Sawyer was still, currently, an active part of the business.

Juliet tried to keep up with his long strides as he headed up the ramp that led off the dock and onto the paved path outside Boys of the Bayou. But between her short legs, the hip waders, and the fact that she just didn't do long and hurried very well, she was several feet behind him before he noticed and stopped.

Though the view from behind Sawyer Landry was nothing to be upset about.

The man was big. As in tall and broad and with big muscles. Really big muscles. Like oh-my-god-I want-to-squeeze-those biceps. That had actually been her first thought when she'd seen the soft green cotton of his Boys of the Bayou T-shirt wrapped lovingly around those upper arms. She wanted to squeeze them. Feel them bunching. The way they would if he were to lift her up and—

"You comin' or what?"

She blinked and jerked her thoughts away from Sawyer

Landry's wet-panty-inducing biceps. There was the rest of him to think about, too, after all—the shoulders, the ass, the scar. A little shiver went through her. That scar was hot. It made his otherwise if-I-was-a-model-for-hip-waders-everyone-would-own-them face and body a little less perfect. More touchable. *Rugged and wounded.* Those were the words that came to mind when she paired that scar with the broody look in his eyes. She wanted to know everything about that scar. She wanted to trace it with her finger, then her lips. She wanted to find out if he only smiled with half of his mouth because he was always only mildly amused, the way he'd seemed on the dock with her, or if it was because there was some nerve damage under that scar.

She stopped in front of him on the path where he was waiting for her. "These are my bayou-wading boots, not my running boots," she told him.

He looked down at the hip waders, his gaze lingering on her upper thighs.

Ooh, tingles. She liked those.

"I can't believe you're wearing hip waders," he said, almost to himself.

Juliet put a hand on her hip. "I was coming down to the bayou. I don't know much about how things work down here, but I understood water and mud." She lifted a foot, turning it back and forth as she studied the boot. "Regular boots didn't seem like enough. So, I went to the local sporting goods and hunting supply store, told them what I'd be doing, and this is what they recommended."

Sawyer nodded at her. "Good thinking."

For some reason that surprised her. He didn't seem like the type who gave a lot of compliments. She already had the impression that he liked things a certain way—his way. And that he expected most people to fall short. Surely a girl showing up out of the blue—apparently Josh, Owen, Maddie, and Bennett hadn't only neglected to tell *her* about *Sawyer*—

without a clue as to how to build a dock but insisting that she teach her brother a lesson, could be a tad irritating.

But she *really* needed to teach her brother a lesson.

Chase wasn't a bad guy. He'd just had a really easy life and hadn't needed to make a lot of hard decisions or take responsibility for much. Their father was wealthy and connected, their older brothers Ryan and Rhett were all about success and power and had no qualms about using their father's influence to get ahead. They were four and six years older than Juliet and until she'd turned ten, they'd been okay big brothers. But after her hospitalization, things had changed. At fourteen and sixteen they hadn't had the patience to deal with her and her new limitations and they'd given up quickly, leaving her behind more often than not. Chase had been younger by three years and, being the baby brother, had already been left behind by the older two a lot. He could keep up with Juliet and so they'd grown closer. Now, though, since he'd been at college and in their older brothers' fraternity, he was showing signs of being infected with the Dawson family asshole-itis.

She was going to do whatever she could to put a stop to that.

Owen and Josh Landry had seemed like the perfect hard-working, blue-collar, fun-loving, responsible, and *nice* guys to be a good influence on Chase.

Yeah, she really did think that Chase needed some dirt under his nails and a few blisters.

Now, looking up at Sawyer, she wondered what he'd think of Chase and if Sawyer would give him a chance. What she knew about building a boat dock had come from Brandon and a few YouTube videos.

Chase knew even less than she did.

"You think me getting hip waders was good thinking?" she asked.

"I like a girl—a *person*—" he corrected, "who does their homework and prepares," he said.

Then you're gonna love me. Thankfully, she didn't say that out loud, but if homework and preparation got him going, he was going to be *into* her. Not that she'd want that. Not that she'd expect that. Not that it was even worth thinking about. She was here for two weeks to build a dock—but mostly to make her little brother work hard for a change and hang out with some good guys rather than his spoiled rotten, idiotic, frat brothers— and there was no reason to get caught up in some guy.

But yeah, if Sawyer liked preparation, he was going to go gaga over her accordion files.

She'd learned over the years that she'd rather be *over* prepared than surprised, or worse, embarrassed. Shit happened, and she'd found that expecting that and having a plan for when it did, served her well.

"Well, I can assure you that, if nothing else, I have a plan," she told Sawyer.

He studied her for a moment. Then he said, "I guess a girl doesn't show up with safety goggles on a whim, huh?"

Juliet felt her mouth tug up on the left in a little smile. "That's a pretty good assumption."

He let out a breath that seemed resigned. "Cora better have sausage gravy this mornin'," he said.

"Sausage gravy will make it all okay?"

"Well, sausage gravy never made anything *worse*."

She was going to have to take his word for that.

Sawyer turned and started across the road toward the rickety-looking building.

"Um...where are we going?"

"Oh, the rundown shed has you worried?" he asked.

"Maybe a little."

He gave a soft chuckle. It was a low, rumbly sound that made her shiver again. But it was a warm shiver.

"Well, you can stay down here while I go talk to them," he said. "Just watch out for the snakes."

Juliet picked up her pace. She couldn't do much. She didn't walk quickly to start with and when she tried, she was at risk for dragging her right foot and catching her toe. The heavy boots made it even worse. But until she could look up more about the snakes in this part of Louisiana, she was just going to avoid them. And keep these cover-almost-everything boots on. "That's okay. I think I'll risk my luck in the shed."

"Okay, but you should know that sheds and garages and outhouses and stuff are the perfect spots for black widows."

He sounded amused, but Juliet's shiver was definitely cold this time. She definitely knew that black widows were spiders.

"What is wrong with you?" she asked him. "Trying to make it so I won't sleep at all while I'm here? Between the alligators and the snakes and the spiders, what the hell are you all doing down here?"

He actually outright laughed at that, and for a second Juliet thought she'd risk a few spider bites to hear more of that. They surely had antivenom in the hospitals around here, right? She'd look that up, too.

"I guess we don't know any better," Sawyer said. He stopped in front of the door to the shack. He looked down at her. "I should say that I'm sorry for scaring you, but..." He lifted a shoulder. "I'm not. I'd rather someone be scared and think I'm an asshole but *not* have a black widow bite than think I'm a nice guy and end up in the ER."

She met his gaze. "For what it's worth, I'd think you were *more* of an asshole if you *didn't* warn me about spider bites."

For a second, a little warmth flickered in his eyes. Then he said, "We're gonna get along just fine then. I can scare the hell out of you about hangin' out down here and I won't even have to exaggerate."

"Um, yeah, the whole scenario with me strangling with the

rope I would use to tie myself to the dock? Not something I would have even thought of and I'm a *pro* at the What-If game and Yeah, But game. You're good."

"The Yeah, But game?" he asked.

"For instance, someone says, 'I'll be sure to put my seat belt on in the car' and I say, '*Yeah, but* if your car ends up in the river and is going under, you would wish you *didn't* have it on.'"

His eyes widened. "Wow."

She nodded. "That's what I'm saying. You might have met your worst-case-scenario match, Sawyer Landry."

Again, that little spark of warmth flickered in his gaze. "Maybe we'll have to make that into a drinking game or something."

She grinned. "Hey, maybe. Though I'm a lightweight."

Sawyer's gaze ran over her body again. "Do you get more morbid or less when you're tipsy?"

"Oh, more. For sure." Yes, she tended toward the macabre, but she could keep it under control, for the most part. Liquor changed that.

He nodded as if that was the right answer and gave another almost-smile.

He took his hand off the door handle for a moment, seeming to be pondering something. Not going in? Not confronting his family and partners?

"You do wear your seat belt, though, right?" he asked.

"Of course. Unless I'm driving near water."

He opened his mouth to reply, but she cut in. "Just kidding. I wear my seat belt and always carry a multi-tool."

Sawyer seemed surprised, but she was certain he knew what a multi-tool was. A guy who lived and worked on the bayou, fishing, hunting, and boating for a living, probably had one of the handy metal tools that included everything from a knife to a can opener to scissors in one of his pockets at all times.

"What if you can't reach your purse when you're in the car and it's goin' under?" he asked.

The *what-if* from him made her smile. "I don't keep it in my purse when I'm driving."

"What if you can't reach your pocket?"

"I don't keep it in my pocket, either."

"Okay, where do you keep it?"

"In the front of my bra."

His eyes, predictably, dropped to her breasts—okay, in fairness, to the front of her bra that she'd just mentioned—then came back to hers. "Oh? Think you can always reach that?"

"I think I could shimmy it up to my mouth and then drop it to a hand if I couldn't move my hands for some reason."

His gaze went back to her chest and she knew he was trying to imagine that.

Yes, she'd practiced it. It took a lot of shimmying and some hunching and great neck range of motion, not to mention a certain bra, but it was doable.

"I don't have it in there right now, if you're wondering," she said, after a few seconds of him studying her breasts.

"Oh, I was definitely wonderin'," he said, his drawl a little lower and longer.

She wondered what else he'd been wondering about. "I'm not driving right now," she said, as an explanation.

"You had it in there on your way down here?"

"There's a lot of water around here."

He just nodded, seemingly accepting that explanation. "Right."

"I know that seems like I'm a huge worrier."

"Just seems prepared to me."

She gave him a big smile. "Thank you."

Then he blew out a breath and grabbed the door again.

"Well, as prepared as you seem to be for bein' down here, I

33

don't think you could really be ready for what's about to happen."

Juliet felt her eyes widen. "What's about to happen?"

"You're about to meet my family."

She relaxed a little. "Oh, I've met them, remember?"

He gave a short laugh. "Uh, no. Not even close."

Then he pulled the door open.

It wasn't even eight a.m., but the building was seemingly full of people. And it was loud.

There was conversation and laughter, the clinking of silverware against plates, bowls, and cups, and the morning news coming from the two TVs mounted on the wall.

But all the noise stopped, except for the TV, as everyone in the place turned to look at them. Juliet felt completely conspicuous, as if someone had just shined a spotlight on her. She swallowed hard and gave the room a wobbly smile.

The place looked like a shed on the inside, too, but a shed that had a hodgepodge of paraphernalia on the walls—from a New Orleans Saints poster to a banner that read 1992 B League Fast Pitch Champs to a variety of photographs hung in mismatched frames. The only pattern to the wall décor seemed to be "stick it up wherever."

The room was full of tables and chairs, had a few booths on the west wall, and a wide wooden bar running along the east wall. Clearly there was more to it than this one room—there was a set of swinging doors that seemed to lead to a kitchen and an alcove at the back that likely led to restrooms—but it seemed very much like it had been a simple square building and whoever owned it had slowly added stuff to it as needed.

The tables and chairs didn't match, the light fixtures didn't match, most of the bar stools did, but where the majority were covered in black vinyl with silver legs, there were three oddballs. One had a cherry red seat with silver legs, one had a blue seat with black legs, and one had a bright yellow seat with each leg painted a different color. All of the stools were occupied.

Even on first glance, it seemed that the people inside the building were also a mishmash of styles and ages. Seemingly, everyone was in blue jeans and T-shirts, a few in flannel. There were only three women by Juliet's count. Two sat at the far end of the bar and even they were a mix of styles. One, a pretty brunette, wore cutoff shorts and a baby blue T-shirt, and her eyes widened when she saw Sawyer and Juliet come in, giving them a big smile. The woman next to her was in a black tank, black skirt, black combat boots, and heavy black makeup around her eyes. She looked curious, even dropping her one foot from where it had been propped on the bar to sit up straighter. The only other female was behind the bar. She had snow-white hair that hung in a long braid down her back, deeply tanned and wrinkled skin, and bright eyes that Juliet could feel taking in every detail about her. She was also wearing a T-shirt that said: *IOWA, for some reason you have to come here to be President.*

"This is a restaurant?" Juliet asked Sawyer, nearly whispering. The entire place had gone quiet when they'd stepped in.

"My grandma's place," he said. "It's mostly a bar, but they do food, too, and seems everyone in town comes in for breakfast before heading out for the day."

"Well, damn, Kennedy," the man perched on the bright yellow covered stool said. "Guess you're gonna have to be the next kid in the family to walk in here with a hot girl now that Josh, Owen, and Sawyer have all done it."

"I'll see what I can do, Grandpa," the woman with the goth look called back.

"My sister, Kennedy, and my grandfather, Leo," Sawyer said to Juliet.

"I'm..." Juliet wasn't really sure how to describe what she was at the moment.

"I completely understand." Sawyer put a hand at her lower back and nudged her further into the room. "Let's get this over with."

"This?"

"Them gushing all over you."

"They're going to *gush*? They don't even know me."

"That won't keep them from it. I'm pretty sure they know a lot *about* you," he said dryly.

She let him lead her into the room. "They do? You didn't."

"I'm probably the only one. I'm also sure that was very intentional. My family is a lot of things, but good at keeping a secret is not one of them. Just because they didn't tell *me* you were coming, doesn't mean they didn't blab all about it."

Oh boy.

Sawyer stopped in the middle of the room, his hand still on her lower back, and Juliet found herself inching closer to him for some reason. He smelled good. That was certainly part of the reason. Oh, and this incredibly intimidating collection of characters who was looking at her like she was about to say something astoundingly important and extremely entertaining.

She wasn't. Not at all.

"Everyone, this is Juliet Dawson. Juliet, this is most of my family and a good portion of the work force in Autre, Louisiana."

"You already made her put a life jacket on?" Sawyer's grandfather asked him.

Sawyer moved his hand from her back to tuck it in his pocket. "This is how I found her."

The older man swiveled on his stool and looked her up and down. "Those hip waders yours?" he asked.

Juliet nodded.

"How about that hard hat?"

She nodded again. They didn't need to know everything

was only about two days old. Truth was, she probably should have owned a hard hat a long time ago.

The man shook his head slow and gave a low whistle. "Wow." Leo looked at Sawyer. "Don't think I could have described your perfect woman until I saw Juliet here."

Juliet's eyes widened. "Oh, no. I'm here to—"

"We know why you're here, honey," the older woman behind the bar cut in. "Let's just say the life jacket is kind of a cherry on top."

Juliet opened her mouth to reply but Sawyer sighed.

"I'm sincerely offended that you all thought it would be this easy," he said to the room at large.

No one replied, but there were several looks exchanged.

"What would be this easy?" Juliet asked him softly.

He looked down at her. "Distracting me."

Juliet lifted a brow. "Distracting you? From what? With what?"

"From being on their cases. And with you," he said.

His voice was lower and a little husky suddenly, and she felt another shiver dance down her spine. After a long moment, he lifted his head and looked around.

"I'm kind of a hard-ass and I worry too much and I harass them—according to everyone here anyway. If I told *them* about the potential to accidentally hang themselves with a rope off the edge of the dock, they would just roll their eyes."

Juliet looked around, too. "But that's a pretty serious risk."

"The chances are about a million to one. Maybe more," Sawyer said, looking at her again.

"Still, there's a *chance.*"

He gave her a smile that *almost* tugged that other corner of his mouth up. "Exactly." He glanced at the group again. "But they don't see it that way, so they recognized the perfect opportunity to get my attention on the new girl traipsing around my boat dock with an electric saw she doesn't even know how to use."

Juliet opened her mouth to protest but the truth was, she did *have* an electric saw and she did not have any idea how to use it. It was still in the box.

"I'm sure they're imagining me following you around and giving you detailed instructions with drawings on a white board and begging you to wear safety goggles."

She narrowed her eyes. "You carry a white board around?"

"I would if I thought it would make someone listen."

"I have no intention of *not* listening," Juliet said. "But I don't need white board drawings and I already have safety goggles."

"Exactly," he said. Like before.

Then he gave her another very pleased look, but this time with a nearly full smile, and for a second Juliet found herself staring at his mouth. Damn.

"They know *me* very well," he said. "But they didn't plan on *you*."

He seemed almost triumphant. Like maybe he'd won a round with his siblings and partners.

She wasn't sure what he meant by that, but she liked that he was smiling about it.

"So how much *do* you know about building a boat dock?"

"On a scale of one to ten?" she asked.

"Sure."

"Five and a half."

He gave her a slightly amused look. "A half?"

She shrugged. "I've done some research. I know the best woods to use for boat docks, I know that the closest place to rent a backhoe is Newton, I *own* an electric saw *and* safety goggles. But never having used that saw probably only gets me a half."

His eyebrows were nearly to his hairline. "You're going to rent a backhoe and then do what with it?"

They were just going to move past the never-used-a-saw-thing then. Okay by her. Juliet shrugged. "Dig stuff up. Move debris. Move dirt around. I haven't gotten into the details of that."

"I can drive the backhoe," Leo piped up.

"No." Sawyer shook his head. "Nobody's driving any backhoes. *I'll* handle any heavy machinery that's needed."

Juliet fought a smile. Looked like his siblings *did* know him. If they wanted him distracted, all she had to do was throw around terms like "backhoe." Imagine if she'd just had one delivered like she'd considered.

"I've driven a backhoe before," Leo told him.

"You have a bus to drive," Sawyer said. "Isn't that enough?"

Leo shrugged. "I mean, you can't dig shit up with a bus."

Juliet grinned. It was obvious these people loved teasing, and teasing Sawyer seemed like fun. "What about pile drivers?" she asked. "I know that we'll need those."

Sawyer groaned. "Definitely not. Good lord, if you can't even take a video of the underside of the dock without almost breaking your neck, I can't let you near heavy equipment." He pointed a finger at her nose. "Don't look anything else up about large pieces of construction equipment. I don't want to hear about dump trucks or anything from you."

That was fine with her. She had no desire to drive a back hoe or a dump truck. She nodded. "I'll do whatever you tell me to do."

"I like the sound of that."

For some reason, a wave of heat rolled over her at that. Why did the things Sawyer Landry said sometimes sound dirty?

"You're really going to help with it?" Kennedy asked.

"With the big stuff," Sawyer said with a shrug.

"You're really going to take a couple weeks off to hang out and...nail stuff?" Kennedy pressed.

Juliet gave the other woman a quick glance. She hadn't

meant that the way it sounded, surely. Juliet looked up at Sawyer.

He had simply lifted one brow at his sister. "Seems likely at some point."

That definitely sounded dirty and Juliet shook her head. What was wrong with her?

"Really?" Kennedy's expression shifted from sly to surprised.

"Watch this," he said. He looked down at Juliet. "I guess I *could* let you drive the backhoe. That could be something that might come in handy sometime."

Juliet did *not* want to drive a backhoe. Her usual lack of coordination already had her nervous about things like power tools and sharp edges, honestly. A piece of heavy machinery that was often used to knock stuff down? That was *not* a good idea.

"Yeah, but what if I end up taking out one of the other docks and then we have to rebuild two?"

Sawyer gave her a satisfied grin. "Exactly." He looked at Kennedy. "I think it's going to be okay."

Ah, they'd just played the Yeah, But game. Juliet felt like she'd just passed some quirky test.

Kennedy looked downright stunned now, but she nodded slowly. "That's...great."

"Okay, time for a partners' meeting," Sawyer said, looking toward the back table where Owen and Josh Landry were sitting with a couple of other guys.

"Oh, good," Ellie said. "Cora!" she called. "Partner meeting."

"No," Sawyer said, steering Juliet toward the bar. "I've got something better for you."

"Oh?" Ellie asked.

"Her."

Ellie's eyes lit up as she focused on Juliet. "I can feed her and ask her everything I want to know?"

Juliet looked up at Sawyer and saw him nod. "Yep."

She turned wide eyes on Ellie, who looked like Sawyer had just given her a shiny new toy for Christmas.

"Juliet, this is my grandmother, Ellie. Ellie, this is Juliet."

He nudged Juliet forward, and the men at the bar, in a seemingly choreographed move, all shifted one stool over, leaving an empty one dead center.

Juliet dug in her heels instantly.

Sawyer noticed her resistance and gave a low chuckle she could *feel* at her back almost more than she could hear it.

"Smart girl to be cautious around this bunch," he said, his voice low. "But once you taste Cora's sourdough bread with her strawberry-rhubarb jam, you'll be thanking me."

"Cora?"

"Ellie's best friend and business partner. She does most of the cookin'."

"Okay, now, for fuck's sake, let's get you out of all of...that," Ellie said, waving her hand up and down to indicate everything Juliet was wearing. "I'm sweatin' just lookin' at ya."

Come to think of it, she was a little hot. "I don't have any shoes on under these." The guy at the sporting goods store had told her she could buy this kind, with the built-in boot, or buy the kind that went over boots—and then buy the boots sepa-rate. She'd thought these seemed easiest, but they didn't fit as well as she'd like. Her right ankle was a little wobbly some-times, especially on uneven terrain, so she was going to have to be careful in them. Once she took them off, though, she'd be without support at all. She rarely went barefoot and the bayou seemed the last place to start.

"That's okay," Ellie said. "The health department won't cite us if you go barefoot in here for a bit."

Juliet hadn't even thought of that. "You sure?"

"The last time the health department was down here was 2004," Leo said. "And the guy said he'd forgive anything as long as he could have a third helping of Cora's red-eye gravy and grits."

Well, okay then.

Juliet braced a hand on the stool to remove her boots. She always liked to have something solid nearby in case she wobbled. She was really very steady and rarely had falls. If she got tired or too hot or was sick with the flu or something, she noticed her weaker right side more and had to be more careful, but most of the time she was fine and no one around her could tell she had about thirty percent less strength on her right side compared to her left. But she was always prepared and didn't push her luck. Standing next to solid objects when she would be partially balancing on one foot was just smart.

Juliet pushed the top of the left boot down first, keeping her right foot booted and therefore more stable. It wasn't until she'd pulled her right foot out of its boot that she noticed there was very little conversation going on around her. She looked up to find everyone watching her. Was she doing something wrong? Was there a wrong way to take boots off? She glanced at Sawyer. He was also watching her, unblinking, a weird look on his face.

Juliet glanced down. What the hell? She was wearing shorts and no socks or shoes, as she'd told them. She figured out quickly that the boots would be a hundred times more comfortable with socks on and would definitely add them next time, but the guy at the store hadn't mentioned that. She looked back up to Sawyer, frowning slightly. "What are you staring at?"

Sawyer cleared his throat and looked up at her. Almost as if he hadn't realized he'd been staring. He glanced around and scowled at everyone. Several turned away and went back to their breakfasts and conversation. Then he focused back on her. "Just thinkin' that you probably weren't in danger of overheating in those boots after all."

"What do you mean?"

"You don't have much on under there."

She looked down again. She had on denim shorts. They seemed pretty simple and basic. She wasn't an outdoorsy girl, so she didn't have a lot of work-outside-in-the-heat-and-dirt type clothes. Hiking, boating, skiing—all things her older brothers had loved—were a little tough for a girl who couldn't trust her endurance and balance. Not to mention that her packing strategy was driven by the careful, always-be-prepared, you-better-take-it-just-in-case voice in her head rather than any attempt at minimalization and efficiency.

"Is there a dress code in here?" she asked him, putting a hand on her hip.

Everyone in the place had denim on, except Kennedy.

"No...I wouldn't say there is." Sawyer ran a hand over the back of his neck. "Maybe you should keep the life jacket on though." He looked slightly pained suddenly.

Juliet frowned. And unbuckled the front of her life jacket. She shrugged out of it, tossed it on top of her boots, and then reached for her hard hat. She took it off and placed it on top of the bar. She ran a hand through her hair and watched Sawyer take in her whole outfit under the safety gear.

His gaze raked over her and she completely lost track of the fact that there was anyone else in the room with them. She stood in front of him, barefoot, in short denim shorts, a fitted black tank top with spaghetti straps, and...that was it. She had more clothes in the car, of course, but she'd dressed for potentially falling into alligator-infested waters rather than sitting in a bar having breakfast that morning.

She felt her cheeks get a little warm, her nipples get hard, and her skin tingle everywhere Sawyer's gaze touched. And his gaze touched a lot of places. Seemed she did have a lot of skin showing.

It was hot in Louisiana at the end of July. Everyone knew that. Even people who hadn't done research into what the average temps and weather was like this time of year knew that. She knew that the average temperature was ninety-two degrees, rarely dipping below eighty-seven degrees, and that the humidity was around seventy-nine percent.

So, she'd dressed accordingly. She'd thought.

But it was becoming very clear, very quickly, that she *hadn't* prepared fully for coming to Autre.

Because she hadn't expected Sawyer Landry.

Then again, she wasn't sure she *could* have prepared for Sawyer Landry.

"Okay, partner meeting." Josh suddenly appeared at Sawyer's side and clapped him on his shoulder.

"Maddie's not here though," Owen said, joining them. "We'll have to go get her."

"Yeah, you go on," Ellie told him. "Juliet is just fine here with us."

Sawyer just grunted at that, but he did let Josh turn him away.

"Be careful you don't slip in that puddle of drool there by your feet," Owen said to Sawyer, shooting Juliet a grin and a wink, just before Sawyer put his elbow into Owen's side, hard.

Owen grunted then and the men headed for the door.

"So, you're a lawyer here to build us a new dock," Ellie said, pouring a cup of coffee and setting it and a small glass of orange juice on the bar in front of the empty bar stool.

Clearly she expected Juliet to take the seat.

Without any better—or really any *other*—option, Juliet started to climb onto the stool. She felt her left foot stick to the floor for just a second as she lifted it, and she grimaced slightly.

"There's a ninety-eight percent chance that's beer or coffee creamer you just stepped in," Leo told her, swiveling on his stool to face her, his coffee cup in hand.

Juliet settled on the stool beside him. "Do I want to know

what substances might fall into that other two percent?" she asked.

"Maybe not," he said, with a nod. "But I can promise it's not urine. Or floor polish, for that matter."

"Fuck off," Ellie told him.

Juliet gave a surprised laugh.

"Hey, I said it definitely wasn't urine," Leo said. "I know you cleaned that up."

Juliet's eyes widened. "There *was* urine?"

"He's just a piglet!" the brunette who was sitting with Kennedy called. "And he'd never been in a bar before. He got excited."

"A *piglet*?" Juliet asked. "A real piglet?"

"He'll only eat if Tori is holding him," Ellie said. She beamed down the bar at Tori with clear affection. "She's a vet. All of the animals love her. He's still getting used to being without his mama, so Tori keeps him with her a lot."

"Is he here now?" Juliet looked around. She didn't know much about animals, but the pictures of piglets she'd seen were cute.

"I have a sitter for him today," Tori said.

"A...sitter. For your piglet?" Juliet asked.

Tori shrugged. "He's a little needy right now."

"And he pees on the floor?"

"Just that one time," Tori insisted. Then she added, "That one time *here*."

Juliet grinned at her.

"That spot is right behind your bar stool," Ellie said to Leo as she refilled his coffee cup. "So, it's definitely not beer. The last time you let a drop go to waste you were probably..." She shook her head. "Hell, I don't even know."

Leo nodded. "You got that right. And by that logic, it means it's also not gumbo."

"By your seat, it's not mouthwash or cologne, either." This

came from another older woman who had just come from what Juliet assumed was the kitchen. She had short salt-and-pepper curls, and was plumper than Ellie.

Leo chuckled, clearly not offended.

"It's also not blackberry juice," the woman said. "Since you *forgot to pick any blackberries up.*"

"Oh, I'll bet it's frosting," Leo said to Ellie. "From that cinnamon roll Cora threw at me two days ago when I forgot the blackberries." He lifted his cup for a sip, seemingly unbothered by having breakfast pastries thrown at him. And unapologetic about the blackberries.

Cora set a plate of toasted bread, a little dish of jam, another dish of what looked like whipped butter, and a knife in front of Juliet. "Apple butter," she said, pointing at the second dish. "You let me know what else you want, sweetie." Then she looked at Leo. "It actually could be apple butter," she said. "I threw toast at you yesterday when you forgot them *again.*"

"Yep, that's true." Leo just nodded, sipping again.

Okay, so the older generation here had food fights on a regular basis. Interesting. Then Juliet bit into a piece of sourdough bread with strawberry-rhubarb jam and instantly decided that throwing food in here was a travesty. If it was even half as good as the *toast*, it would be downright sinful to do anything but eat it and sob with pleasure.

"You're a lawyer, huh?" Ellie asked.

"I am. Most of my work is as a patient advocate, working with people who were having a hard time navigating the healthcare system and dealing with their insurance companies. I also lobby for healthcare issues in D.C."

"And you're from Virginia?" Ellie asked. "You grew up there?"

Juliet nodded. "In Alexandria. My dad's an investor. My mom was a stay-at-home mom."

"You have brothers other than Chase?"

Juliet shouldn't have been surprised Ellie knew of her brother, she realized. "I do. Two older."

"You close with your family?"

"Um, Chase and I are pretty close."

That seemed like a good enough answer for Ellie because she just nodded and went on. "Do you have a boyfriend?" Ellie pushed the coffee cup in front of Juliet closer.

Juliet coughed slightly, finished chewing, and swallowed. She shook her head. "No, I don't."

"Husband?" Ellie asked. She nudged the little ceramic pot of cream closer to Juliet's cup.

"No."

"*Ex*-husband?"

Well, they weren't subtle here. "Nope."

"Are you heartbroken?" Ellie pushed the container that held sugar and sweetener packets closer.

"Not heartbroken, either," Juliet told her.

She'd dated but hadn't been serious with anyone since her first year of college. The What-If and Yeah, But games got a little...um...tiresome for a lot—okay all—the guys she'd gone out with. Because she was *really* good at both games. She could go on and on and on.

Sawyer had seemed fine with the games though. Like maybe he could even hold his own against her. He intrigued her. She couldn't deny it.

The people in her life were one of two extremes—either they hovered, or they quickly grew frustrated and left her alone completely. Her parents and a couple of girlfriends fell into the first category. Her brothers fell into the second.

Except for Chase. He was right in the middle. He was always willing to help her and sometimes sensed that she needed an extra hand or extra time. But then he just held his hand out or slowed down. He never sighed, or rolled his eyes, or stepped in to do something for her because it would be easier or faster. He just...went along.

"So, you're single and have your own hard hat and you're here to make sure your little brother doesn't turn into an asshole," Ellie said, leaning onto her forearms on the bar top. Once more she nudged the cup of coffee forward.

Juliet nodded. "Yes."

"I approve of all of those things."

Juliet smiled. "You care that I'm single?"

"Well, that way no one here will tell me that I should feel guilty about pushing you toward my grandson."

Juliet choked slightly on her last bite of toast. She frowned at her plate. How had that all disappeared so quickly? And could she ask for more?

"Need a drink of coffee?" Ellie asked.

Juliet shook her head and swallowed hard. "No, thanks. I don't drink coffee."

Everyone nearby paused and looked at her, obviously shocked. And obviously eavesdropping.

She swallowed again. "I like tea," she said, almost hesitantly.

A second later, a glass of iced tea appeared in front of her. She'd meant hot tea, but this would do. She picked it up and took a drink. And nearly spit it back out.

Sweet tea. She should have known. You had to be careful ordering iced tea in the South if you didn't like it sweet. Since she preferred hot tea, she didn't usually have that problem and hadn't thought of it.

Everyone was watching her, and after her coffee comment, Juliet knew better than to say she didn't like sweet tea, either. That might be an even bigger sin. She swallowed, gave them a big smile, and decided that she'd rather turn the conversation back to something they all liked.

Sawyer.

"If I had a boyfriend, you *wouldn't* push me toward Saw—your grandson?" she asked. Okay, so Ellie hadn't said she'd push Juliet toward Sawyer. That had just been where Juliet's mind had gone.

Besides, she didn't want to be pushed toward anyone. That would be ridiculous. She was only here for two weeks.

But on the heels of that thought was another--*Vacation flings are a thing for a reason.*

You were far from home, where no one really knew you, and it was all temporary. Just fun. No big expectations. And the guy didn't even have to know about your penchant for safety plans and traveling with things like ankle braces and bungee cords. Oh, and duct tape. Duct tape was magical.

On second thought, Sawyer Landry very likely knew a lot about duct tape and might just appreciate her appreciation for it.

But the guy didn't have to know about *all* of her...idiosyncrasies. A fling could mean simply having sex with a guy with big hands and a half grin and an interesting scar who seemed to think her life jacket was kind of awesome.

"Oh, I'd still push," Ellie said. "*I'd* have no loyalty to your boyfriend back home. But this way I don't have to listen to anyone tell me I should feel bad about it."

"You'd do it even though it would make you feel bad?"

"It wouldn't make me feel bad," Ellie said. "It would make me feel *annoyed* to listen to them tell me it *should* make me feel bad. But that's no problem because you don't have a boyfriend."

Juliet liked Ellie. "So do I get to pick which grandson?" she asked, suddenly feeling a little sassy.

Maybe it was the sweet tea or maybe it was the attitudes of the people around her—also sassy, and seemingly very accepting—or maybe it was the look in Sawyer's eyes when he'd looked her up and down a little bit ago.

Ellie chuckled. "Well, there's Mitch and Sawyer. Mitch is

the handsome one who's always grinning like he's up to something. Because he is."

Juliet glanced over her shoulder. Mitch had to be the one who was leaning back in his chair, his ball cap on backward, grinning at one of the other guys with a grin exactly as Ellie had just described.

"And you know Sawyer."

Juliet faced Ellie again. The woman was watching her closely, clearly trying to gauge Juliet's thoughts about Sawyer through her expression or tone.

"I assumed Maddie and Owen were together by the way they acted last week when we met," Juliet said. "But what about Josh? He's not an option?"

She wasn't interested in Josh. He was very good-looking and had been very nice last week. But no, it was Sawyer who was the Landry occupying her attention. Just Sawyer.

"No, Josh is not an option." The vet with the piglet that peed on floors was the one to answer.

Ah. He was taken. By the vet. Juliet gave her a smile. "Got it."

"So I guess the question is if you're into the flirty, troublemaker type or the broody, bossy type."

Broody and bossy. No question. At least as of Sawyer Landry saying, "What the hell is going on?" and then grabbing the back of her shorts.

"Honestly?" Juliet asked. "The brother I'm here to bail out of the mess he caused? Flirty, troublemaker type. I think I'm full-up on those."

Ellie gave her a satisfied grin. "No broody, bossy brothers?"

Juliet sighed and was surprised to find herself taking another sip of sweet tea and not hating it. "No. Just impatient, selfish brothers, other than Chase."

Ellie frowned. "I'm sorry to hear that. Are they impatient with *you*?"

"Oh yeah. I'm four and six years younger than them. And I had...trouble keeping up with them." Lord, she'd almost said, "I had a stroke when I was ten." She *never* let that spill. But with this woman, it was so easy to just talk. It seemed that everyone here was just accepted as they were, and Juliet was shocked by how quickly she'd relaxed around them. "They're into things like kayaking and hiking down into the Grand Canyon," she said of her brothers.

"And they didn't want to take you to the Grand Canyon?" Ellie asked.

That one hurt, she had to admit. Some of the things they'd wanted to do, surfing for instance, she hadn't regretted being left out of, but the Grand Canyon...yeah, she'd wanted that one. She shook her head. "They like to go hard and fast. Just not my thing."

Ellie was studying her eyes, and Juliet could tell that the sharp older woman could see that it wasn't because staying home had been Juliet's preference. But Ellie didn't call her on it or press with more questions and Juliet appreciated that.

They were all adults now. Ryan and Rhett were both in their early thirties and Ryan had a serious girlfriend, who went on their ski trips with them. It wasn't just the sports that they'd decided Juliet couldn't keep up on. They'd assumed that a three-week trip around Europe would be hard for her, too.

The truth was, it would have been hard for *them* because she would have needed to research everything and plan a pretty strict agenda and haul along a lot of paraphernalia for all of the what-if scenarios. She could bike around Italy, dammit. She just needed elbow and knee pads. And a helmet. And a first aid kit. But then, she took first aid supplies wherever she went.

"Well, we don't go hard and fast down here," Ellie said. "Long and slow and laid-back is more our style."

Juliet smiled at that. "Sounds like my kind of place."

Just then the door to the bar opened and again everyone turned to look. Juliet wondered if they did that no matter what, or if everyone who was usually here for breakfast was present and accounted for, so they knew it was a stranger coming in.

This time it was Chase.

He was on time for a change. Already a positive difference.

He sauntered in, seeming to not notice that everyone in the place was looking at him.

"Good morning," she greeted him as he stopped behind her stool and she swiveled to face him.

"Hey. So, I saw your car. Where's all the stuff?"

"Being delivered in about a half hour."

"The stuff?" Leo asked.

"The wood and some of the tools I rented and..." She shrugged. "Stuff."

Brandon had helped her by sending a list of materials and tools she'd need and she'd ordered everything from a lumber-yard and supply company. She'd bought a few things. It probably didn't hurt to own a power drill and a hammer and that electric handsaw, for instance. Those seemed like things she could have use for again possibly. But there were wrenches and a nail gun and other tools on Brandon's list that seemed excessive for a woman who was less than perfectly coordinated even with steak knives.

"We've got tools," Leo said, seeming confused about why she would have done that.

"I don't want to be a bother," she told him. "Chase and I are going to fix this and I didn't want to put anyone out." *Don't be a burden* was her life motto, after all.

"Loaning you a hammer or two is hardly putting anyone out," Leo told her.

Juliet shook her head. "I insist on being self-sufficient here."

She had a really good idea about what she was going to do for the dock. Of course, getting it from her head—and the page behind the second tab in her accordion file—and actually out on the banks of the bayou was the challenge. But the worst that could happen would be she'd screw it all up and end up paying Boys of the Bayou back to have it rebuilt by professionals. They'd have only lost two weeks. Hopefully, that wasn't too horrible for them, and hopefully, that would be enough time for Chase to have seen some good role models.

"What do you want me to do?" Chase asked. He seemed bored. Or irritated. He was probably both. But he was here. That's all she needed. These people were hardworking, blue-collar, manual labor types. They'd show him how to buckle down and do the hard stuff, even when they didn't want to.

"I want you to sit your butt down and tell me if you want your sausage gravy on biscuits or chicken fried steak," Ellie said.

Chase looked at her, seeming a little shy suddenly. "I'm okay."

That was new. Was it possible that Chase was feeling sheepish about what had brought him back to Autre, Louisiana for the next two weeks? Was it possible she'd found people who could make Chase Dawson self-effacing?

"That isn't what I need to know," Ellie told him. "What did you eat this morning?"

"Cereal."

Ellie rolled her eyes. "Sit down. You're getting chicken fried steak unless you say the word biscuits in the next five seconds."

"I'm fine," Chase said. "It was Cornflakes. Really nutritious."

"Uh-huh. And that's gonna wear off about the time you swing that hammer the third time," Ellie said. "Cora!" she called over her shoulder. "Need a chicken fried steak!"

"But I..." Chase looked at Juliet.

All she could do was shrug. "They fed me already and if I outwork you today, I'm totally not going to let you live it down."

"Of course you'll outwork me today," Chase said. "You

always outwork everyone." But he pulled out the stool that had magically become empty next to Juliet.

"Does she?" Ellie asked.

"She overthinks and overplans everything and then has to use it all. I think it's so she doesn't feel silly about the accordion files," Chase said.

Juliet elbowed him in the side.

"Accordion files?" Leo asked.

Chase nodded, undeterred by her jab. "Everything in her life is in accordion files."

Juliet frowned. "Not *everything*."

Chase gave her a look. "Every project, trip, event, and hobby has an accordion file."

Juliet lifted her glass of tea. Well, that didn't mean *everything* in her life.

Ellie gave her a soft smile. "So, something like building a dock would definitely have an accordion file, I'm guessing."

But it didn't feel like Ellie was teasing her. Juliet gave her a smile back. "It does."

"What are some of the tabs?" Ellie asked.

"Materials and tools. Building plans. Resources—local. Resources—general. Photos." Juliet knew she overplanned. She overthought. She overdid. But those accordion files were her safety net.

"Sounds like we're in good hands," Ellie decided.

"Did you buy steel-toed shoes?" Chase asked with a smirk, sliding the hard hat on the bar top over an inch. He knew it was hers.

"I did," Juliet said.

"The amount of money you spent on equipment and gear could have probably paid for two docks," Chase said.

"Not the point. And you know it."

"Me ending up with blisters is the point."

She patted his arm. "Yes. Yes, it is."

Chase sighed.

Cora set a plate in front of him a moment later. "Chicken fried steak *and* biscuits," she said. "I have a feelin' you're gonna need it."

He sighed again. But he definitely didn't push the plate away.

Juliet grinned and sipped her tea. Her not-really-completely-horrible sweet iced tea.

———

Sawyer turned in the direction of Cora's house. Maddie was staying with her grandmother. She wasn't a morning person and was likely still in bed or just now nursing her first cup of coffee.

"Uh, this way," Owen said, turning up the first sidewalk.

Ah, Maddie was at *his* place.

But they didn't get all the way to Owen's house. Maddie met them on the street halfway between Owen's and Ellie's. Clearly Owen had texted her a heads-up.

Her hair was up in a messy bun, she wore a baggy T-shirt and shorts with one of Owen's button-down shirts over it all, and slip-on sandals. She had her glasses on and she looked not-quite-awake. Also, not-quite thrilled about the impromptu partners' meeting.

Maddie blinked at them all. "So, she's a morning person, too? That's just great."

Amused, Sawyer asked, "Who?"

"Juliet Dawson."

He nodded. Maddie had definitely been expecting Juliet today.

"Apparently," he said. "She was down on the dock when I got there. And I think she'd been there awhile."

Maddie took a breath. "Okay, before you say anything more,

this is a great idea. We all think so." She gave Owen and Josh a look that clearly said they were expected to agree with her.

"We *all* think so? I don't remember voting. And I thought I was the majority partner," Sawyer said dryly, folding his arms and looking down at her.

"Well, that's what's so great about our arrangement," Maddie said. She squinted up at him, clearly still coming through the not-quite-awake cobwebs. "You can still be outvoted if we all agree on something you don't."

"That's a *great* thing about our arrangement?" Sawyer asked.

"Checks and balances," Maddie said with a nod. "It's good when it's in the best interest of the business. Even more so when it's for the good of one of the partners." She finished with a yawn that she tried to hide behind her hand.

"Juliet and Chase Dawson have no construction experience. They have no experience on the bayou or with boat docks. Oh, and Chase was the one who trashed the dock we're rebuilding. Don't really see how this is good for the business."

"Because you're going to end up firing Skip and Tanner by day three. If they don't quit after day two of you bossing them around," Maddie said.

Skip and Tanner were the guys Sawyer had talked to about rebuilding the dock. He'd intended to do it, but he did need more hands and he couldn't pull Josh and Owen off the boats for that long. They had to keep doing tours to keep money coming in.

"And then where will we be?" Maddie asked. "Still without any help and even farther behind. With Juliet and Chase, you've got two pairs of hands but they'll *listen* to you. They *expect* to be bossed around."

Sawyer shifted slightly at that. Why did every thought or mention of bossing Juliet around sound a little dirty? And why did he think that was a possibility anyway? Because she'd been agreeable out on the dock that morning. She'd acknowledged the risks. She'd admitted he had some good points. She'd been wearing a fucking life jacket and hard hat.

Agreeable.

Someone who admitted he was right.

Someone who took safety seriously.

She was a rare gem around here for all of those reasons.

"They don't know anything about building a dock," he felt compelled to point out. To his business partners. Who'd had a meeting and set this all up *without even telling him*.

Maddie rolled her eyes. "It's not like you're building a rocket ship," she said. "It's a dock."

Not that Maddie had ever built a dock, either. Sawyer lifted a brow.

"Basically, they'll be cutting boards and nailing them together, right?" Maddie asked. "So, you just tell them where to cut and what to nail."

Sawyer shifted again. It was juvenile as hell to think dirty thoughts whenever someone said "nail" or "nailed." He wasn't fourteen. But Juliet and Brandon had been talking about the same stupid thing. There really *were* a lot of construction terms that could sound sexual. It was going to be a long two weeks.

Was he seriously considering going along with this plan?

Yes. Because, other than the thing about these guys going behind his back, it wasn't a *bad* plan.

"So, you set this up to protect Skip and Tanner?" Sawyer asked. "They're big boys. And they're getting paid. They can handle me being picky."

Maddie snorted. "They shouldn't have to. They build docks for a living, for fuck's sake." She sighed. "Listen, Sawyer, you're going to insist on overseeing everything happening with the new dock anyway. Now, instead of worrying about and snapping at the tourists or worrying about and snapping at *us* all day, you've got two people who signed up for it and kind of deserve it and can't quit."

"Juliet deserves it?" Sawyer asked mildly, feeling a little tightness in his chest. Yes, he did worry and snap. He'd been doing it for nine months now.

Maddie lifted a shoulder. "Well, Chase does. And Juliet's here voluntarily. This was her idea. If she's as willing to help her brother out as she seems, then she'll put up with you for a couple of weeks." Maddie gave him a little smile. "I'll handle your portion of the tours and all will be well. Consider it a little two-week vacation."

Sawyer gave her a little frown. "I'm not supposed to *worry* about you out on the bayou on an airboat?"

She'd taken over a tour for him last week and it had ended with her pointing a gun at a gator she thought was going to make a snack out of Owen. All had ended well, but one of the tourists on the boat had been pissed as hell and had caused a huge ruckus about it. They'd smoothed things over eventually, but Sawyer couldn't shake the truth that it had all been *his* fault. Maddie had taken the tour over for him because he'd growled at a boat load of tourists earlier in the day. In fact, that was a relatively regular occurrence. People didn't take safety out on the airboats seriously enough. Maddie had taken the tour over to give him a break. And, okay, to ensure their customer reviews didn't totally tank because he was unable to lighten up and make the tours fun anymore.

But truthfully, he knew that Maddie getting on that airboat —in spite of the fact that was *way* out of her comfort zone and hadn't turned out that well—had been because she was worried about him. She didn't care as much about the customer reviews as she did about *his* well-being. The fact that his emotional baggage was putting the people he loved in uncomfortable, and somewhat dangerous, situations was not okay.

He needed to get his shit together.

"Hey, the only person I almost shot was Owen," Maddie said, giving her boyfriend a huge smile. "And if that does end up happening, he'll forgive me."

Owen grabbed her wrist and pulled her close, kissing the top of her head. "You'd nurse me back to health?"

"I'd make you alligator gumbo out of the fucking lizard that tried to take a bite of you," she said, with a little frown.

"Okay," Josh said, interrupting their...whatever it was. "Anyway, Maddie can take your tours and you can oversee the dock building," he said to Sawyer.

Maddie smiled. "Yeah, you might worry about me a little, but I think you're going to be pretty distracted for the next couple of weeks."

He'd called it. They'd taken one look at Juliet, heard her plan to come rebuild the dock, and had instantly thought "vacation from Sawyer's bitching."

Hanging out with Juliet Dawson in her hard hat and safety goggles? Distracted was one word for it. Turned on. Mixed up. Amused. Those were all definite possibilities as well.

But turned on and amused could be good things. They were certainly things he hadn't felt much of over the past several months.

"Okay."

Maddie blinked up at him, but now it was with clear confusion rather than sleepiness. "What?"

"I said, okay. Let's have Juliet and Chase rebuild the dock."

Maddie's eyes widened. "Really? Just like that?" She looked at Owen. "That's all it took?"

Owen shrugged. "Big brown eyes. I knew her big brown eyes would get to him."

Sawyer didn't deny it. But it wasn't Juliet's eyes that had gotten to him.

Okay, it wasn't *just* her eyes.

Josh gave Sawyer a huge grin. "Sure. Her eyes. Couldn't have been those curves underneath the hip waders."

Sawyer took a deep breath. He and Josh and Owen hadn't joked around a lot lately. Josh and Owen were two of the most laid-back people Sawyer had ever met. They were friendly and fun and knew how to make people feel instantly comfortable. And they'd been walking on eggshells around him, protecting him by taking on more of the tours and dealing with customer issues as much as they could, trying to make things easier on him since Tommy had died. He'd still been worrying too much and bitching at them.

"She had on hip waders?" Maddie asked, her eyes wide.

"And a life jacket," Owen said with a grin.

Sawyer really liked when Josh and Owen and Maddie grinned and teased. He wanted them to joke around and laugh. With him.

Maddie looked up at Sawyer. "You made her put a life jacket on already?"

He was going to relax. Chill out. Show them that he was not a complete emotional wreck and that he could be happy.

Even if he had to fake it every single day for the next two weeks.

It would be easier to convince them if he was on the shore building a dock while they were doing the tours though. They all spent long hours every day together. It was damned difficult to hide anything from anyone around here. But if they were out on the bayou, focused on their customers, and he was on land, preoccupied with Juliet and Chase, it would be a lot easier to fake laid-back and happy when he was with his family after hours.

And he would be with them after hours. In Autre, Louisiana, there was no escaping the Landry clan. They worked, played, ate, fought, laughed, and cried together. For better or worse.

Sawyer tucked a hand in his front pocket and consciously relaxed his shoulders. "I found her that way," he said, as he'd told Leo.

"She showed up in a life jacket and hip waders?" Maddie asked. "No way."

He nodded. "Yep. Seems Ms. Dawson is all about preparedness and safety."

He couldn't help the little smile he felt thinking about that. They'd played the Yeah, But game. Juliet Dawson might be as big a pessimist as he was.

Maybe he wouldn't have to fake *everything* about relaxing and enjoying things with Juliet around over the next two weeks.

"Wow," Maddie said. "I didn't even know that about her." She gave Owen and Josh a conspiratorial smile. "This should be interesting."

Could he let the Dawson siblings try to build a dock, shrug a little, say "sure" a few times to make his family feel like he wasn't a total emotional loss?

Sure.

"And she has her own safety goggles."

There was a long pause and then they all laughed. Sawyer felt a pang in his chest. Fuck, when was the last time he'd made them *laugh*?

Tori and Maddie had made *him* grin a few times. Even Josh and Owen with their stupid jokes and the way they handled the customers made him smile. But *he* hadn't made *them* laugh in far too long.

"She also has on very short shorts," Josh filled in for Maddie. "Under the hip waders, of course."

Maddie grinned at Sawyer. "You would go for someone who was capable and cautious."

Yeah, it seemed to fit. He could admit. But that was the thing. He wouldn't have gone for that type typically. Wearing hip waders and a life jacket on a boat dock when she had no intention of getting in the water and was doing it as a just-in-case measure was an overreaction. A year ago, he would have seen that. That would have been his first impression, in fact, rather than thinking it was the hottest thing he'd seen in forever. He would have been all about her stripping it all *off* rather than thinking about her putting safety goggles *on*.

A year ago, he would have been flirting his ass off rather than talking to her about potentially strangling herself over the edge of the dock. Okay, that had felt a little flirtatious—strangely—but that was *not* sexy. Hell, a year ago that wouldn't have even occurred to him.

A year ago, he would have thought this whole plan was great, in fact. He would have thought that Chase Dawson *should* rebuild the dock, and he would have thought Juliet wearing those hip waders was hilarious. He would have loved the idea of torturing a spoiled frat boy with manual labor and would have already asked Juliet out.

That would have been normal. His usual.

If he embraced it all now, it would surprise his family. But it would also make them happy. Relieved, even.

"Well, if she comes out in steel-toed boots, I'm a goner," he joked.

Joking.

He remembered that. Vaguely.

He took in the slightly stunned, but very pleased, looks on Josh, Owen, and Maddie's faces and felt like he'd just given them a fucking gift.

God, had he been that bad? That wound up? That hard to be around?

Yeah, he had.

The last few months had been hell.

He thought about Juliet again. Gorgeous, worst-case-scenario pro, worried-big-sister, willing-to-get-her-hands-dirty-to-make-things-right Juliet. She was out of her element here, clearly. If she was a worrier by nature—and the pocket knife in her bra indicated she was...and then some—the bayou was going to give her all kinds of things to fret about. Cottonmouths and black widows were only the beginning.

But he had a feeling she was going to be a step or two ahead of him.

He smiled thinking about that. Again.

Smiling.

Yeah, he vaguely remembered doing a lot of that, too.

3

AN HOUR LATER, SAWYER WAS NO LONGER SMILING. HIS FROWN
was going strong though.

It was probably because of the huge truck blocking the road
in front of Boys of the Bayou.

Or maybe it was the ridiculous amount of wood and equipment that truck had delivered.

Possibly it was the three young guys who were unloading
said wood and equipment, and making asses of themselves
over Juliet.

Though it could have been that Juliet was now dressed in
work clothes. Or what Sawyer assumed she thought were work
clothes. She had a long-sleeved white tee paired with khaki
work pants and her hard hat. She also now had safety goggles
on. And steel-toed boots.

Holy fuck. He'd been right. He was a goner. Even without
the tiny tank and short shorts. He was *all in* on her current look.
She was wearing the damned goggles even as she watched the
guys unload the truck and directed them where to put everything. Which was ridiculous. She didn't need the things
on *now*.

And then there was the neon green safety vest she wore. Was she afraid the guys were going to back over her with the truck or whack her with one of the wooden planks they were carrying?

But it made him freaking *like her*.

Even as he was annoyed by it. There was no way this woman, with that body, needed to add neon, look-at-me green to the ensemble. All the men were definitely looking.

For his part, he was hard as a rock looking at her in her goggles and vest and boots. She was the epitome of the fantasy he hadn't even realized he had.

"Just need you to sign right here," one of the guys told Juliet, turning the clipboard he held slightly so she could see it but not enough that she didn't have to lean in a little. Enough that there was no way the guy wasn't going to catch a whiff of that lilac scent from her hair. Probably enough that one of those encased-in-glow-in-the-dark-green breasts would brush against his arm.

Sawyer didn't even realize he was stalking across the expanse of dirt and grass between his vantage point from the path to where the over-the-top amount of wood and boxes of bolts, screws, and nails sat until he was nearly on top of them.

Juliet smiled at the man. "Great. Thanks. I appreciate you guys coming out with such little notice."

She leaned in to sign, and Sawyer noticed the guy looking down the front of her vest.

Jesus, how did she not realize she looked like the star of an online erotic story that started, "When I hired *Building Babes* to put in my man cave, I had no idea that they were going to send Juliet over to do the pounding and screwing."

Okay, maybe that was just him.

Also, maybe he'd been without sex for too long.

"I assume you guys will come back and haul the extra away at no cost?" Sawyer asked the guy.

He had no reason to think they'd do that. Why the hell would they? But it caused the guy to look up from Juliet's cleavage into Sawyer's face. So that Sawyer could give him a *hands-off* look.

The guy caught the meaning of his look, but he didn't seem to buy that Sawyer had a claim here. He smirked. "I'll do whatever Juliet wants me to do with my wood."

No. He hadn't said that. Looking straight at Sawyer like that? It wasn't very fucking subtle, that was for sure. It also wasn't all that clever.

"Oh, I'll definitely let you know if I need anything smaller," Juliet said, handing the pen back to the guy.

"Smaller?" the guy repeated.

"Well, *smaller* is the only reason I can think that I'd need to call you," Juliet said.

Sawyer studied Juliet's face. Did she realize what the guy was implying?

"Oh, honey, we've got bigger, too," the guy said. "A lot bigger. As big as you can handle."

Juliet lifted a brow and Sawyer felt satisfaction expand his chest. Oh yeah, she knew what the guy was insinuating.

"I really think we have *big* covered," she said. She cast a look at Sawyer, then back to the guy. "I mean, it could be too much, honestly. But I'll need to give it a try before I know for sure." Yeah, there was no question what *she* was inferring, either.

Holy hell, he liked her.

Yeah, you'll need to give it a try, Sawyer thought. *No worries. It will be exactly how much you need.*

He wasn't even shocked by the thoughts. He hadn't had any like them in months, but he welcomed them. This was normal. When a hot girl talked about big wood, especially with a little gleam in her eyes, it was *normal* to think dirty thoughts. This was good. Maybe faking being okay for his family wasn't going to be that difficult. Maybe it wouldn't all be fake.

Sawyer didn't even bother to cover his grin as he met the other man's stare.

"Yeah, okay, well, whatever." The guy tore the top page off his clipboard and handed it over to Juliet. "You have my number."

She handed it to Sawyer. "Sawyer will give you a call if we have any problems."

The guy finally gave a resigned sigh. "You Sawyer?" he asked.

"Yep." Sawyer tucked the number into his front pocket.

"Great."

Yeah, Sawyer thought so, too.

The guy headed up the incline toward the trucks, and Juliet turned and started toward the pile of wood.

That was it? No more flirting? No more wood innuendo? How about some direct comments about the size of the wood around here?

Sawyer grinned. Totally normal thoughts.

Before he could start that conversation, however, Chase came ambling down the hill, a cookie in hand, and Juliet gave him a smile. Sawyer watched the siblings for a moment. Juliet looked so affectionate when she looked at Chase. Clearly she was exasperated with him, but it was also obvious that she loved him.

Damn, he knew that mix of feelings well. Very, very well.

Sawyer went to join them.

"Do you have work gloves?" she asked Chase as he stopped in front of her.

"Uh, no." Chase finished off the cookie and looked his sister over. "I don't have any of that, either." He grinned. "But I'm guessing there's a bag with my name on it in your rental car."

Juliet nodded. "There is. Behind the driver's seat. Hope the vest fits."

Chase laughed. "I'm not wearing a safety vest."

She frowned. "You should. They're not used to having us around down here. It doesn't hurt to be sure they see you."

Chase rolled his eyes. "Jules, these guys *all* see you. Trust me. And I'm not wearing a bright green safety vest."

Sawyer glanced around. Were there other guys gawking at Juliet?

"You'd prefer yellow?" she asked dryly.

"I'm not wearing a vest," Chase said again.

Juliet sighed. "Okay, if you get run over, don't complain to me." She shrugged out of her safety vest and pulled on the life jacket that had been hanging on the end of the sawhorse. Then she pulled the safety vest on over the life jacket.

Overkill. For sure.

Sawyer grinned.

"If that happens, I'll only expect the small balloon bouquet, not the large," Chase said with a nod.

Sawyer almost chuckled. Chase had a sense of humor. That was going to be handy down here.

Juliet reached for an accordion folder on top of the closest stack of wood planks. She flipped it open and pulled out a sheet of paper. "Here are the plans. I figure we'll cut and weather treat the boards here, get enough for the first section, and then do the framing closer to the shore."

Sawyer looked from her to the paper she spread out on top of the wood. She knew about the weather treating and framing, huh? Okay that was good. He squinted at the paper. That actually looked like true plans for a boat dock. With specific measurements and everything to scale. He leaned in. "Did you do this?"

She cleared her throat and Sawyer realized he was essentially leaning *over* her. He straightened but didn't step back. He didn't mind being in her personal space and she smelled good. If she wanted more room, she could ask for it.

"I did," she said, looking back at the plans. "I based it off of what was here before. But if you want it shorter or longer or wider or whatever, just say so."

"You had the measurements of the original dock?"

"Yes."

"How?"

"Owen."

Right. Sawyer had to quit forgetting that everyone was in on this but him. He let out a breath and focused on her plans. "Looks good," he said, surprised to find he actually meant it.

She gave him a dazzling smile, and Sawyer realized in a flash that a smile like that could get him to agree with her on pretty much anything. He needed to tread very carefully around Juliet Dawson and her smiles. And her safety vest.

She leaned and grabbed the tool belt that had been draped over the woodpile. She strapped it around her waist, settling it on her hips. Then she plucked a pair of safety goggles from the front pocket and put them on.

She smiled up at him behind the plastic lenses.

Dammit.

He turned to Chase. "You need to get suited up?"

Chase grinned. "I think I'm good."

"At least wear work gloves," Juliet protested.

"Jules, I'm good," Chase insisted. He gave her a little frown. "Sawyer's not wearing work gloves."

Juliet squinted up at Sawyer. "That's because Sawyer probably has calluses that are two inches thick." She looked at her brother. "Or did you develop calluses from the keg stands and video game controllers?"

Sawyer felt the corner of his mouth twitch. His callouses weren't *that* thick but, yeah, he worked with his hands, and yeah, his palms could probably leave a few tiny abrasions on Juliet's smooth skin.

He felt his lower body tighten and *almost* pushed those thoughts away. But, no, that was okay. Getting turned on by the thought of touching a woman, leaving faint marks, was normal. He was fine.

Safety goggles, no. Running his rough hands all over Juliet's body, yes.

Chase sighed. "Where are the gloves?"

"Here." She pulled another pair from another pocket on her tool belt.

"You had a backup pair?" Chase asked.

"Of course."

"Of course," Chase muttered.

"You guys start over there," she said, pointing toward the farthest stack of wood. "I'll start here."

There were sawhorses set up in both locations and there were already boards resting on top of them for cutting and staining.

"We're working separately?" Sawyer asked her.

She glanced at Chase and said, "The guys already hooked the extension cord to the saw and got it all set up," she said. "But be sure you read the safety instructions."

Chase opened his mouth, then shut it, and nodded. "You got it."

Juliet waited until he was a few yards away, then said to Sawyer, "I haven't gone over any of the plans or anything with Chase. I'd love it if you'd do that."

"They're your plans."

"But you can review them with him."

"Why wouldn't you do it?"

"Mostly because I think it would be nice for him to learn it from you. But also because he'll think I've overdone it all."

Sawyer nodded, fighting a smile. "Have you?" He already knew the answer. He didn't know her well, had really just met her, and yet some things about Juliet were very obvious.

"Probably," she admitted.

One was that she went a little overboard on things. Another

was that she was aware of it and was adorably self-deprecating about it.

Adorably. There was that word again.

"Why do you want him to learn it from me? Isn't it a good thing for him to realize his sister knows how to use power tools and stuff?" Sawyer had been raised around extremely capable women. It had never occurred to him that his grandmothers, mom, sister, aunts, or really any of the women he knew, could *not* do something they wanted to do. But some men needed to be whacked over the head with the idea that women were as capable, if not *more* capable, than men.

"Oh, Chase is very aware of what I can...and can't...do," Juliet said. Her gaze flicked away from Sawyer's for a moment, then came back.

"Does he give you a hard time about things you can't do?" Sawyer felt himself frowning. Did Juliet need him to teach Chase some manners?

"What? No," she said, shaking her head. "Chase is awesome. We're close. He's always been great about...everything."

There was a little pause before "everything." Just like there had been before she said "can't" before. "What's everything?"

"Just...everything," she said. "How things are. He's always been my ally. Always been there with me. But I know he wants to do more. He does more with his stupid fraternity brothers and Ryan and Rhett..." She trailed off and then gave a little shrug. "I'd like him to have some more down-to-earth experiences."

Sawyer felt a little lost. Chase wanted to do more. What did that mean? He'd been Juliet's ally? That was a strange word to use. Wasn't it? "Who are Ryan and Rhett?" Sawyer wasn't sure why that was the question he'd finally settled on asking. But he sensed the rest of it had to do with something personal with Juliet. He didn't need to get personal with her. Or Chase. He was personal with more than enough people. His people were a handful and he knew more details about all of them than he really cared to, honestly.

He knew about the side effects of Leo's cholesterol medication, Ellie's issues with her now-ex boyfriend, Trevor, about how Ellie and Leo were hooking up again, after being divorced for several years but remaining best friends, and how doing it on the crappy couch in Leo's trailer was bad for Ellie's hip. And that was all just his one set of grandparents. Yeah...he knew more than enough details about his people's lives. His dance card was full.

"Rhett is our oldest brother," Juliet said. "Ryan is second. They love to ski and go hang gliding and scuba diving. I think now that he's been off at college, Chase is realizing that he's missed some things and wants to be a little more adventurous."

"Honey, I'm not takin' your brother hang gliding," Sawyer said. Fuck no. Even if he knew how or had the means, there was nothing about that that sounded good to him. Now he flashed to all the dangers of it, but even before he'd become a safety-obsessed wacko, nothing about hanging thousands of feet over the ground sounded fun.

"Good," she said. "I don't want him to hang glide."

She gave a little shudder, and Sawyer assumed that she felt similarly about being that far up in the air without a solid airplane around her.

"I want him to have some more down-to-earth experiences. Everything about Autre is different from what he's used to and there's a lot of..." Again she trailed off.

Sawyer chuckled. "There's a lot of *a lot* of stuff down here. Critters, humidity, bullshit, moonshine...just for starters."

"I was going to say testosterone," she said. "There's a lot of testosterone down here."

That caught Sawyer off guard, but he laughed again. "Well, yeah, there's that, too."

He wasn't going to pretend that he didn't know what she

was talking about. What he and Josh and Owen did for a living required strength and stamina, being good with their hands, and a willingness to get dirty and sweaty. He knew from the boatloads of tourists they took out every year that even the outdoorsmen from up north found the hunting, fishing, trapping, camping, and boating on the bayou interesting and different. Then there were the guys who wore suits to work in offices every day. They loved the stories about living and working on the bayou. And then there were the women. It wasn't hard to get the impression that people found what he and the guys did down here...manly, for lack of a better word.

"I'll tell you what," he said, letting his southern drawl really hang out. "I think drivin' airboats and huntin' gators is way manlier than hang gliding." He did. He really did. So was fixing those airboats and butchering those gators and well, pretty much everything else he did down here on a daily basis. Fuck hang gliding.

Juliet *almost* rolled her eyes. He could tell it had almost happened. And it made him grin.

"Yeah, well, based on his recent escapade with the airboat and all," she said, "I think maybe Chase wants a little more of the bayou experience. He could definitely use some time around hardworking testosterone instead of golfing testosterone."

Sawyer appreciated her admiration. Okay, she hadn't *said* she admired him and what he did for a living, but she obviously was more a fan of *his* influence on Chase than their own brothers' influences. Interesting. He wanted to know more. But he was *not* going to ask. He also wasn't going to flex his muscles in front of her. Much. That urge was as juvenile as thinking of sex anytime someone said "nailed."

Tommy would have done the same damned thing though.

The thought hit him out of the blue.

But it was true. Tommy would have loved hearing about

how masculine Juliet thought they all were and he would have strutted for her for sure. He would have definitely thought of sex with "nailed" and "pounded" and "drilled." He probably would have said something flirtatious and inappropriate to her about it, too.

Because it was all just in fun. It just meant that he wasn't taking things too seriously. It was just a dumb way to make a beautiful girl laugh and maybe blush a little.

There was no harm in that.

Maybe having a few juvenile urges wasn't all bad. Maybe it meant that the good old boy inside Sawyer hadn't completely disappeared.

"Okay, you want some *real* men hanging out with your brother, you got it," Sawyer said, giving her a grin that felt surprisingly easy. "And if there's anything you can think of that *you* might need from a real man with plenty of testosterone, you just let me know."

It was a dumb, cocky thing to say and Sawyer was shocked by how much he loved having said it. Especially when that *did* get a little blush from Juliet.

He also vaguely remembered flirting. And being dumb and cocky. It was all coming back so quickly, he was a little shocked.

She cleared her throat and shook her head. "Am I going to regret having my baby brother hang out with you all?"

Sawyer laughed and said honestly, "Maybe. But I promise that even if he builds up a tolerance for moonshine, falls in love with fried gator, learns to swear in French, and ends up knowing all the words to 'Jambalaya,' he'll also know how to build a dock and maybe even how to catch and clean a catfish."

Juliet blew out a breath. "There's plenty of that moonshine to go around, right?"

Sawyer was nearly overcome by the urge to kiss her at that moment. "*Always* plenty of moonshine," he promised.

Then he headed for Chase. The Dawson he was supposed

to be spending time with and influencing, before he ended up kissing the one who was feeling like a pretty damned good influence on *him*.

———

TESTOSTERONE. FREAKING. EVERYWHERE.

Juliet risked a glance in Sawyer and Chase's direction.

They were cutting boards. As they had been for the past hour or so. Just as she'd asked them to do. Exactly according to plan.

So why did everything about coming to Autre feel unexpected?

Juliet flipped her long ponytail over her shoulder and focused on the board in front of her. She bent and traced a line in pencil along the edge of the ruler. She was behind where Chase and Sawyer were with cutting the boards, but there were two of them, one of whom had done this before. And she had to measure everything five times. But still, the point wasn't how many boards they could cut in what amount of time, it was Chase actually cutting boards with his own two hands.

She hadn't been exaggerating or kidding about wanting him around men who worked for a living rather than men whose idea of manual labor was lifting their skis on and off the top of their SUV.

Was she bitter toward Rhett and Ryan because they'd left her out of all of those ski trips? Yep. She owned that. She loved her brothers, but she didn't really *like* them much. They hadn't given her a lot of reasons to like them. They'd left her behind. Rather than slowing down and making some adjustments for her, they'd gone on without her because taking her along had been too much work. That was hard to like.

But she'd had Chase. He'd been her travel and adventure buddy. That meant more things like sightseeing tours and hot-air balloon rides rather than rock climbing and hang gliding. But he'd been okay with it.

Well, he hadn't *really* known what he was missing.

The past four years had been a little different. He'd been in college and she'd been in law school. He'd been in the fraternity with guys who skied and scuba dived. She hadn't come home to visit as often once she was buried in law school work, so he'd had some time with Ryan and Rhett without her. They'd started inviting him along, first for beers, then ball games, and then, yes, skiing.

"You need to do something with your hair."

Sawyer's deep voice startled her and the pencil line veered sharply to the right as she looked up quickly. She'd been lost in thought about Chase and hadn't even noticed that their saw was quiet. She looked over but didn't see her brother.

"He headed into Ellie's for a break," Sawyer said.

"Oh." She frowned and glanced at her watch. They'd been working for a while and it was getting warm. "Okay."

"You need to do something with your hair," he said again.

She had her long hair in a ponytail hanging down her back. Well, when it wasn't slipping forward as she bent over. She flipped it over her shoulder again. "What do you mean?"

"It's too long to just pull back. It keeps blowing in your face. Or it's going to get caught in the tools or something."

Juliet glanced at the circular saw that lay to one side. "You think so?" Could her hair get caught and twisted around the blade? That was a scary thought. "Wouldn't the saw just cut it off?" she asked, truly curious.

Sawyer looked at the saw then back to her. "Maybe. But it keeps blowing in your face. What if it does that while you're using the saw and you don't see how close to you are to your finger and you cut the tip off?"

Okay, *that* was terrifying. Her eyes widened and she dropped her pencil and shook her work gloves off. She pulled the hard hat off and grabbed her ponytail, pulling it up and wrapping it around the base into a bun. She didn't have anything to secure it with, but she grabbed the hat again and put it on, tucking the hair up underneath it. She dropped her hands and looked up at Sawyer.

"Bend over," he said.

Her eyes got wide again but not for the same reason. That sounded…

"Bend over the board and pretend you're measuring or cutting," he explained, almost as if he knew what she'd been thinking.

Juliet wasn't sure if she should grin or blush at that. She wasn't used to her mind wandering into dirty territory so easily. Then again, she wasn't used to being around men like Sawyer Landry. At all.

It was the testosterone all over the place. Had to be.

She did what he suggested, bending over to pick up her pencil. The hat wasn't sitting fully on her head with her long hair piled up under it and it tipped, her hair slipped, and the hat fell off with her hair swinging free again. She sighed.

"You have a pair of scissors?" she asked him, straightening.

"Scissors? No. I can get some."

"You want to help me chop it off?"

"Your hair?" he asked, eyebrows up. "Uh, no."

"You think Kennedy would do it?" she asked, bending to retrieve the hat and setting it on top of the board she'd been drawing on.

"I do," he said. "But you're not cutting your hair."

"It's in the way."

"Don't overreact."

"What do you suggest?"

"Braid it," he said, lifting a shoulder. "A French braid would keep it at the back of your head and out of the way."

Juliet blinked at him. "You know about French braids?"

Sure, she supposed he'd *seen* them. His grandmother's hair had been braided that morning. He had a sister. But she didn't think men paid all that much attention to hairstyles or at least what they were called. Or realized that sometimes they were just functional and had nothing to do with the men looking at them.

"I do know French braids." He stepped closer. "I know lots of things."

She couldn't help her grin. He was flirting with her. Again. He also seemed a little startled by it. Again. It was as if it was happening accidentally.

"Well, that's not a bad suggestion," she told him. "But I can't French braid."

She knew the basics. She understood how French braids were formed. She *might* have been able to do it on someone else. Maybe. But the problem doing it on herself was two-fold. Her right hand struggled a little with fine motor movements at times and without being able to see the back of her head, she was unable to go by feel.

"I do."

Again, she just blinked up at Sawyer. That seemed to happen a lot. This man surprised her a lot. "You know how to French braid?"

"I do." He studied her hair. "I mean, we could just put it up in a twist and secure it with that pencil, but you seem to need that pencil." He gave the board she'd been drawing on an amused look. "A lot."

"Measure twice, cut once," she said. "That's a well-known rule in construction."

He nodded. "Where's the measure five times come in?"

He'd apparently been watching her. She'd been trying *not* to watch him—unsuccessfully—but she hadn't noticed him watching her. That gave her a surprising tingly feeling. She was used to people watching her, actually. Her parents had downright hovered, especially when she was handling sharp objects. But Sawyer hadn't hovered. He'd let her work. This whole thing with her hair was the first thing he'd really commented on, period. And he wasn't wrong about it.

Her parents, on the other hand, were also pros at the What-If game. It wasn't like she'd fallen into that habit on her own. After Juliet had fallen off the slide at the water park, broken her arm, and nearly drowned, Patricia Dawson had become an expert at assuming the worst would happen. It was what had created Juliet's penchant for safety and protective gear and her elaborate planning ahead. Those were the only things that had made her mother back off even slightly.

Juliet decided to ignore Sawyer's comment about her measuring repeatedly. "You could put my hair up in a twist and secure it with a pencil?" she asked. That seemed very practical and yet something that she was surprised Sawyer would even think of, not to mention be able to *do*.

He nodded, studying the top of her head again. "But that would make that hard hat not fit. And I assume you want to keep that on?" His amused gaze was on her face now.

"I do," she said. "Head protection is important."

"Especially when everything you're working with is on the ground."

"Something could happen," she protested. "What if I'm cutting a board and a bird suddenly swoops in and startles me and I jerk the saw and bump into the board and it goes flying?"

Sawyer shook his head, almost as if amazed by her What-If scenario. "The board is going to fly *up* rather than falling to the ground?"

"If I jerk and bump it just right." She wasn't saying it was *likely*. But it was possible.

"Okay. So, the hard hat stays on," Sawyer said easily.

He wasn't going to make fun of her or argue. She liked that.

"That means a French braid," he concluded.

It wasn't a *bad* idea. In fact, it was a pretty good idea. But he was going to have to do it. Suddenly she realized that meant Sawyer was going to put his hands on her. Tingles tickled down her spine and she swallowed hard. "You're going to braid my hair?"

His eyes darkened slightly. Was the whole his-hands-on-her occurring to him, too? And affecting him?

"Guess so." His voice was a little gruffer.

"Well, okay then."

He moved in closer. "Turn around."

She did, preparing herself for his touch. *It's just your hair. It's a braid. This isn't sexy.*

Sawyer dragged the hair elastic from her ponytail and then combed his fingers through her hair.

Yeah, she'd so been lying to herself. This was very sexy. Sawyer started at the base of her skull and raked his fingers up through her hair, rubbing along her scalp, then pulling them through her hair, tugging slightly, and Juliet felt her nipples beading.

Wow. She crossed her arms over her chest and tried to focus on...anything else.

It was impossible, of course. All she could really think about was how big Sawyer's fingers and hands were, how the roughness of his skin caught on her hair slightly, how confident he was even when braiding hair, how he'd come over in the first place because he was concerned.

It wasn't just his hands, either. He was standing close, obviously, his huge body right behind her, emanating heat and bigness and hardness. No, hardness and bigness didn't seem to be things that could be emanated, but dammit, Sawyer Landry did.

As he started braiding her hair, his fingers and the backs of his hands skimmed over her neck and upper back and she knew he noticed the goose bumps. He didn't comment, but then, he didn't really have to, did he? She was just grateful that she didn't actually shiver.

It didn't bother her that Sawyer might know she was attracted to him. It was more that something as simple as having him braid her hair made her horny was a little embarrassing.

It had been a while since she'd scratched this itch. Quite a while, actually. And it wasn't her fault that nature made women react to the big, alpha protectors with the urge to strip naked. It was just science. Yes, she was attracted to men's minds and hearts, too. Sure she was. At least until a particularly gruff and rugged one put his big, hot hands on her and made her not care if he knew anything about anything other than all the best places to put those hands. For an hour or so. Then she'd go back to caring about the other stuff. Probably.

She felt Sawyer loop the elastic ponytail holder around the end of the braid.

"There you go."

His voice was so deep anyway, but she could have sworn it sounded a little huskier now.

Juliet tried to pull herself together and turned to face him with a great-thanks-for-the-help smile that would hopefully cover the fact that she was nearly panting. She reached back and felt the braid. It seemed perfect.

"Thanks. I appreciate it."

He leaned in suddenly and Juliet sucked in a quick breath. But he was simply reaching past her to grab her hard hat. He put it on her head. But his fingertips trailed down the side of her face and down her neck before he stepped back.

Okay, *that* hadn't been an accident.

She blew that air out. Holy. Crap.

"How do you know how to do that?" she asked.

"I don't know if you'll believe me."

An ex-girlfriend. It had to be. "Bet I will."

"Kennedy."

Juliet frowned. "Really?"

"Really. And I can do a lot more than French braid." He grinned at her surprised, confused look. "Ken was a beauty queen until she was thirteen. Was in tons of pageants."

Juliet felt her eyes growing rounder.

"She competed regularly. It was a family affair, and Josh and I not only had to listen to her practice *hours* on the fiddle, but we learned to do hair and makeup."

"Wow." This family was...just wow.

He nodded.

"She fiddles?"

"She's awesome."

"Why did she stop at thirteen?"

"She read a biography of Ruth Bader Ginsburg and decided to become a feminist outspoken against the superficial and unfair standards we put on women and their bodies."

Juliet stared at him, taking all of that in. "That's..."

He nodded. "I know." He looked over her pile of boards. "You ready to take a break, too?" he asked.

Juliet shrugged. "I'm okay."

"You need to stay hydrated and take time to cool off once in a while."

Yeah, cooling off was probably a good idea, but it had nothing to do with the Louisiana sun. If Sawyer would just move his big, hot body away from her, she'd be fine.

"I'm good for right now." She gestured toward the water jug she had sitting on the dirt a few feet away. She squinted up at the sky. "I was thinking about putting a tent thing up though. What do you think?"

"A tent thing?"

"You know, one of those portable canopy things that people take to ball games and picnics for shade?"

He also looked up at the sky, then ran his gaze over her from head to toe. "You're pretty well covered."

She looked down. She was *very* well covered. "No fear of flying debris, bug bites, or sunburn," she said with a nod.

"Guess that's true."

"But the shade?" she asked. "For some relief from the heat?"

He shrugged. "I guess when we need relief from the heat, we go, you know, into the actual shade." He looked amused. "Among other things."

"Other things?"

It wasn't so much that she needed to know other ways to keep cool. But she really liked the way he looked when he was mildly amused. It was a very good look on him.

"Lots of water and sweet tea," he said.

She gave an involuntary shudder.

His amused smile grew. "No to sweet tea?"

"Not my favorite," she admitted. "But don't tell Ellie," she added quickly.

He chuckled at that. "I would never."

Yeah, the chuckling was nice, too. "I've got the water covered though," she said.

"Good."

"Anything else?"

"Well, when we get hot there *are* a couple of other things we do," he said.

Had he moved closer?

Juliet swallowed. "Like what?"

"We take clothes off," he said.

Yeah, his voice was definitely deeper now.

"I gue—" She cleared her throat. "I guess that makes sense, but there are bugs and sunburn to consider."

He gave her a nod. "Sunscreen and bug repellent are important. Cora makes bug repellent that's amazing."

Huh. Homemade bug repellent. She might have to give that

a try. These people intrigued her, she had to admit. "What about the flying debris?"

Sawyer glanced at the boards behind her. "Yeah, well, I guess we do take some risks down here."

Ah, ha. "I'd rather be a little hot than dealing with an infection from a piece of wood imbedding itself in my skin and muscle tissue."

Sawyer paused, then shook his head, almost disbelievingly. "Okay, girl. Then that only leaves one other thing to do when you get too hot."

"What's that?"

"Swimming."

For a moment, looking into Sawyer Landry's eyes, for the first time since she'd been ten years old, Juliet wanted to take her clothes off and jump into a body of water.

That lasted about twelve seconds. But that was twelve seconds longer than she'd considered doing it to that point.

"I don't have a swimming suit."

"You don't need one. The fewer clothes the cooler you get."

"Skinny-dipping?" she asked.

"Skinny-dipping," he confirmed.

"You actually skinny-dip?" she asked.

"Of course."

Sawyer Landry naked.

She just took a few seconds to relish that thought...and the images that went with it. Skinny-dipping with Sawyer might be the *one* way she would ever even possibly consider any of that. "Do you have a private pool with lots of chlorine and a maximum depth of three feet?" she asked.

She wondered if being naked but with a life jacket on still counted as skinny-dipping.

"Don't need a pool when I've got a whole bayou in my backyard."

She shuddered. "There is *no way* I'm jumping in *there*. Clothes or not."

"So, the naked part of skinny-dipping isn't the problem?" Sawyer asked. "It's the water?"

"It's absolutely the water," she said. It was actually *all* water, but water where she could see the bottom, *touch* the bottom, and that was pumped through a filtration system was tolerable. Maybe. For a short period. With plenty of floatation devices within reach. "I mean, other than just the dirt, there are snakes and alligators and fish...and fish and alligator *poop* in there." She frowned. "Do snakes poop? I mean, they probably do, right?"

Sawyer blinked at her. "I've never really thought about it."

She nodded. "They almost have to. And they probably do it in that water, too." She shuddered again. "No, thank you. There are just places I do *not* need dirty bayou water."

"It's the poop that's keeping you from skinny-dippin'?" Sawyer asked, clearly trying not to laugh. "You are *really* thinking about the wrong thing when it comes to bein' wet and naked, darlin'."

Okay, well, wet and naked sounded like a great idea, and when he called it "dippin'" with his Louisiana drawl and added the "darlin'," dirty water sounded like a lot more fun, she had to admit.

It was absolutely crazy how easily this man made her body heat and her pulse race. Had she packed her vibrator? Because she might need to get something delivered if not.

"But there are *so* many other places to be naked," she said. "Cleaner places. Where you don't risk having important things bitten. And that don't involve poop."

She was flirting. Kind of. Referring to poop might detract from the flirtatiousness, but it was closer than she'd been in a long time. Maybe that was why she hadn't had sex in so long.

Flirting would probably help with that. Also, not referring to poop would also probably help.

But, seemingly undeterred by her use of the "p" word, Sawyer's eyes darkened, even as he grinned, and he leaned in slightly. "You have a point. Though getting naked isn't always the best way to *cool off*."

Maybe flirting with *Sawyer* would help with that no-sex thing she had going on.

"Hey, Jules!"

Chase broke into their...whatever it was.

They both straightened as if they'd been caught telling each other secrets. Or about to kiss.

She looked to where her brother was standing on the edge of the road at the top of the slight hill where they were working. "Yeah?"

He was holding what looked like a sandwich. She hadn't ever seen him eat this much. He looked...happy. She frowned. It wasn't as if Chase wasn't a happy guy. He definitely was. But she knew he was put out about being here. Mostly because he knew she intended this to be a couple of weeks of life lessons and he thought she was overreacting.

"I'm going to go to New Orleans with Mitch," Chase called. "He's dropping a busload of people off at the hotels and then he needs to pick up a bunch of supplies for his grandma."

Juliet frowned and looked at the pile of wood he and Sawyer had cut that morning. "You've got work to do here."

"We got a lot done," Chase said. "And I'm still helping out."

"But you—"

"Let him go."

She looked up at Sawyer. "What?"

"Let him go with Mitch," Sawyer said. "You wanted Chase to come here to help us out. If Mitch needs to do a pickup for Ellie, he could use an extra hand and this will keep one of us from having to go along."

"But..." She looked at her brother again. "We have to finish the dock while we're here and we don't have a ton of time."

"Mitch is a good guy. You want a positive influence on Chase, Mitch can be one, too," Sawyer told her.

"Ellie said that he's a troublemaker," Juliet told him.

Sawyer shrugged. "He is."

"Chase is already a troublemaker. I don't think he needs more influence in that department."

"Yeah, well, Mitch has something Chase probably doesn't."

"What's that?"

"A grandma that he's afraid of."

Juliet gave a little surprised laugh. "Ellie can catch him?"

Sawyer shook his head. "No, but she's got a ton of people who would catch him and hold him down for her."

"She'd actually smack him?" Juliet asked.

"Smack him? Nah. Not that she's above that. But she's found something that works better for disciplining us boys."

"I have to know," Juliet said.

"He'll have to sit in a chair behind the bar for a full day and she'll read Ralph Waldo Emerson to him, talk to him only in French—and will respond only if *he* speaks French."

Juliet stared at him. "She'll read Emerson?"

"Well, she'll recite a lot of it. But yeah, as she works, she'll have her book of his poems open on the bar top and she'll read out loud."

"And will communicate only in French?"

"Yep."

"To torture him."

"To—and this is a direct quote—instill some ever-lovin' class and higher thinkin' in him." He grinned and both corners of his mouth went up slightly. "Apparently, if we got into trouble—especially at school—we were displaying a horrible *lack* of class and higher thinking."

Juliet loved this. She narrowed her eyes. "How many poems do you know by heart?"

"Most of them."

"You must have gotten into trouble a lot."

He winked. *"J'ai adoré chaque minute."*

Juliet stared at him.

Damn.

A big, rugged man with a scar and a panty-warming smile who could speak *French*? She was in big trouble here. "What's that mean?" she asked after she'd swallowed hard.

"And I loved every minute."

Oh, she bet he had.

"The thing about Ellie is," Sawyer went on. "If we *hadn't* gotten into *some* trouble, she would have worried about us."

"But you all got into *a lot* of trouble," Juliet pointed out.

"Yeah. But we were all straight-A French students. Plus," he said, tucking a hand in his front pocket. "We liked hanging out with her. Cora slipped us samples of whatever she was making that day. We learned to swear. We heard stories from all the fishermen and everyone else who worked around here and developed a real appreciation for how hard they worked and how much they loved it."

Wow. He spoke French and loved his grandmother. She really liked him. All of these people. But especially Sawyer. "So, Mitch's troublemaking isn't *trouble* trouble."

"All I can promise is if Chase ends up sitting behind Ellie's bar as a punishment, it'll make him a better guy."

"She *still* makes you guys sit back there?"

"She would," Sawyer said. "But we've gotten a little better at hiding our troublemaking." He leaned in. "The trick is to get in trouble all together...then there's no one left to tell on ya."

Juliet laughed. "You all are crazy, you know that?"

"Oh, for sure," he said with a nod.

"Does it rub off?"

"If you're lucky."

She swallowed hard. She'd never had this kind of cama-
raderie. Her family was a lot less...all of this.

"Anyway," Sawyer went on. "Could be good for Chase to see
other parts of our business. What goes into everything here
beyond just having docks for people to get on and off the
boats."

She thought about that. It *would* be good for Chase to
realize that he'd impacted an entire business and a number of
people, not just a boat dock. "But the dock..." she said, one
more time.

"It'll get done," Sawyer said. "Somehow. It's just one thing
we've got going on though."

Maybe he had a point. The better Chase knew these people
and saw what their daily lives were like, the more it would sink
in that a series of bad decisions by him and his idiot friends
combined with a moment of stupidity had really affected other
people.

She nodded. "Okay, fine." She looked up at Chase. "See you
later."

He gave her a grin and a wave and headed back for Ellie's.

"And now you can take a break," Sawyer said to her.

"I've still got wood to cut."

"But you're here working with Chase, right? You didn't bust
up the dock. You don't have to work when he's not here."

She frowned. "Of course I do. We made a promise to rebuild
the dock. If he can be helpful otherwise, that's great, but there's
no reason I can't keep going."

Sawyer opened his mouth to reply—or argue—but finally
he just said, "Okay. Don't overdo."

"I'm safe from sunburn, bug bites, my hair getting caught in
a saw or blowing in my face so I hack off a finger," she said with
a smile. "I'm good."

He clearly wanted to say something more, but he nodded.

She fired up the circular saw and tried to concentrate on cutting along the line she'd drawn. She could feel him standing there, just watching her for several long moments, but eventually he moved off, and she let out a little breath.

Sawyer was damned distracting and she found herself thinking it would be fun to have him around. A lot. Talking in that low drawl, telling her about his family, teasing her about skinny-dipping.

Maybe *insisting* she go skinny-dipping with him.

Or at least insisting she do the first step of skinny-dipping— stripping down to nothing—with him.

Juliet scowled at the board she was cutting. She needed to pay attention. If she got distracted, she could cut something crooked. Or cut something *off* after all.

4

He hadn't hovered *at all*. Over anyone. For three days.

That was...fucking amazing.

Sawyer stepped back from the workbench, wiping his hands on the rag he pulled from his back pocket.

Owen had asked him to look at the motor on their backup airboat and Sawyer had jumped at the chance.

He'd been working on paperwork and running errands for the last two days, but he hadn't had as much to do as he'd hoped. That was all Maddie's fault. Since she'd come home, things had been running much smoother. Files were organized, invoicing was caught up, and their vendors—the guys who delivered bottled drinks, snacks, and T-shirts, and who spent inordinate amounts of time shooting the shit with Josh and Owen and flirting with Kennedy—were suddenly a lot more efficient with Maddie around. Which was helpful from a business standpoint but made things difficult when Sawyer was trying to stay busy and act nonchalant about the dock building going on.

Truthfully, he was trying to act nonchalant about the woman who was doing that dock building.

He'd walked down to the dock yesterday morning, seen Juliet running a circular saw underneath a blue nylon canopy, and been glad that she'd had her hard hat on—if the wind caught the flimsy tent, it could have collapsed right on her. And turned on. Turned on by the hat *and* the fact that he was sure she'd thought of the danger of the tent whacking her in the head. Thankfully, also by how gorgeous she looked in the morning sun in her long-sleeved blue shirt and the blue jeans that made her ass look amazing when she bent over to measure a board. Because wanting her because of that ass in those jeans was normal. Wanting her to wear a hard hat in bed wasn't.

Juliet was quirky, but that shouldn't even be a blip on his radar. Quirky was par for the course around here. In fact, it was a polite term for what the people around here really were. But he'd had a hell of a time walking past her and into the office.

After he'd decided her hair needed to be French braided so it wouldn't get caught in the saw—for fuck's sake—and had then flirted with her over skinny-dipping and fish poop—for fuck's sake—he'd realized that he also wanted to be sure she was completely covered in sunscreen and that the area was fully cottonmouth-free.

Sunburn and snake bites were real threats.

For a woman without long sleeves and pants and steel-toed boots.

That was not Juliet.

He and Chase had been working a few feet away from her for a little over three hours, and it had been clear from the first minute that Juliet had everything handled. A plan. The right tools. Protective wear from head to toe. Literally. Then, instead of just being impressed and happy to have someone so well prepared around, he had made up a stupid excuse to What-If about her circular saw and had French braided her hair.

He'd quickly realized that the only way to be nonchalant

about her and to try to break his new attraction to neon green and yellow plastic was to avoid her.

The old Sawyer would have never come up with that bit about her hair. Of course, the old Sawyer wouldn't have been turned on by her steel-toed boots, either.

He was determined to remember old Sawyer. To show his family that he remembered him. Among other things, old Sawyer knew how to take time off. So that's what he'd done.

Kind of.

He'd taken his crazy, steel-toed-boots-are-hot, can-I-play-with-your-hair self away from Juliet, at least.

Which had turned out fine. The dock building itself was going great. He'd swung by every day after hours and checked things over. Not because he'd been concerned about how things were going, but just because the stacks of wood were on his way home.

Okay, maybe he'd been a little *curious* about how things were going.

Juliet really did seem to have it all covered though. The boards were cut and treated. There weren't as many boards ready to go as he would have expected after three days of all-day work, and they didn't seem to be preparing to frame it up any time soon, but Juliet and Chase were amateurs. Sawyer, Owen, and Josh could have had it half done by now. Skip and Tanner definitely would have been framing it by now. But what was done, had been done well.

Bottom line, him hanging out around Juliet's work site would have been a complete overreaction and he was done doing that.

It really was nice to walk away from it knowing that Juliet was being cautious, keeping an eye on Chase, and doing a good job even without Sawyer being on top of her. Things. On top of *things*.

Because being on top of *her* was a whole other thing.

It was also something he'd been thinking about more and more, even without having so much as a conversation with her over the past two days.

He seemed to be thinking about her almost constantly.

Talk about getting back to old Sawyer.

As he tossed the wrench into the toolbox, Sawyer thought about his "normal" state. In particular, how women had figured into that.

He loved women. He'd had his share of dates and overnight guests—maybe more than his share. He'd never been the playboy Josh and Owen had been before Tori and Maddie, but he enjoyed flirting with the tourists and entertaining the ones that decided to hang out in Autre for the weekend crawfish boil that happened at Ellie's every Friday and Saturday.

But he hadn't been to a crawfish boil, not to mention making nice with the out-of-towners there, in months. He just hadn't been able to pull up a sense of fun or a desire to drink and dance. Both of which was required at Ellie's crawfish boils. He hadn't wanted to pull anyone else's mood down, so he'd just stayed away. Of course, he'd been able to hear the zydeco music and laughter from his house just a couple of blocks over from Ellie's. It had made him miss Tommy even more at first. Then, slowly, he'd started opening his windows on purpose to hear it. That sound was as much a part of his life as the sound of his mother's voice or the crickets and frogs out on the bayou. It was home. It was part of him.

It was time to get back to it.

He still needed a part for the motor and he'd have to head over to Mountville in the morning to get it, but his stomach was growling and, honestly, he wanted to see what Juliet was up to. Maybe even flirt with her a little. Not enough to find out anything too personal, but just enough to get a blush and a smile. Harmless fun.

Just like old Sawyer would have.

When he stepped out of the workshop, however, there was no one around. It was nearing dusk, and they didn't have any bayou tours booked tonight. He looked around. Huh. He'd been inside working longer than he'd thought. He never lost track of time like that.

The light in the front office was on though.

"Oh, of course, Mr. Baxter, I'll get those right over to you."

As he stepped through the door, Sawyer saw Kennedy nearly roll her eyes right out of their sockets as she listened to Bennett Baxter's response.

"Would you like those color-coded?" Kennedy asked Bennett with feigned sweetness. Very feigned. "Or should I just put them in the same folders from last week. You know, the ones labeled *You're A Grown Man and Can Do This Yourself for Fuck's Sake* and *Fishing, Frogs, and other F words* and *I'm Not Your Secretary But My Ass Does Look Amazing in a Pencil Skirt.*"

Sawyer rolled *his* eyes. Those were actually the file folder names she'd sent Bennett. Sawyer had seen them.

Bennett Baxter was the fourth partner in Boys of the Bayou. The very *new* fourth partner. He'd just bought in a little over a week ago. Apparently, Kennedy had decided to be offended that she was attracted to a guy who wore a tie and had manners. According to Maddie, it irked Kennedy immensely that she had chemistry with a stuck-up suit. It amused everyone else. Sawyer tried very hard to ignore it.

Bennett was a good guy, and it was always kind of fun to see Kennedy *not* have the upper hand, but she *was* his little sister.

"Be nice, Ken," Sawyer told her. For all the good it would do.

"It's amazing to me," she said to Sawyer, though clearly Bennett could hear every word, "that a man with a law degree and a master's degree in conservation and biodiversity, can't figure out how to put things into an Excel spreadsheet."

So, Kennedy had kept track of Bennett's specific advanced

degrees. Sawyer wasn't sure Kennedy even knew that *he* had a biology degree.

"You agreed to send him whatever reports he needs," Sawyer reminded her. "He's just trying to get caught up on things."

"I don't remember agreeing to that," Kennedy told him.

"I told you five days ago."

"I remember you telling me to do it. But I don't remember saying yes."

"You don't have to say yes. You just have to do it." Sawyer gave her a knock-it-off look. "That's what *employees* do when their *bosses* tell them to do things."

"You're going to fire me if I don't?" she asked.

She knew the answer to that. He couldn't. Boys of the Bayou had been Leo's before it had been Tommy's and Sawyer's, and part of the agreement they'd made with their grandfathers was to employ anyone in the family who wanted a job. Thankfully, that only meant Kennedy full-time and Mitch and Leo both part-time. They couldn't have afforded a much bigger payroll, for one thing. For another, working with family was its own particular brand of hell.

Especially mouthy family with sassy attitudes.

Leo entertained the tourists from when he picked them up at their hotels in New Orleans until he let them out on the path that led down to the dock. He was often mentioned in the online reviews on the travel sites. Mitch mostly did the work because it was a great way to meet girls. Most importantly, *tourist* girls—i.e., the kind that didn't stick around and get attached.

Kennedy was the only one who worked full-time besides Sawyer, Owen, and Josh. She was also the only one who got a regular, full paycheck. The owners took out of the profits and, obviously, the amount of those profits determined how much they each made. Kennedy, on the other hand, got the same amount each week.

"Worse," he said. "I'll tell Leo on you."

Everyone knew that Kennedy had Leo wrapped around her little finger. Especially Kennedy. It had been that way for twenty-five years. As the only girl in a family of boys, and the youngest of his grandchildren, Kennedy had been Leo's favorite from the second she was born. But he'd get on her when it came to the business. Boys of the Bayou meant a lot to him. Which was why he rarely had to get on Kennedy about it. She knew it mattered to him and she liked making him proud.

"Fine. I'll send them," she said to both Sawyer and Bennett. "They'll be in the email with the subject line *You'll Never See Me In a Pencil Skirt.*"

Sawyer couldn't hear Bennett's response, but he did note the tiny smile on his sister's face. The tiny, not sarcastic, he-actually-kind-of-amuses-me smile.

He did *not* need to know that Kennedy and Baxter were flirting. He couldn't fire Baxter, either. The other man owned seventeen-and-a-half percent of the business. There was no policy against employee fraternization in their handbook. Mostly because they didn't have a handbook. But also because the guys who owned Boys of the Bayou and employed Kennedy were all related to her, or, in Tommy's case, had been family-by-association and had thought of her as nothing more than an annoying little sister. They'd given each other a lot of shit. Maybe that's what this was with Baxter. Maybe she was looking for a new place to direct her sassiness.

Or maybe she wanted in Baxter's definitely-not-denim pants. Sawyer shook that off. He didn't want or need to know that.

Kennedy disconnected with Bennett with a, "Sorry, I can't hear you. The cell reception down here in Hicksville is shit. I'm losing you... I...can't..." She hit the END button on her cell.

Bennett Baxter did not think of Autre as Hicksville. That was Kennedy putting words in his mouth. He might be from Savannah, but he loved everything about their little town and the bayou. He'd been born into a wealthy family and golfed and went to horse races, but he was like a little kid down here and had romanticized everything about the bayou from the crawfish to the voodoo legends. But Kennedy refused to give the guy any slack.

"You know what I think?" Sawyer asked her. "I think you don't send those reports to him until he calls because you *want* him to call so you can flirt with him."

Kennedy gave him a bored look. "Of course I want him to call so I can flirt with him."

Sawyer blinked at her. "You admit that?"

She lifted a shoulder. "He's hot. And he's got a great phone voice. And he flirts back really well."

"I thought..." Sawyer frowned. "I thought you didn't like him."

"I don't."

"But, you're flirting with him."

She shook her head as if Sawyer was just too slow. "He's hot."

"You mentioned that."

"And he's got a great phone voice."

"That, too."

"But he's not good for much else," she said, almost regretfully. "What's he gonna do? Fix my car? Build me a she-shed? Get rid of the bats that are living in Ellie's attic? I don't think so." She shrugged. "So, I'm just enjoying what he *can* do for me."

"Be a target for your sarcasm?"

"Yeah," she agreed with a grin. "And give me stuff to think about at night when I'm in bed and—"

"*No*," Sawyer said firmly and loudly. "You are absolutely *not* going to finish that sentence."

She gave him a mischievous smile. "Okay."

"Wait, you have bats?"

Kennedy lived with Ellie where she had taken over most of the second floor.

Kennedy made a disgusted sound. "Yeah. Little bastards."

"He could learn that stuff," Sawyer suggested.

Kennedy shook her head. "I've already seen him in the suit and know about the law degree and that he speaks a second language and established some foundation to save snow leopards." She frowned. "I think it was snow leopards. Something endangered like that. Anyway, any hope of Bennett Baxter being down-to-earth and manly is already shot."

"He's a really good, smart guy who dresses well," Sawyer said. "What's the problem?"

"I like men who work with their hands and know how to *do* shit," she said. "I mean, snow leopards are great and I'm glad someone's saving them, but I need someone to get the fucking bats out of the attic, you know? Little bastards," she added again in a grumble.

Sawyer looked at his sister with affection. It was most likely that Bennett Baxter intimidated the hell out of her. She liked the "manly" men down here because she knew how to handle them. She was smarter than most of them and knew what made them tick. None of them would ever surprise her or have the upper hand.

The truth was, she could get the bats out of the attic herself.

"What about you?" she asked.

Sawyer lifted a brow. "You want me to come get the bats out? I will, but it will cost you monster cookies."

"That's it?" she asked. "Consider your payment already in the oven."

Kennedy was also an amazing cook. She worked for the

guys because it kept her from having to work with Cora and Ellie, both of whom had taught her to cook and bake, but they drove her nuts. They bickered almost constantly and could never agree on recipes. Which had led to Kennedy putting in her earbuds and figuring out the recipes on her own growing up. She was better than both of them now.

"But no," she said. "When I asked what about you, I was talking about the new construction worker." She jabbed her thumb in the direction of the window that looked out over the area where Juliet had been working.

Kennedy smirked at him and Sawyer sighed. He'd had his mind off of Juliet for a whole five minutes there.

"What about her?"

"There's a woman you barely know operating power tools out there on your property, but you've been leaving her alone, letting her just do whatever she wants," Kennedy said.

"Yeah. So?"

Kennedy tipped her head. "So that's not like you."

"It is," he said. "It's like the old me, anyway."

"The old you, huh?" Kennedy narrowed her eyes. "I remember him. He was pretty cool. He gave me a five percent raise, if I remember correctly."

"He did," Sawyer said. "Great guy."

"If you need something to jog your memory…"

"I'm not giving you another raise."

"Fine." She wrinkled her nose at him. Then she said, "But I don't remember the old you bein' like *that* though."

"Generous?"

"I mean with Juliet."

"You don't remember him being laid-back? Unconcerned about the little things? Levelheaded?" he asked.

"I don't remember him being willing to walk away from a gorgeous woman."

Sawyer gave her a quick grin. "You might have a point there."

"Though you do *look* a little like him," Kennedy said, studying him.

"Yeah?"

"Yeah. You don't look..."

"Stressed? Uptight? Angry?"

"Constipated."

He gave a short bark of laughter. He should have expected that. She chuckled. "God, it feels good to tease you again."

He focused on her. "What do you mean?"

"You haven't been in a teasing mood for a long time, big brother," Kennedy said. "And there hasn't been much to tease you about. I mean, I've *wanted* to tease you about your freak-outs with the tourists and with Owen, but...it hasn't felt funny." She looked at him seriously. "It's been scary."

Sawyer's heart twisted. "I'm sorry, Ken."

"I know." She reached out and covered his hand with hers. "I don't blame you. I just want you to be happy."

He nodded. He knew that. Losing Tommy had been hard on them, too, but it was even harder because they'd also lost Sawyer a little bit.

"Can I tell you something?" he asked. "About Juliet?"

Kennedy, predictably, perked right up. "Yes."

Okay, he could do this for her. It might get him more teasing, from her and from the guys who she would undoubtedly tell, but he understood that would make them all feel better. To feel like they *could* tease him would help.

And what he was about to say was true. He just hadn't intended to share it.

"I'm actually a little worried about..." He trailed off, aware of how this would sound. Yeah, Kennedy was going to really enjoy teasing him about this.

"Yes?" Kennedy asked, leaning in, clearly eager.

"I'm a little worried that maybe Juliet's *too* careful."

It was true. It had been in the back of his mind since he'd first met her. At first it had been funny. Then it had given him some peace of mind. Then he'd found out that she'd not only never skinny-dipped, but she was adamantly against it. For safety reasons. Reasons that made sense.

Natural water, be it bayou, river, lake, or ocean, was dirty. Full of critters. And critter poop. He grinned thinking about that. Had a woman ever turned him on talking about if snakes pooped or not? That would be a very definite no.

But the point was, skinny-dipping was fun. Spontaneous. Not something to be over-thought. He wondered if Juliet ever did anything like that—just did something because it felt good without a whole accordion file for it.

He wanted to take Juliet Dawson skinny-dipping.

More specifically, Juliet Dawson was making him want to go skinny-dipping again, in spite of the possible dangers.

That was huge. Really huge.

Kennedy blinked at him. She leaned in. "Excuse me? Could you repeat that?"

Sawyer felt satisfaction slip through his chest. He was making Kennedy happy. Could he give her this much? For that smile? Absolutely.

"I'm worried Juliet is maybe *too* careful. I think she needs to lighten up a little."

Kennedy slowly shook her head back and forth. "Hallelu-jah. Praise the Lord," she said, still with a note of disbelief in her tone. "He really is back."

Sawyer felt a kick behind his breastbone at that. "I don't know about that," he said, meeting what she'd said, and meant, head-on. "But maybe he's on his way."

He was shocked to see Kennedy's eyes fill with tears. She

leaned over the counter and wrapped her arms around his neck. "I'll take it," she said, her voice raspy.

He let her squeeze him, actually blinking rapidly himself as he felt his eyes stinging.

Fuck. He knew that he'd been stressing them all out, but he hadn't realized he could bring his tough-as-nails sister to tears.

Kennedy sat back after a long moment. She sniffed. "So, what are you gonna do about her?"

If Kennedy's tears had shocked him, the impressively long list of things he'd like to do with—and to—Juliet Dawson that tripped through his mind actually took him aback.

Wow. He hadn't realized just how subconsciously filthy his thoughts had gotten.

"I'm going to...keep my eye on her," he said.

Kennedy gave him a knowing wink.

"And maybe get her to have a little fun."

"*Yes,*" Kennedy said enthusiastically. "You should totally do that."

"You think?"

"Come on," Kennedy said. "She's only here for a few days, right? So you flirt a little, have a little fun, remember what it's like to laugh and kick back and be not-a-pain-in-the-ass, but it's nothing serious for you to get all worked up about. Then maybe some of that will stick after she leaves."

For some reason that made Sawyer's gut twist a little. Juliet was leaving.

She'd been here for four days and he'd barely seen her over the last three, for fuck's sake, yet he was already feeling like her leaving might be depressing. What the hell was that?

Stupid. That's what it was. But yeah, maybe the two weeks with her could snap him out of his funk, remind him how to have fun, prove that he didn't have to be on top of everyone and everything all the time.

He could just be on top of Juliet.

And not in the if-I-leave-her-alone-she-might-die way. Instead, it could be in the I-really-need-to-get-her-naked-in-water-of-some-kind way.

"Yeah. Okay, maybe."

Kennedy lit up at that. As would the rest of his family when she told them that he was not just smiling more, but that he wasn't breaking out in hives at the idea of having fun. Hell, he'd even used the word and hadn't choked on it.

They'd probably build a statue of Juliet and put it right in front of Ellie's. Or on the end of the dock Juliet and Chase were building.

If he got laid, they might declare an annual holiday.

Was it weird that the Landry family cared about everyone getting laid? Maybe. But they were a weird bunch. Who all thought getting laid regularly was a really good thing. Right up there with homemade cornbread and live music on Friday nights.

"You goin' up to dinner?" he asked.

"Yeah." Kennedy quickly closed down the computer, pocketed her phone, switched off the little lamp on the counter, and slid off the stool. "Let's go."

They headed up to Ellie's. It was the gathering spot for his family at the start of the day and the end. He'd never thought twice about it because it had been that way all his life, but it was nice to know there was a place he could always go and there would be friendly faces and good food. They didn't *all* show up there *every* morning and night, but everyone stopped in often enough that they kept tabs on one another and knew if anyone needed help with anything. He was certain there had been *many* conversations about him over the past few months.

It wasn't just his brother and sister and Maddie that needed reassured that he was getting better. He knew his mom and dad were worried, his grandparents, hell, most of the town.

Sawyer pulled the door open and stepped inside with a big

smile. He took a huge breath of the Cajun-spiced air and looked around.

His mom and dad sat at a table near the bar. His grandma was behind the bar, of course, and his grandpa was perched on his stool—the one with the bright yellow seat—and Josh, Tori, Owen, and Maddie were sitting at a table near the back. Chase and Mitch were with them.

Kennedy headed for the back table after blowing her parents a kiss, but Sawyer crossed to his mom first. "Hey."

Hannah Landry smiled up at him. "Hey yourself."

He bent over and kissed her cheek. "You look pretty tonight."

His mother tipped her head. "And you look...different."

He nodded. "I'm relaxed."

Her eyes widened slightly. "Yep, that would be different."

His dad chuckled. "Looks good on ya."

"Thanks. I might try to keep it up."

They both grinned and he felt good about making someone—two important someones—happy.

He headed for the table at the back. Not because he necessarily needed to see any of those people, but he found himself curious about how Chase was doing. And if anyone wanted to drop any information about Juliet.

Sawyer pulled an empty chair away from another table, turned it, and straddled the seat.

"How's the engine?" Owen asked.

"Not great. But I can get a part in Mountville tomorrow and finish it."

Owen nodded. "Want me to go over and get it?"

"Want me to do your first tour of the day?" Sawyer asked him.

"No," Maddie inputted, before Owen could say a word. "It's been *really* nice having *four* full days without anyone talking about the Doom and Gloom tour."

Sawyer cocked a brow. "The Doom and Gloom tour?"

"Well, that's just what *we* call it," Maddie said. "Behind your back," she added. "But it's those tours you take out where you talk about which poisonous snakes and spiders live on the bayou and the statistics on alligator attacks and how much damage hurricanes and storms can do."

Huh. He did do that. He hadn't realized he'd done it *a lot*. But the bayou wasn't a place to fuck around.

That was what had been going through his head for months now.

The thing was...fucking around on the bayou was a very popular pastime down here and something he and his family had been doing all his life.

"Maybe we should market that," he said, reaching for a shrimp on his brother's plate and popping it in his mouth. "We call it that up front, tell people they're going on a ride into the dark and dangerous bayou, throw in some voodoo and ghost stories...we could sell a shit ton of tickets to that."

Maddie looked at him, clearly stunned.

He swallowed the spicy shrimp. "What?"

"That's..." She glanced at Owen and Josh. "That's not a terrible idea."

Owen snorted. "It's not?"

"People take ghost tours in New Orleans all the time. People go through haunted houses and to horror movies. The New Orleans cemetery tours sell a ton. People love to be spooked," Maddie said.

"There are lots of creepy stories from down here," Mitch said. "Hell, there was a supposed serial killer for a while in the thirties or something."

"And there are the legends about the rougarou," Kennedy said with a little gleam in her eye.

The rougarou were fabled werewolf-type creatures that prowled through the small towns and rural areas of Louisiana.

Maddie sat up a little straighter, clearly excited. "If we specifically *tell them* that's what's going to happen, rather than, you know, Stan and Betty from North Dakota coming down to see cypress trees romantically draped in Spanish moss, learning about how they could find a brown recluse in her purse when they get back to the Hilton Garden Inn, then it could be great."

Sawyer grinned at her. That was pretty funny. "We might not sign a lot of Stan and Bettys up." He looked over at Chase. "But dumb college kids down on vacation might eat that up."

Chase grinned back. "Sounds like fun."

"I'll start working on it," Maddie said. "*But*," she added. "We're not there yet, and you don't need any practice scaring people, so why don't you work on the motor and Owen will take the tours."

Sawyer nodded. "Fine by me." He even shrugged. Just for good measure.

Again there was an exchange of surprised looks around the table, but no one said anything like "what the hell have you done with Sawyer Landry?"

"I've gotten a lot done these last few days," he said. "I'm feeling very relaxed."

"That's fantastic," Maddie said.

"Things with the dock look great, too," he said to Chase. "You guys are doing a good job." It was a *slow* job, but it was good.

"Uh, thanks." Chase gave a little grimace.

"What?" Sawyer asked.

"He's not building the dock," Kennedy said, jumping in readily to tell on Chase. "He's been messing around with Mitch. Juliet's doin' that all by herself."

Sawyer looked at Chase. "Oh yeah?" What the hell was this?

"Hey, Juliet is cool with it," Mitch said quickly. "Chase helped me with some stuff for Ellie, we checked Leo's transmission, he did a couple of hotel pickups with me, and then Ellie sent us out with some boxes for Otis."

Otis was an old guy who lived in a cabin on the bayou and was essentially a hermit. Ellie knew him from back in the days when he'd been a shrimp boat captain, but after his wife had died he'd retired to his cabin and was rarely seen now. Ellie sent the boys out about once a month with supplies and, in her words, to make sure Otis was still alive and even needed the supplies.

"And then you went fishing," Kennedy said.

"Juliet thought that was great," Mitch protested.

"You took Chase fishing?" Sawyer asked. "While Juliet worked?"

"Well, it started out with me showing him how to drive the airboat," Mitch said. He shoved Chase in the shoulder. "Obviously, he doesn't know how or he and Juliet wouldn't be here building us a new dock in the first place."

Chase nodded. "Mitch was helping us cut some of the boards and we were talking about it and he said he could easily show me, and Juliet encouraged it."

Sawyer frowned. He wasn't shocked. He knew that Juliet thought Chase was looking for some new adventures and that she liked the idea of him doing it down here instead of on the ski slopes with his fraternity brothers. But she was also all for Chase getting his hands dirty with good male role models who were *working*, not cruising around, fishing and goofing off.

Fixing Leo's truck and the hotel pickups and God knew what they'd done at Ellie's could all be considered work, he supposed, and the trip to check on Otis was nice and definitely representative of the culture and lifestyle down here, where they took care of their neighbors, even when it required a boat ride down the bayou to enable a guy in remaining a recluse.

"And look." Chase held his hand up, palm toward Sawyer. "Blisters."

Sawyer nodded. "Nice."

"Even got a sliver in there yesterday. Ellie dug it out for me."

Everyone at the table winced at that.

"Man, always have Cora do that stuff—stitches, slivers, relocating stuff—she's way gentler than Ellie," Owen said.

Chase looked at him. "Cora puts in stitches and relocates *stuff*? As in dislocated joints?"

Owen shrugged. "A couple guys here have shoulders that need put in once in a while. And she's relocated at least three fingers that I can think of."

"She splinted up Jerry's broken leg that time, too," Mitch said of Sawyer's dad. "I'll never forget the way he yelled."

Chase frowned. "Holy shit. She shouldn't just be splinting broken legs. Did she send him to the hospital after?"

"What for?" Mitch asked.

"To x-ray his leg," Chase said.

"He didn't need an X-ray. It was *obviously* broken," Owen said. "Anyone could see that."

"What if he needed pins or something placed? He definitely needed to have the bone set. And casted." Chase was looking at them all with disbelief.

"She did set it," Josh said. "Moved the bones back where they were supposed to be before she splinted it. Geez."

Chase looked at them as if he couldn't tell if they were kidding or not.

They weren't.

He looked down at his hand. "Ellie put some ointment on my hand after she got the sliver out. She wouldn't tell me what was in it. She said it's because I'm going off to med school and I might give the recipe to some big pharma company and they'd sell it for a hundred bucks a bottle when it only costs her three seventy-two to make it."

"She's completely serious about that," Kennedy told him.

"It's safe, though, right?" Chase asked.

"She's been putting shit like that on us all our lives and we're...basically okay," Owen said with a smirk.

"She's used this same stuff on you?" Chase clarified.

"Well..." Owen looked around and they all shrugged. "She doesn't tell us what's in it, either. I guess we wouldn't really know."

"Might be nothin' but good old mud or something, honestly," Josh said.

"Though, makes sense to experiment on the new guy," Kennedy said thoughtfully. "I mean, it's possible the side effects won't kick in until you're long gone and can't prove it happened here."

"Ah, good point," Josh said with a nod.

Sawyer watched Chase. He wondered if the kid realized they were fucking with him. And that them fucking with him meant that they liked him and that he was an adopted part of the family now.

"And I suppose that Ellie has about a dozen alibis in case I would try to turn her in?" Chase asked.

Sawyer grinned. Yeah, the kid knew they were messing with him. That was good.

"Who ya gonna turn her in to?" Josh asked.

"The cops? The health department? The FDA?" Chase asked. But he was smiling.

Maddie snorted. "They're gonna believe that little old lady held you down and smeared you with some strange potion against your will?"

"Well, she didn't really *ask* if it was okay," Chase said.

They all laughed.

"Just fyi," Maddie said. "Don't waste your time 'turning her in' to the local cop. George swears by Cora's homemade face masks."

"The local cop uses face masks?" Chase asked.

"Oh, sure," Owen said. "But he *really* loves her foot soaks."

"What's in *those*?" Chase asked.

"So you've been off messing around with Mitch, and Juliet's been working by herself?" Sawyer broke in, bringing the conversation back to the original subject. Or at least the one he was most interested in. These tangents could go on for hours and hours. And hours. He knew that for a fact.

"Well, yeah," Chase said, a little sheepishly, letting Sawyer change the subject. "But I promise you, she's fine with it. She's glad I'm having some fun and learning some new things."

Chase obviously knew Juliet better than Sawyer did and he'd been here with her every day. It was entirely possible that she *was* completely fine with it. Still, it seemed wrong that she was out there doing it alone.

No, she wasn't *alone*. Kennedy was right inside the office, Ellie and Cora were just across the street, and Maddie, Owen, and Josh were coming and going on the docks all day. It was also possible Juliet liked the alone-ish time. It was actually damned difficult to *be* alone here. It was one of the things he loved best about Autre and his family. None of them knew much about being alone, and Sawyer, for one, preferred it that way.

Still, it bugged him to think of Juliet out there working by herself.

But he had to be cool here. No overreacting. No *worrying*. No hovering. She was a grown woman with a hard hat who, from what he could tell, was doing a great—if slow—job cutting boards. What the hell did he have to worry about anyway?

"Learnin' some new things like what? You've never heard the word fuck used so eloquently? Or you've never been fishing before?" Sawyer asked.

"No to the fishing thing," Chase told him.

"Seriously?" Josh asked. "You were never on a boat before you stole ours?"

Chase looked around as if he wasn't sure he should admit what he was about to say. "I've been on boats."

"Just not fishing? Waterskiing or something?" Josh asked.

Sawyer could tell his brother thought he knew what Chase was going to say. At least, pretty close. But he was going to make the kid say it out loud.

Chase sighed. As if he knew what was coming. "Just...boats. Big boats."

"Like pontoons?" Josh asked, grinning.

"Like...yachts," Chase finally admitted.

Everyone at the table laughed. Clearly they'd been expecting the answer.

"Yeah, guessing the airboat ride was a little different than drinking mimosas on the deck of your daddy's yacht," Kennedy said with an eye roll.

"I prefer Bloody Marys, actually," Chase said, with a feigned haughty air.

Kennedy laughed.

Obviously, no one else was all that concerned about Juliet feeling left out or working while Chase was playing. Sawyer shouldn't be, either. She was actually getting exactly what she wanted—Chase spending time with guys who were very different from his brothers and college friends. She wasn't here for her. She was here for her brother and the dock.

She was probably thrilled with Chase going off with Mitch and spending time up at Ellie's. Besides, surely she knew she could *ask* for an airboat ride or a tour or to go fishing or any other damned thing she thought sounded fun.

"Did you at least invite her along?" Sawyer heard himself ask.

"Invite who?" Mitch asked.

"Juliet," Sawyer said with a sigh.

"Oh. Of course I told her she could come," Mitch said.

"She said no?"

"She did. Pretty adamantly actually."

Sawyer looked at Chase. "Adamantly? She doesn't like boats?"

Chase shook his head. "Not at all."

"Even the yachts?" Sawyer asked dryly.

"The yachts are better."

Juliet was a snob? She didn't seem like a snob. "Because of the mimosas?"

He could get her mimosas on the airboats if that would make her like them more.

Sawyer frowned at that thought. Why did he care if Juliet liked the airboats? It didn't matter to him if she wanted an airboat ride or not. Hell, she'd be one less person he'd have to lecture about staying safe out there.

Then again, she was one less person he needed to lecture about safety in the first place. It was one of his favorite things about her. He knew she'd freaking sit where she was supposed to and wouldn't try to stand up or reach out for a snapping turtle or some dumb thing.

"Nah, she'd like the yacht better than the airboat because on the yacht she's farther away from the water," Chase said, picking up his beer. "Those airboats are *right there*." He took a drink.

Sawyer frowned. "Right there? You mean down on the water?"

Chase swallowed and nodded. "Yeah. She's scared of the water."

Sawyer sat up straight and everyone around the table seemed to pause. "What?" Sawyer asked.

Chase nodded again. "Yeah. She's scared of the water. Being in it. She almost drowned when she was ten and ever since—"

Sawyer was out of his chair and on his feet.

"—she's nervous around water," Chase finished, his eyebrows up.

"She's scared of the water because she almost *drowned*?" Sawyer repeated. "But she's here building a fucking *boat dock*?" He stared at the younger man but was picturing Juliet.

Working down by the water. Alone.

In her life jacket.

Jesus.

"Yeah." Chase shrugged. "That's what she does. She just... pushes through."

Everyone was quiet for a moment. Then Tori said, "Wow."

"So that's the deal with the life jacket and everything," Kennedy said, for once not being a smart-ass.

"She's just a *really* careful person," Chase said. "It's not just water." He looked up at Sawyer. "You've seen it. The gloves and the boots and everything. My mom used to freak out about all the bad things that could happen, and Juliet learned to counter all of that by being overly prepared and taking every precaution."

Sawyer pushed a hand through his hair. Juliet was here, rebuilding the dock, to help the Boys of the Bayou and her brother, in spite of being scared enough to wear the life jacket nearly twenty-four-seven. He shoved his chair up against the table.

"Where is she right now?" When he'd stopped in the last couple of nights and she hadn't been here, he'd been relieved. It was easier to act nonchalant about her presence in Autre if he didn't *see* her.

That was over now.

"She's just been going back to Cora's at night," Chase said. "She's pretty sore and tired at the end of the day. Cora told her to help herself to whatever."

Sawyer paused. "You guys are staying at Cora's?"

How had he not known that?

Because he'd been *nonchalant*. He'd been *not* hovering. Not needing constant updates. Not asking how things were going.

And this is what he got. He hadn't known Juliet was fucking scared of the water she was working right next to every day. He hadn't even known that she—they—were staying at Cora's.

"Yeah. We were going to go over to the motel, but as soon as Ellie and Cora heard that, they insisted we stay with Cora."

Sawyer nodded. That was no surprise, but he liked it. He looked at Maddie. "Where are you staying?" Maddie had been staying with her grandmother since she'd come home.

Maddie sighed dramatically. "I was homeless until Owen swept in and saved the day." She leaned into Owen who kissed the top of her head. "I'm staying with him for the next two weeks."

"You're a freaking hero," Sawyer told Owen.

"I always step up," Owen agreed.

Sawyer watched Maddie grin up at Owen and felt warmth fill his chest. Damn, he loved these people. He was so fucking glad Josh had found Tori and that Owen and Maddie had found their way back together.

"So Juliet hasn't even been coming over here to eat?" he clarified.

Which meant she also hadn't been over here socializing or, more accurately, showing up so that everyone could check on her, make sure she got some of Cora's muscle cream for her soreness, feed her, and to just generally see if she needed anything.

Dammit.

What was wrong with everyone? They were involved to a fault at times. But with Juliet? They were just letting her work alone every day and then go back to Cora's, also alone, at night?

What the fuck?

He frowned at the people around the table, but they weren't the only problems. What were Cora, Ellie, and Leo doing? Taking care of people even when they didn't need it—or didn't *think* they needed it—was their freaking specialty.

"Cora's stocked the fridge," Maddie said, giving Sawyer a look that said clearly that he was definitely *not* acting nonchalant now. "And Juliet said that she wants to be sure she doesn't get over-tired so that she can't do as much the next day."

"Cora gave her some of her muscle cream, too," Tori said. "I took it over last night."

"Is that what's in the jar that says *Sprains, strains, and automobiles*?" Chase asked. "I saw it sitting on the kitchen table."

"Yep," Tori told him. "Amazing stuff."

That name was the kind of thing that happened when his grandparents and their friends drank together. Which happened often. They were hilarious. Or thought they were anyway.

"Ignore the automobiles part," Sawyer said. "That's just a joke."

"No, it's not," Kennedy said. "Leo put it on the hinge of my car door. Lubed it up and it hasn't squeaked since."

"Yep, we used it on the window track of an old Chevy to get the windows down," Owen said. "Worked like a charm."

Sawyer shook his head as everyone laughed.

"What is it?" Chase asked.

"Some kind of balm Cora and Ellie make. They have all kinds of homemade creams and potions for stuff," Josh said.

"Good lord," Chase said. "Maybe I need to come back here after med school and show you all how *real* medicine works."

"Or maybe you need to come back here after med school and use Cora and Ellie's stuff in your practice and actually *help* people," Maddie tossed back.

Chase grinned. "Maybe."

The new guy seemed to be fitting right in. His plate had clearly held red beans and rice and fried catfish. He was drinking the local beer, laughing and giving everyone crap, as if he was one of them. And even talking about coming back.

That made Sawyer feel good.

Chase wasn't his problem, he reminded himself. But seeing him like this would make Juliet happy.

And yeah, Juliet being happy mattered to him. Just like it mattered a lot to him that she was scared of the water.

So much for being nonchalant.

Juliet was over at Cora's, alone, sore and tired because she had been building a dock *by herself*, and battling her fear of the water. Which, by the way, was a very healthy fear down here. The bayou water was full of stuff she should be afraid of.

But it bothered him that she was.

He *wanted* people to be cautious around the bayou and to recognize its threats. Even before Tommy had died but definitely since then. Now there was a gorgeous, worry-wart here, and he was bothered because she was afraid of the water and *didn't* want to go out on an airboat?

He was going crazy. That was the only explanation.

He turned on his heel and headed to the kitchen, grabbing to-go boxes and filling them with the night's special. Yes, he was going over to Cora's to check on Juliet. He was going to insist she eat something substantial, ask about her sore muscles, and tell her she didn't need to finish the dock.

He was going to do what he'd have expected all of *these* people to have already done.

Ellie waved at him as he came out of the kitchen and Cora blew him a kiss. He gave them both a little wave, but he was annoyed with them. He wasn't going to get into it, but...

Wait, fuck that. Yes, he was.

He crossed the room to his grandmother first.

"Hey."

She looked over her shoulder at him as she slid two mugs of beer across the bar. "Hey."

"Why haven't you been taking care of Juliet?"

Ellie turned to face him fully, propping a hand on her hip. "Pardon me?"

"She's been working her ass off and then going back to Cora's alone and you're all fine with that?"

Ellie narrowed her eyes at him. "What makes you think we're fine with it?"

"Well, she's *over there right now alone*," he said, sweeping his hand in the general direction of Cora's house.

"You wanted us to hog-tie her and bring her over here against her will?"

He was aware that the nonchalant answer was not "yes." Still he said, "Let's just say that wouldn't have surprised me."

Ellie studied him for a moment and then said, "Juliet is something we don't see a lot of around here."

"What's that?"

"Fully independent."

Sawyer frowned. "Come on."

"She's also a bit of an introvert. That's a rare breed here," Ellie said, lifting a shoulder.

"Tori's really quiet." He cast a look at his brother's girlfriend. Tori was sweet and much preferred animals to people.

"She's quiet, but she loves to be loved," Ellie said, the look on her face as she looked at Tori full of affection. "She loves to be with all of us, surrounded by the noise and the crazy, even if she's not as loud as the rest of us." Ellie looked back to Sawyer. "Juliet takes care of herself. Not only does she not need to be taken care of, it makes her a little uncomfortable to be fussed over."

"Maddie is really independent and doesn't need to be taken care of," Sawyer pointed out. "She takes care of us more than we do of her."

Ellie again got a loving look in her eye when she glanced over to where Maddie was laughing with the group. "Madison was like a flower that hadn't been watered in far too long when she got back down here to us. But how long did it take her to bloom? Two or three days?" Ellie asked. "She can *survive* without us, but she wasn't really living. She needed to be loved our way, too."

"You don't think Juliet needs to be loved?" Why was he having this conversation with his grandmother anyway? Juliet was leaving in a week and a half, and he was simply concerned that she wasn't alone to face her fear of the water, not whether or not all of her emotional needs were being met.

"Of course she needs to be loved," Ellie said with an eye roll. "Everyone does. But she needs to be loved *her* way. Which is not exactly what we're all used to."

"And what's her way?" Sawyer didn't doubt for a second that Ellie knew what she was talking about. Juliet had only been here for a couple of days but Ellie was amazing at reading people. She'd been around a lot of them over the course of her life and she seemed loud and like she was always commanding the room, but the truth was, she was an observer. She watched people and their interactions and reactions. She definitely tested those reactions with the things she said and did, too.

"We need to let her take care of herself."

"Why do you think that?"

"The life jacket," Ellie said.

"She's afraid of the water."

"Huh."

Ellie didn't look impressed—or concerned—by that.

"She's wearing a life jacket twenty-four-seven because she's afraid of falling in the water," Sawyer clarified.

Ellie smiled. "I don't think so."

"No?"

"If she fell into the water down there, she knows there are always at least four people who would jump in and save her."

"Okay," Sawyer said slowly.

"The life jacket means that she can save herself."

That hit him directly in the chest.

Juliet was afraid of the water, but she was making sure that if the worst happened, she could take care of it. Herself.

Sawyer studied his grandmother. "Leavin' people alone isn't really what we do down here." *He'd* been leaving her alone, but he'd assumed other people would be in her business.

"No. It isn't. But that girl spends a lot of time and energy being prepared for anything. She plans it all out. She makes sure she has everything she needs so she's not reliant on anyone else." Ellie frowned. "I don't know who made her feel like she's trouble, but we need to be sure she doesn't feel that way here."

Sawyer felt a surge of protectiveness go through him. Exactly what he *didn't* want to feel for anyone else.

"So if we're not helping her and taking care of her, what are we doing?"

Ellie smiled at him. "Enjoying her."

Sawyer paused a second. If Ellie was a typical grandmother, or even anyone else's grandmother, he'd know for sure that she did not mean that in all the not-so-innocent ways his mind took it. But she was not a typical grandmother and the chances that she'd meant that, at least a little dirty, were good.

"What does that mean?" he asked carefully.

"We show her that even if she doesn't need our cooking or our power tools or even us hauling her out of the bayou if she falls in, that even if she's scared of the water that we need to make a living, we like seeing her smile and we'd love to hear her stories and we want to have her around."

He'd already enjoyed her.

Sawyer couldn't deny that.

And he hadn't been all that helpful to her really. He'd made up the French braiding thing. Other than that, she'd been well prepared and he'd...yeah, enjoyed her. He'd love to play more of the What-If game with her. He'd love to see more of that sassy sense of humor she'd displayed when she'd told the wood delivery guy that she didn't need anything bigger. He'd love to just watch her work through a plan, doing all the research and sorting things into her accordion files.

Sawyer blew out a breath. If he was *actually* a laid-back kind of guy, he'd let this all lie. He'd just leave it alone.

But he wasn't going to let it lie.

Because he was not actually a laid-back kind of guy.

"She's only here for another week and a half," Sawyer told his grandmother. And himself. Saying it out loud helped remind him as well.

Ellie shrugged. "I've found that a lot of times when people come down here, or come *back* down here"—she cast a glance in Tori and Maddie's direction again—"they often stay."

"She's a lawyer in Alexandria."

"There are patients who need advocates in Louisiana, too."

Sawyer smiled and shook his head. "So you *are* tryin' to set me and Juliet up."

"A beautiful safety-freak who will face her fears in order to help her brother and who *doesn't* need anyone hovering over her and making sure she's safe and sound every second? Nah, there's nothing there that would be good for you at all." She gave him a soft smile and then reached up and cupped his cheek. The one with the scar. "Be happy, Sawyer. For one minute, for one day, for one and a half weeks. Grab whatever you can get."

He took a deep breath, then leaned in and kissed Ellie's cheek. "I love you, Jelly."

They never called her Grandma or Gram or anything like that. She had always been Ellie. Growing up in a town where they'd had two grandmas and two great-grandmas it had just become habit to call them all by their first names. But when he'd been little, he'd thought they called Ellie Jelly. The name had stuck until he was about five.

Her eyes filled with tears—also something that rarely

happened—but she grinned. "Get out of here. I'm not the one who's off by herself." She looked around the bar with a fake sigh. "God knows, I'm never the one off by herself."

Chuckling, Sawyer turned and headed for the kitchen—and the back door. He was heading over to Cora's, but the fewer people who knew the smaller the chances that someone would come up with some reason to also stop over and see how things were going.

He didn't mind letting Juliet know they liked having her around.

But he kind of wanted to do it alone.

5

JULIET WENT TO ANSWER THE KNOCK ON THE FRONT DOOR OF Cora's house.

This was the first time anyone had stopped by when Cora wasn't home. Juliet assumed that everyone in Autre knew the best place to find Cora, almost always, was at Ellie's. Why would someone be stopping by when Cora wasn't here?

So Juliet took a knife with her.

Sawyer Landry was on the other side of the screen when she pulled the heavy inner door open, however.

A breath of relief rushed out of her lungs and she let the hand with the knife, that she'd been hiding behind her back, relax at her side.

"Hi," she said with a big smile.

Damn, he looked good. He had his hands braced on either side of the doorframe. A plastic bag filled with what looked like take-out boxes dangled from one thumb, his T-shirt had a streak of grease on it, and the jeans he wore had clearly had the pleasure of being molded to his hard body many times before.

"Hi." He, of course, noticed the knife. "Everything okay?"

"I'm not used to people knocking on this door while Cora's gone."

"You could have just ignored it."

"What if the person decided that meant no one was home and broke in to steal something?" she asked.

His mouth quirked up on one side. "What if it was Leo sneaking in to snag leftover food?"

"I don't know Leo well, but he doesn't strike me as the type to sneak," Juliet said, also letting her mouth turn up at one corner.

Sawyer chuckled. "Fair point. What if it was Maddie coming over to get something she forgot to take to Owen's and she's trying not to disturb you? Trust me, *she* can sneak."

"*Yeah, but* she probably knows better than to sneak in here."

"Why's that?" He seemed to be enjoying this.

"Because she's smart. And I'm clearly already a little...over-reactive. A girl like me wouldn't be in a house alone *without* a weapon nearby, right?"

"Overreactive?" he repeated. "Is that what it is?"

Juliet propped a hand on her hip. "Isn't it?"

"Wearing a life jacket when you're afraid of water makes sense to me."

Oh. Juliet felt her mouth drop open. But she shut it, pressed her lips together, shook her head, then said, "Chase told you?" Of course he had. It was bound to come up.

Sawyer nodded. He straightened, his arms going to his sides, but he didn't step back. His eyes were still on hers when he said, "I can't believe you're here building a boat dock when you're afraid of water."

Something in his voice made her pause. It was rough and a little softer and...sounded like admiration.

Juliet wasn't sure she wanted admiration. She was doing something she felt like she needed to do and she was...coping.

She was doing the job in the way she needed to do it to get it done. She wasn't being brave. She was just being her.

But she did like that soft gruffness in his voice.

The gruffness that also made her very aware of the fact that she was wearing only a tiny tank top and a pair of short cotton shorts. The less clothing the better around here. He'd said so himself. When it got hot, they took clothes off. She was fine with that when she was inside and out of the sun and away from bugs. Very fine. But she hadn't been expecting a visitor. Especially one that made her all too aware of every inch of her skin whenever he was around, even when she was fully clothed and wearing a life jacket.

She crossed her arms, trying to hide her nipples that seemed to want Sawyer to be especially aware of *them*. "It's really hot tonight."

"It is," he agreed. "But I gotta say, I'm on the side of no AC if that means you'll keep dressing like that."

She gave him a little smile that felt shy and flirtatious at the same time. "I'm okay," she told him. "If you're here to check on me. I'm fine."

"That's not totally why I'm here," he said. "But yeah, I'm glad to hear that." He frowned. "Actually, that *is* why I'm here."

"To be sure I'm okay?"

"Yeah." He looked puzzled.

"Are *you* okay?" she asked, a little amused.

"Me coming over here to be sure you're okay is ridiculous. As ridiculous as it would be for me to hang out and supervise you with the tools. You don't need any of that at all, do you?"

Juliet lifted her shoulder. "Not really."

"Damn," he said quietly. "She was right."

"Who was?"

"Ellie."

Juliet smiled. She loved Sawyer's grandmother. Ellie let Juliet just do her thing but also definitely gave the impression

ERIN NICHOLAS

that she was there if Juliet needed anything at all. Juliet had been looking for someone like that for a long time without even consciously realizing it.

"What was she right about?"

"That we don't need to help you or take care of you," Sawyer said. "That we should just...enjoy you."

Juliet felt her heart trip in her chest and warmth flood through her. It was partly because that was a nice thing to say. She liked the idea that they might enjoy having her around.

But again, the way Sawyer said the words made it sound like something else. Something more.

Something a lot dirtier. Her nipples thought so, too.

She swallowed. "Oh." She really didn't know what else to add to that. Other than "get in here and take your clothes off."

"You don't have to build the dock, you know," he said. Almost as if he couldn't help saying it. "Not if you're scared."

"I'm good if I have my life jacket on."

"You sure?"

"Yeah. Just like anyone with a disability, I need to do what I can the way I need to do it."

"Fear isn't really a disability, is it?" he asked with a frown.

"Isn't it?" she asked. "If it keeps you from doing things you want to do. Things that other people do without trouble."

Sawyer just stood, looking at her for a long moment. Then he said, "Yeah, maybe it is."

He looked like there was a lot swirling through his mind.

And he looked really good standing there just being him.

And the bag he was holding was clearly full of food and it smelled amazing.

"Do you want to come in for some iced tea?" she asked.

He nodded slowly. "I really do."

She smiled and moved back, giving him space to step into the house.

He headed straight for the kitchen, clearly comfortable in

Cora's house. He got plates and forks out while she retrieved a glass for him and filled it, along with her spill-proof cup, with iced tea.

They set everything on the table and Juliet took her seat, pulling in a deep breath. "That smells amazing."

Sawyer pushed a plate toward her. There was shrimp, sausage, rice, and a savory sauce. She didn't even care what this was specifically called. Her stomach rumbled.

"You haven't eaten?" he asked, picking up his fork.

When was the last time someone cared if she'd eaten? Maybe when she was six. She grinned. "I did, actually. But I think Cora uses voodoo or something to make you hungry even if you were completely full five minutes ago."

He grinned and picked up his tea. "There is very little I'd put past the women in my family." He took a drink and grimaced.

Juliet laughed. "Oh yeah, regular iced tea. No sugar."

"That just isn't right." He got up, returning with Cora's sugar container and proceeded to dump three spoonfuls into his glass before stirring.

Juliet lifted her completely non-sweet tea and took a long drink. "We're going to have to agree to disagree on this."

He took a long draw of his as well and then said, "It's actually a relief to know there's one imperfection."

"In what?"

He gave her a steady look. "You."

She snorted at that. "Oh, sure, safety-obsessed, water-fearing, addicted to accordion files." She lifted her spill-proof cup. "Klutzy. Total picture of perfection."

He was still looking at her, almost studying her. "Klutzy?"

"I knock cups and glasses over all the time," she said. "I use accordion files because they make it easy to organize things but also because I love the elastic band that goes around the outside. When I drop them, everything stays together."

He nodded, then took a bite of food. As if all of that made total sense.

Which it did, of course. If you spilled a lot, it made sense to use a spill-proof cup.

At the same time, it wasn't exactly *normal* for a twenty-seven-year-old woman to spill a lot.

"In Chase's defense," Sawyer said, after swallowing his bite of rice, "I started the conversation about you and airboats and the water."

"Oh?"

"I wanted to know why they hadn't invited you along on the ride and Mitch said you'd declined. Adamantly."

She nodded. "Definitely."

He took a breath and set his fork down. "I've spent a lot of my life taking people out on the bayou. The tours have always been about giving people a little fun and an appreciation for this part of the world. I used to love the big grins and the people who wanted to learn more, come fishing and hunting, camp, hang out for the crawfish boils, get more immersed in everything here." He sighed. "Over the past few months, I've been the opposite. I've been all about emphasizing how dangerous and dark the bayou can be. When people get that excited, wow-this-is-awesome look in their eyes, I try to... squash it. I haven't taken a fishing or hunting group out in seven months. Ever since I freaked out on a guy who wandered off from the group." He paused and swallowed. "I've stopped loving it. But now, with you, I want nothing more than to put you on an airboat and see the wind whipping your hair around and see you grinning and looking around with amazement."

Juliet knew her eyes were big and round. She hadn't been expecting any of that. "*Nothing* more?" she finally asked, trying for flirtatious. Because God help her if this man wanted her to get into the murky waters of the bayou, she might actually do it.

"Well..." He gave her a sexy little grin. "Maybe not *nothing*, but I'd love to see you on an airboat."

"Why?" she asked quietly.

He shook his head. "Not totally sure. Maybe because I get the impression you don't have a lot of fun and, no matter what's happened, deep down that damned bayou and those boats are the epitome of fun for me."

Juliet studied him. "I think it's great that you love what you do for a living."

He seemed to think about that for a second. "That *fucking* bayou," he said. "It really does mean fun for me. Also, hard work. And family and friendship. It's brought me closer to the people I love, given me a sense of who I am and where I come from. I've also wanted to get as far away from it as I can. It's made me happy. And it's broken my heart."

God, she wanted him. The realization rocked through her.

Sawyer Landry was hot. Period. But he had this sexy, flirtatious side that was mixed with protectiveness. A loyalty and love for his family that was mixed with exasperation. A sense of humor that was mixed with self-deprecation. A strong work ethic that was mixed with a fun, charming side.

He was wounded. Not just his face but something else. She wanted to know everything.

And kiss it all better.

"I don't know if I'd say I don't have any fun," she said. "But I don't have a lot of *physical* fun." She blushed almost instantly hearing that out loud and scrambled to correct her words. "I don't have a lot of fun that requires my body to do..." She realized she wasn't really making it better, "...things," she finished weakly.

Sawyer was grinning widely now. "Yeah, I think your body is definitely part of my interest in all of this."

She blushed even harder but smiled in spite of her embarrassment. "I don't do strenuous things that require a lot of strength and stamina," she said carefully. "So hiking and skiing and fishing and boating and stuff like that is out. And just water in general."

"So basically, everything about the bayou," he said.

"Kind of."

There was a beat of silence. Then he said, "You were at least a little into the water idea with the skinny-dipping. Not in the bayou but in a pool."

She nodded. "But that was pretty much all about *you* being naked."

Heat flared in his eyes. "I guess you did mention there were lots of *other* ways to be naked."

"There *really* are."

"But skinny-dipping..." He blew out a breath. "See, you're showing me that while I love a good hard hat and life jacket, being *too* careful means you miss out on some things."

Juliet sobered a little at that. She couldn't argue with that. She sat back in her chair and chewed on her bottom lip. They were talking about being naked and that could go in some really great directions. But, this was her chance to share. If she was going to. How much was she willing to tell him?

All of it, she realized quickly. She wasn't embarrassed about her situation. It was what it was.

"I had a stroke when I was ten," she said.

Sawyer's gaze went from hot to concerned in a snap. "*What?*"

She nodded. "I was at the water park with my brothers and mom. I was at the top of one of the slides, and the next thing I knew, I'd fallen into the pool below. I don't remember a lot of it, except the terrifying feeling of not being able to figure out how to move my arms and legs to swim back up. I couldn't think clearly. I couldn't make my mouth work to blow air out instead of sucking it in."

Sawyer's gaze was intense. He sat, not moving or even blinking.

"My brother, Rhett, pulled me out. If he hadn't been right there and paying attention, I don't know what would have happened." She took a deep breath. "I was unconscious when he pulled me out and they rushed me to the hospital, assuming it was because of the near-drowning. Later they determined that I'd had a stroke and that was what had caused me to fall. The near-drowning was a symptom."

"You had a *stroke*?" Sawyer clarified. "As a kid?"

"It's more common than you think," she said. "Mine was mild and, since I was young, I was able to recover more of my function than older people sometimes can. But I have a thirty-percent weakness on my right side and poor fine-motor coordination. I trip often, I knock things over and spill. Most people think I'm just a klutz, and that's okay, but I have to be aware of those things and I've made adjustments." She gestured to her cup. "I'm not great with fine motor on either side because I was right-handed before the stroke and had to relearn to do a lot with my left to compensate. So neither hand is perfectly coordinated. I have balance issues and feel weaker if I overdo, so..." She shrugged. "I have to be more careful and plan things out and take my time." She gave him a little smile. "It makes adventurous, spontaneous fun a little difficult."

"Wow." He stared at her for a few long moments. Then he shifted, hanging an arm over the back of the chair, angling his body toward her. "Does all the protective gear make you feel safer?"

He seemed truly interested.

"It actually *makes* me safer," she corrected.

"Okay," he agreed.

That was it. No more questions about her stroke, no questions about should she really being messing around with power tools, no sudden excuses to get up and leave.

She tipped her head. "When I was turning eleven, about ten months after the stroke, I wanted a bike for my birthday. But I knew my mother would say no. For the first couple of months, I was unsteady and weak and scared and I didn't want to do a lot of things like play at the playground or even run and play around the house. But I was ten. I got over all of that. I *wanted* to play. I wanted to go down slides and swing on swings. Except, I often fell because of my weakness and balance. It freaked my mom out. She got more and more careful with me and more and more restrictive in what she'd let me do. By the time that birthday rolled around, there was no way she was going to go for a bike. So, I decided I had to do something to reassure her."

Sawyer was watching her with rapt fascination. She hadn't talked about her stroke and physical deficits in a long time, and she didn't think she'd ever shared the bike story with anyone.

"I asked Rhett to take me to the local bike shop. I got a helmet, elbow and knee pads, a bright orange shirt that would make it easier to be seen, a bell, and all kinds of reflectors for the bike. I even took a bike safety class online and got this pretty certificate that I printed out to show her. I presented all of this to her when I asked for the bike. I figured if I took every safety precaution, it would make her feel better and more likely to go along with it."

"Did it work?"

"It did. I got the bike."

He smiled. "And that's where the protective gear addiction comes in."

She nodded. "It was always for other people. At least for a long time. The more *I* was conscious of the risks and worked to prevent them before they were even a problem, the more likely it was that people would trust me and let me do my thing."

He gave her a look that was a mixture of admiration and affection. "Worked on me."

She grinned. "Exactly." Then she shrugged. "But—"

"There's a but?"

"Yeah."

He sighed. "Okay. Hang on."

He seemed to actually want to know all of this. Juliet marveled at that a little as she watched him get up and cross to the bag he'd brought from Ellie's. He dug for the final box and brought it to the table. Inside was a huge piece of cake. It had six layers of cake with alternating layers of custard.

"What is *that*?"

He grinned and handed her a fork as he took his seat again. "Cora's version of a Doberge cake."

"Wow."

"It tastes even better than it looks."

Juliet took a bite and moaned. He was right.

Sawyer cleared his throat and shifted on his chair, and Juliet looked over at him. He was watching her and without thinking, she licked the frosting off her fork. Slowly. Her eyes on his.

"Fucking love this cake," he muttered, almost to himself.

She smiled. He was so much fun to tease. She loved the flirtatious chemistry between them. He'd made her smile every single time they'd spoken. When he wasn't making her aware of her nipples in a way she hadn't been in a very long time. But even that was...fun. See, she could have fun. Just not airboat-on-the-bayou fun.

She'd missed seeing and talking to him over the past couple of days. That was weird. She didn't know him well, and it wasn't as if they'd established any kind of pattern or habit of seeing one another. But yeah, she'd missed him and had found herself looking for him throughout the day.

"Okay, so go on," he said, after he'd taken a few bites. "You said all your safety gear and preparedness makes people more likely to leave you alone, *but*..."

She nodded and swiped one more bite of cake before going

on. "*But* all of that takes a lot of the spontaneity out of things," she said. "And it just takes time and effort. I learned that I could either be fully prepared and safe, *or* I could be fun-loving and adventurous. But it was hard to be both. If my brothers wanted to go on a bike ride, I couldn't just plop on my helmet and go. I had to take time to get everything on, lace up my shoes with triple knots so they didn't get caught, put on long sleeves and pants so I didn't get scraped up if I fell, make sure I had my backpack with my first aid kit, flashlight, phone, mace—"

"Mace?" Sawyer broke in. "To go on a bike ride?"

She nodded. "The more stuff I had, the farther my mom would let me go and the longer I could stay out. I thought of *every* single What-If I possibly could."

Understanding flickered in his eyes, along with a smile. "No wonder you're a pro at that game. You've been playing it for a lot of years."

"Exactly."

"But it made your mom feel better about it all," he said.

"But," she said, "my brothers got really frustrated. Waiting for me to pack up, make sure I had everything, and get dressed with all my gear took forever. Plus, I think they worried. They didn't really want to be out on a bike trail with me if something happened."

Sawyer frowned. "They told you they were frustrated?"

"A couple of times. Then they stopped telling me about the bike rides all together," she said. The little pang of hurt in her chest surprised her. It had been a long time. But that first time they'd left without her was still vivid in her mind.

"Wow," Sawyer said sympathetically. He paused, then said, "They didn't invite you to go skiing, did they?"

He really was paying attention. They'd talked about skiing that first day in regard to Chase and Ryan and Rhett, and Sawyer was putting it all together.

"No. Not skiing, or scuba diving, or hiking, or even on their trip to Italy."

"Assholes," Sawyer muttered.

Juliet smiled. But she shook her head. "And now you know that *I'm* kind of an asshole, too."

He frowned. "How so?"

"I don't want Chase going off with them and doing things they didn't let me do with them."

"Chase didn't go on bike rides and stuff with them?"

"He was quite a bit younger. He ended up stuck with me a lot, especially after the stroke and everything."

"That's how you got so close."

She nodded. "Like you and Josh and Owen. We did almost everything together." She sighed. "But I should let him go. He's way beyond needing to keep up with me and I shouldn't make it hard on him to go with them."

"But they're assholes. He's better off hanging out with the great guys down here." He gave her a wink.

She couldn't deny that she really liked Mitch, and that Owen and Josh and Kennedy and Maddie—for a little extra female influence—had been great to Chase. He was having a good time, smiling a lot and yes, working hard. And eating a lot. Eating *a lot*.

"Well, maybe they're not completely assholes. Maybe I just felt left out."

"Because they left you out," Sawyer said with a frown. "That's an asshole thing to do to someone. Especially their little sister." His frown deepened. "They basically made you pick between keeping your mom happy and being safe and having fun with them."

They had. That was true. "But should they have to give stuff up because their little sister had a stroke?"

"Yes," he said, without hesitation.

Yeah, she wanted him. For sure. "Of course, I'm talking to a guy who knows how to French braid because *his* little sister was into pageants and couldn't do that herself."

He winked. "Fake eyelashes, too. For the record."

"Your family is so great," she said, with a happy sigh.

His smile died but he nodded. "They really fucking are."

Something in his tone grabbed her by the heart.

"I really want them to know I'm okay," he said after a moment.

Juliet frowned. "Are you not okay?"

"I'm..." He took a deep breath and shook his head. "No. Not really." He met her gaze. "I think..." He stopped, then started again. "I think I'm scared of the bayou, too."

She sat up a little straighter. "Really? How is that possible?"

Juliet realized, at the back of her mind, that she should *not* like that Sawyer had some kind of trauma or something in his past. She didn't, exactly. But it made her feel like they were bonding. He hadn't freaked out about her having a stroke. Maybe that was because he had something, too.

"Has anyone told you about my scar?"

She shook her head. "I haven't asked."

He gave her a little smile. "I should have known."

"What's that mean?"

"You wouldn't pry into someone else's stuff."

She shrugged. "I've mostly just been hit by how hot it is. I haven't thought about asking anyone else how you got it."

He leaned in slightly. "You think it's hot?"

She nodded. "Very."

"How's that work?"

"Hell if I know," she said honestly. "Why does having a day's worth of stubble and callouses on your hands and grease on your shirt work? I'm not sure, but it does."

He lifted a hand and ran it over his jaw, almost absentmindedly. "No kidding."

Juliet laughed. "I am *not* the first woman to tell you that she finds you attractive."

"No," he said, again almost as if he was thinking out loud. "But you're the first to lay it out like that. And the first with the scar."

"I'm not," she said, with absolute confidence. "I might be the first to *say it*, but no, Sawyer, other women have found that hot, too. I promise you."

"Huh."

She smiled. "Not sure I should have told you that about the other women."

He reached out and snagged her hand, surprising her but spreading warm tingles up her arm as he ran his thumb over her knuckles. "All I heard was that *you* find me hot."

Juliet laughed. "Good recovery."

"I've never been turned on by hip waders. Until I found *you* on my dock."

Those warm tingles danced up her arm again and then down to her we-love-Sawyer-so-much nipples, and lower. "Oh yeah?"

"And the life jacket and the safety goggles and the bright neon green safety vest and the fucking steel-toed boots."

"Aw," she said teasingly. "I knew we'd get along the second you jumped in on the What-If game."

He nodded, still stroking her knuckles. "I haven't always been like that."

"What happened?"

"My best friend, Tommy, died out on the bayou about nine months ago."

Subconsciously, Juliet's fingers tightened on his. She hadn't been expecting an answer like that. "What?"

"He was out checking traps alone, wading in the waters like he'd done a million times, but this time he pissed off a bull shark."

Juliet felt her mouth drop open. "A *shark*? In the bayou?"

He nodded. "It's rare, but bull sharks can swim up from the gulf. They've been found in the Mississippi, Lake Ponchartrain, and down here in the deeper waters."

"Holy crap," Juliet breathed. "I had no idea."

"A lot of people don't," he agreed. He was staring at their hands. "But Tommy did."

"He was attacked?" she asked quietly.

"Yeah. They can be aggressive if they feel threatened, like most things down here. They're hard to see in the murky waters. They blend in, look like logs." He swallowed hard. "The bigger ones don't usually end up down here. But the babies can since they're smaller. This one shouldn't have done much damage, but it hit his femoral artery. He lost a shit ton of blood pretty quickly."

His voice was softer and she could tell he was seeing it as he told the story. She squeezed his fingers.

"He called me, but he was a ways out and was unconscious by the time I got to him. The fucking shark was still there and when I was trying to get Tommy into the boat, it charged me. I slipped and fell and his tail lashed me across the face."

God, she wanted to kiss him. He was clearly in a lot of pain and she had no idea how to help. But the need to do something tugged at her.

"The ambulance was already there by the time I got him back to the dock, but he died en route to the hospital. He'd just lost too much blood by then. It was too late."

"Sawyer." Juliet could hear the raggedness in her voice.

He looked up. "He was like my brother. We had plans to grow the business, to expand. We'd expected that our kids would grow up together, that we'd teach them to fish and boat on that same bayou. We were supposed to get old, pass the business on to *our* grandsons, and sit our asses on the stools at Ellie's every day and give stupid advice and tell stories that were taller every time we told them. But now...I can't imagine taking my kid out there and teaching him to fish and hunt without thinking about Tommy every damned time. I don't know how I'll ever feel like it's safe, like I can trust someone out there. Because he should have fucking known better than to go out alone. He should have been watching better, been more aware. He should have known that shark was there. But the bayou, the place I love more than anywhere else, took him away. And now I have to deal with loving and hating it equally, depending on it and *wanting* to be here, but also being pissed off...at the bayou *and* Tommy...every fucking day."

He sat, just taking in deep breaths, his hand still curled around hers.

Finally, after several long moments, he looked up.

She just met his eyes and nodded. "I get it."

She did. Circumstances that were totally out of her control had changed everything about how she lived her life.

He swallowed and nodded, too. But then he surprised her. Again.

"I'm just like your mom," he said. "I want everyone to wear hard hats and life jackets and come to me with safety class completion certificates and carry cans of mace in their backpacks," he said. "Metaphorically." Then he paused. "And literally."

Juliet smiled. At least he was aware of it. "It's because you care. That's not *bad*."

"But it's holding them back," he said. "They're missing out on metaphoric spontaneous bike rides because they're trying to make *me* feel better."

Her heart almost couldn't handle this guy. The stubble and the self-awareness? Come on.

She squeezed his hand.

Sawyer blew out a breath. "I really want to get over it. I didn't until recently. I wanted to wallow in it all. I didn't fucking care if people were upset about how I was acting. But now, I see that I really want to be the guy I used to be again."

"Oh, Sawyer," Juliet said softly. "That's not going to happen."

His gaze locked on hers. "No?"

"No. What happened with Tommy changed you. Just like my stroke changed me. The stroke changed my brain. Tommy's death changed your heart. And those aren't things that can be *fixed*." Juliet paused, then said, "It's part of you now. Stop waiting for it to be better or demanding that it *get* better. You have to adjust."

He dragged in a deep breath. "Compensate somehow. Like you do with the spill-proof cups."

"Yeah. Figure out a way to do the things you want to do inside this new reality."

"*You* started coping by getting knee pads and mace," he said. "For your mom. *You* compensated. She didn't."

Juliet knew that he was relating to her mom, so she admitted, "It took a little while for her to realize that it wasn't going to go away. That this was how things were going to be. But there was this time—" She hadn't talked about this with anyone before, either. But she'd never met anyone who needed her stories like Sawyer did. It was kind of amazing, actually, that she knew exactly what he and his family were going through. "I did finally fall off my bike. Of course." She eyed him. "I mean, we can all admit that it was inevitable, right? Eventually, the girl who'd had a stroke, no matter how much protective gear she wore and how many classes she took—and how much her mom worried—was going to fall off her bike?"

He nodded slowly.

"I cut up my shin badly. Even though I had knee pads and long pants on. I hit just right and tore my pants and ended up with this deep gash. So, I sat by the side of the road, pulled out my first aid kit, and cleaned it up and bandaged it. When I got back to the house, Chase distracted our mom while I went upstairs to my room and changed my clothes, got rid of the pants and everything. By the time she found out about it, the cut was already healing."

Sawyer was watching her, his expression unreadable.

"She told me later that all of that helped her," Juliet went on. "It helped her to see that something had finally happened, but that I was okay and that it was healing—even without her intervention. Without her even *knowing* about it. The anticipation of something going wrong was awful, but once something *did* go wrong, she realized that she had two choices—never let me do anything again, or accept that no matter what precautions we take, bad things would still happen sometimes and that there are still things we could do afterward to make them better."

Sawyer didn't say anything.

"And you know what *I* learned?" Juliet asked. "The overprotectiveness wasn't all bad. If I *hadn't* had those knee pads and long pants on, that injury would have been even worse." She paused, letting him think about that for a second. Both she and her mom had learned from something bad happening, and it had changed things between them for the better. "And that even though I *could* do it myself, it was nice to have her help me bandage my knees after that."

"So she totally lightened up and felt fine and never worried again?" Sawyer asked after a long pause.

Juliet could tell he knew what her answer was going to be. She smiled. "No. But it was easier for her to let me go. Instead of keeping me away from the things that might make me need the first aid kit, she took it upon herself to make sure the kit had everything I needed. She bought me a bigger one and just made sure it was always fully stocked."

He nodded slowly, clearly thinking that over.

Juliet smiled. "And because of that, I told her when I did get hurt, which meant that I got stitches the time I needed them and got a tetanus shot the time I needed that. I might not have if I'd still been afraid of her reaction and things would have been worse then."

He didn't say anything for a long moment. Juliet just let him sit until he was ready.

Finally he said, "A few days before you met Maddie and Josh and Owen and Bennett, Maddie took over one of my tours to try to give me a break because she was worried about me. She hadn't driven an airboat in years and she hadn't been on one of the tours in forever. They got down to an area where Owen knows there are gators. In fact, they're kind of trained to expect him. But Owen hadn't told Maddie. One of them got really close to him and Maddie panicked. Pulled out the rifle and took a shot to scare the thing off."

Juliet stared at him. "Wow."

"Yeah. Scared the shit out of me. She could have shot Owen. Or one of the tourists." Sawyer shoved his free hand through his hair. "She was out there trying to help me and it was almost a disaster." He took a deep breath. "But after I calmed down, I realized that she handled it. It wasn't great and I hope it doesn't happen again, but she and Owen were there together and they figured it out. Maddie ended up down at the police station and we lost a lot of money on that tour, but, they—we—handled it."

Juliet loved these people and if they were navigating a life change that left everyone questioning their roles, she could definitely help. Things had been complicated with her and her family for a long time, but they'd figured a few things out over the sixteen years they'd been doing this.

"You're not wrong, you know," she told Sawyer.

His gaze intensified. "What do you mean?"

"To worry. The bayou is a dangerous place. You want them to be safe. You're not wrong to think things could take a bad turn, especially after what happened with Tommy."

He swallowed hard.

"And they get it," she said, her voice softening. "Your family gets why you feel this way and why you react the way you do to things. They don't *blame* you, I promise."

His gaze dropped to her mouth. "Damn," he said quietly.

"What?"

"I really want to kiss you right now."

Surprise rippled through her. That hadn't even been in the top ten of things she would have guessed he'd say.

"Really?"

He met her eyes with a crooked smile. "I am *not* the first man to tell you that he finds you attractive."

She laughed as he used her own words on her. "You haven't actually *told* me that."

"You don't know anyway?" he asked, his voice a little gruffer.

She wet her lips. "I've felt the chemistry," she admitted.

"Yeah. There's a lot of that."

"But why now? In this moment in particular?"

"Because..." He cleared his throat. "You're the first person to make me actually believe that things will be okay."

Juliet shook her head. "I didn't say that." She'd never say that. *Okay* really depended on the person and their definition. "Things will always be different now."

"You didn't have to say it," he told her. "You *showed* me." His voice softened. "Because you're okay. Different than you were before the stroke, yes. But definitely okay. Amazing even."

Amazing. Huh. She wasn't sure she'd ever been called that. She smiled. "Well, when you put it that way..."

He chuckled lightly but quickly sobered. "Really, though, you might be the first person to truly get it. To get that if the bad stuff still has to happen, I really want to be part of the bandaging. They're...taking turns distracting me while the others cover up the torn pantlegs and bloody knees."

"Because you haven't had that moment—the one where

things went terribly wrong but it all turned out okay, even without you."

"But... I have." He said it slowly as if it was just fully occurring to him, too. "I have. Maddie and that alligator. That was the moment. Everything was out of control, but they handled it. Without me. And then..." His eyes narrowed slightly. "Your brother. Taking that boat, crashing it into the dock—that was another moment. Owen and Maddie jumped on an airboat, chased your brother down, and got everyone off the boat before it smashed up the dock so no one was hurt. All without me."

Juliet stared at him. Well, wow. Her brother had been a reason for one of Sawyer's moments. The moments that were going to help him heal.

"That's great, Sawyer," she said sincerely.

"And you helped me realize it."

She nodded. Bandaging other people's knees was really nice sometimes. "You should definitely kiss me for that."

He looked surprised but only for a second. "Come here, Juliet."

6

STANDING, STEPPING TOWARD SAWYER, AND SLIDING INTO HIS LAP, straddling his thighs, took absolutely not one single extra thought. Juliet rested her hands on his shoulders as his big hands settled on her hips. The heat of his palms quickly spread warmth everywhere—up to her belly, down her legs, *between* her legs. She shifted on his lap. The worn denim of his jeans was soft against her bare skin but made her even more aware that her skin was *bare*.

"I'm a little dirty," he said huskily, running his hand up and down the outside of one of her thighs. "I washed up but should have showered. Didn't expect this."

"You probably should have expected this." Her voice sounded a little breathless.

"Yeah," he agreed, his eyes darkening. "I probably should have."

"It's okay," she told him. "I'm washable." Images of showers and soap bubbles tripped through her mind and she hoped through his as well.

He gave her a little grin. "Good to know. Means I can get you *really* dirty."

Juliet felt her breathing quicken. She put her hand against his face, over his scar. "I *really* want that."

Sawyer slid a hand up her back and into her hair. He urged her closer until her lips were nearly against his. "Me, too."

Then he kissed her. It was slow, lips only. He just tasted her. Lingering with a long press, then a brief retreat, then another long press.

Juliet wiggled on his lap, arching closer, thrilled to feel the hard length of his erection against the middle seam of her shorts and his fingers digging into her hip in reaction.

She tipped her head to the side slightly, hoping he'd deepen the kiss. She heard his quiet groan, but he kept kissing her softly. She ran her hands up under his shirt, her fingertips bumping over the hard contours of his abs. His groan was a little louder and deeper now. That was better.

She sat back and pushed his shirt up to his chest, exposing a lot of hot, tanned skin and hard muscles. She ran her flat palms over his pecs, feeling *his* nipples harden under her touch.

"Juliet," he said gruffly.

She met his gaze and pushed the shirt up farther, clearly indicating she wanted it off. He lifted his arms and let her strip his shirt over his head and toss it to the side. He was a gorgeous sight, and she ran her hands over his shoulders and down his arms, relishing the feel of his biceps and triceps bunching. She didn't have time to fully explore before he brought her in for another kiss, this time opening slightly and deepening it a bit. But still no tongue.

She sighed when he retreated a little longer the next time. It was nice. Sweet. Not what she'd been anticipating.

"I expected you to be..." She stopped talking. This was not a time for talking.

"You expected what?"

Yeah. She hadn't really thought he'd let that go. "Just..." She swallowed and pulled back a little to look at him. "I expected you to just take over and go for it and be...dominating."

He gave what sounded like a gruff half laugh-half groan. "Yeah. That's what I do."

"So, why not now?"

"Because you need to time to go through the What-Ifs." He was still holding her hip and had his fingers sunk into the back of her hair. He was also looking at her with a combination of heat and amusement.

He knew her and he was accommodating her quirks. Wow.

"And you're going to reassure me about each one?"

"I'm going to make sure you get them all and add the ones you miss."

She grinned.

"You do the What-If thing with sex, right?" he asked.

Juliet nodded.

"Do the guys play along?"

She shook her head. "When I think a relationship is maybe to that point, whenever we go out, I just make sure I've shaved my legs, I have on nice panties, I have the birth control thing handled—IUD *and* condoms—and I have a toothbrush in my purse. I also make sure I don't drink so I'm fine to drive home if I don't want to stay after."

He blew out a breath. "Wow."

"I happened to shave this morning, I've got the IUD and condoms, my toothbrush is, obviously, upstairs, and since this is where I'm staying, I guess I'm not the one leaving after."

"You've got condoms?"

"In my purse. I'm pretty sure."

"And the panties?" His voice was rough.

"Definitely no worries there. I'm not wearing any." She gave him a mischievous grin.

His fingers gripped her hip again. "Then I guess that's all set. Anything else?"

Her heart was hammering and she really just wanted to take her clothes off. But she also wanted to play with him. This whole thing felt intimate. He understood—and tolerated—her in a way no one else had before. "What if someone walks in?"

"That's a very real possibility," he admitted. "Though I doubt they'd be surprised." He glanced around. "I'd grab that dish towel to cover you up."

She glanced over at it. "That's not very big."

He looked down at her breasts. Her nipples rejoiced at his attention.

"Yeah, we're going to need a couple at least."

She grinned. "What if this table isn't sturdy enough?"

Heat and humor flickered in his gaze. He glanced at the table then back to her. He nodded. "It's old," he agreed. "Might need to just stay here on this chair. Or I could put you up against the wall."

Want washed through her and Juliet had to take a quick breath. Her inner muscles clenched and the urge to press hard against his cock was nearly overwhelming.

"Or we could go upstairs. Closer to your toothbrush and"— his gaze flickered over her—"the condoms, unless you have a hidden pocket in there somewhere."

Juliet wet her lips. "What if you try to sneak out the window afterward and fall off the roof?"

He laughed. "I'm not sneaking out the window." He pulled her in for another long, slow kiss, this time dragging his tongue over her lower lip. "I'll be staying and going out the front door after Cora heads back to Ellie's for the breakfast crowd," he said, when he let her go. "But only because I'll be wanting to stay in that bed next to you for as long as possible. I don't care who knows where I spent the night."

Juliet took a gulp of air. "What if the headboard bangs against the wall and wakes everyone up?"

Sawyer's eyes were nearly black with desire now. "Yeah, *that* is going to happen for sure. Along with a lot of creaking springs. Not to mention the gasping and groaning and 'Oh Sawyers.'"

She laughed even as desire pounded through her. "I guess we should maybe get up there and get going before anyone comes home then."

"But you missed a couple of What-Ifs," Sawyer said.

"Did I?" That was very unlike her.

He leaned in, his mouth brushing over hers. "What if I make you come so hard you can't move for several hours after?"

Air whooshed out of her lungs and she just stared at him. That was a risk she was very willing to take.

He met her gaze intently. "And what if you ruin me for all other women?"

She wanted to do that.

That was a terrible thought to have. She wasn't staying here. Sawyer wasn't leaving here. He belonged on this bayou no matter what had happened and how he felt about it now. And she...didn't. She couldn't even swim. Anymore. That was a complicated result of her fear and water phobia after nearly drowning, but it certainly wouldn't make living near a big, sometimes dangerous body of water a good idea.

"What if we *don't* do it?" she finally asked softly. "Then we both spend forever wondering what it would have been like." She could handle squeaking bedsprings and not being able to move from orgasms so intense her muscles all turned to goo. But she wasn't sure she could handle never knowing what being with Sawyer Landry was like.

Without another word, Sawyer stood swiftly, his hands cupping her ass. Instinctively, she wrapped her legs around him, linking her ankles, and grabbed his shoulders. Unable to resist, Juliet put her lips to his neck. She kissed him, flicking her tongue over the hot, salty skin. She felt the rumble of his groan as he started in the direction of the stairs, climbing them smoothly, as if he didn't have his arms full of a woman wiggling to get her aching clit against his hard body. Really *any* hard part of his body would do at the moment.

At the top of the stairs, he headed down the hallway with long strides, turning into the bedroom she was using, without asking. It didn't matter how he knew which room was hers. It mattered that there was a bed in there.

But he stopped abruptly in the doorway.

Juliet pulled her lips from his neck and looked up.

"What if," he said slowly, "someone put a mosquito netting over their bed?"

Oh yeah, that. "We can just push it back."

"What if there's a bat caught in it?"

Juliet pivoted in his arms so quickly that his grip on her slipped and she felt herself sliding to the floor. Abruptly. She was still against him—and he was big and hard and strong and all of that—so she didn't *fall* exactly, but neither did she have time to really enjoy the slide down the Sawyer-pole.

Because there was a *bat* in her bedroom. Caught in the mosquito netting she'd hung over her bed.

"Oh my God!" she gasped. "What the— Oh my God!"

"Not exactly the way I'd been expecting to hear *oh my God* up here," Sawyer said dryly.

Juliet, her eyes wide and fixed on the flapping brown *thing* trapped in the white netting, slipped around behind him, putting his big, used-to-critters-and-not-freaking-out body between her and that bat.

"What if I'd been up here *sleeping* when that *thing* got caught up like that?" she whispered in an admittedly horrified-sounding voice.

"Guessing I'd have been coming over to get it out a lot like I'm going to do now," Sawyer told her.

She looked up at him. "You're going to get it out?" But of course he was. He was a big, strong bayou boy. He'd probably grown up playing with these things like they were puppies. She shuddered.

"You would have come over?"

"Of course," he said. Then he shrugged. "If I didn't wake up to your bloodcurdling scream, Cora would have leaned out of her bedroom window and shouted at me."

Juliet frowned. "Where do you live?"

He pointed through her window at the house next door.

He was her neighbor? Or Cora's neighbor, anyway. "Oh."

He grinned. "You have another of those nets?"

She did. She'd brought one for Chase, too. Who had laughed and said no thanks. She nodded, a bit sheepishly.

Juliet wasn't shocked Sawyer had assumed she'd have a second one.

"Okay." Sawyer entered the room and Juliet backed *out* of the room.

The next thing she knew he was out again, the net and the bat in hand.

In. Hand.

He was holding onto the thing. It was wiggling but Sawyer seemed to have it under control.

With wide eyes, Juliet followed him down the stairs and out the front door.

Sawyer crouched and set the thing, net and all, on the grass. The bat was clearly trying to bite him, but Sawyer flipped the net back and the bat crawled a few inches away and then took off.

Juliet shrieked as it swooped up into the air. She hated that she'd screamed, but dammit, bats were not an everyday occurrence for her.

Sawyer got to his feet and held up the net. "Good news. I didn't have to cut it."

She stared at him. Yeah. Good news.

Sawyer looked at her, then handed the net to her. "Need help hanging this back up?"

"No." She'd gotten it up there herself the first time.

"I assume you're gonna put it back up?"

She wasn't sure. It wasn't supposed to *catch* things. "The net was supposed to keep things *out*," she said, her voice a little shaky.

Sawyer nodded. "What are the West Nile stats down here?"

She peered up at him. Was he teasing her? But he seemed sincere. It made her feel a little warm—in a different way than his wide, naked chest did—to think that he'd figured her out.

"Louisiana had the highest number of cases in the country last year," she said.

"Figured it was something like that."

She frowned a little. She'd overreacted with the netting, and it was the reason she was not riding the high of a Sawyer-induced orgasm at that very moment. Yeah, she was sure it wouldn't have taken him long to get her there. "Only twenty percent of people infected actually show symptoms," she said.

"So eighty percent of those infected are walkin' around without even knowing it," he said. "Weird."

"Well, only one percent of those infected actually get West Nile encephalitis."

"Still, that would suck," he said. "What if you were that one percent?"

He didn't laugh. He didn't even smile as he said it. He seemed to mean it.

"You're not going to tell me I'm overreacting with the mosquito netting?" she asked. "You're not going to tell me that those of you who live down here don't use mosquito netting?"

"Nope." He tucked a hand into his front pocket.

That pulled the waistband of his jeans down a little and she couldn't help but note that sexy-as-fuck V that dove into the waistband on either side of his abs.

She wet her lips and pulled her eyes away from his lower abs. "You actually think me sleeping with mosquito netting is no big deal?"

"I really do," he said. "It's totally harmless, and if it makes you feel better and keeps you from getting a mosquito bite— West Nile infected mosquito or not—then great."

"It wasn't exactly *harmless*," she said. "I did catch a *bat* with it."

He lifted a shoulder. A big, naked shoulder. "Made it easier to get him out of there. And no one, including the bat, got hurt."

Juliet couldn't name the emotion that went through her with that. Relief? Maybe. Gratitude? That was maybe more accurate. Sawyer's simple acceptance of the whole thing made her feel...good. Her safety tendencies usually brought exasperation, teasing, or worry.

"And," he added. "I kind of got to bandage this situation up at the end. So I'm good." He gave her an almost shy smile.

The emotion that coursed through Juliet's chest at that was something she hadn't expected at all. She felt a bond with Sawyer that was hard to explain. He got her. He understood her, even supported her overreactive tendencies, but she also felt almost proud of him and pleased to have helped *him*, too. She'd done the safety thing by hanging the net and he understood why that was important to her, even if it had resulted in an unexpected consequence. A consequence he'd calmly and capably fixed—bandaged   for her.

Maybe that meant that Sawyer wouldn't worry about her or treat her as if she was fragile like so many men had before. She and her mom had come to some understanding about everything, but men—Ryan and Rhett, her father, her boyfriends— had a hard time not being careful with her once they knew about her stroke and how accident-prone she could be. It was exhausting. To the point she didn't date much.

But with Sawyer, he seemed to appreciate her What-Ifs and Yeah, Buts, and just rolled with it all. If Sawyer could accept everything like he had the mosquito netting, then they could maybe...

Juliet frowned. She was leaving in just over a week. She hardly needed to worry about how he would react to her situation long-term.

"And," Sawyer said, leaning closer and breaking into her thoughts. "I'm thinking that net will also keep out the black widows."

Juliet stared up at him, her mouth open. "I can't believe you just said that," she told him. "I need to *sleep* tonight."

He chuckled. "I'm kiddin'. Cora sprays around the house with her homemade repellent."

"You're just saying that to make me feel better."

"Nah, it's true. It's amazing stuff."

"But it's homemade? Shouldn't she buy some extra toxic chemical stuff?"

Sawyer grinned. "She and Ellie don't do that stuff. They don't want to kill them, just keep them out of the house."

Juliet shuddered. "I think we should kill them. All of them. With fire."

"They eat mosquitoes," he said with a wink.

She groaned. "Not fair." She sighed. "But the repellent works?"

"It does. How did her muscle cream work for ya?" His gaze tracked over her shoulders and then dropped to her breasts but bounced back up to her face after only a second.

Her muscles all felt hot and melty at the moment. As did the rest of her. "Um, good." She rotated her neck. She hadn't realized until now that she wasn't sore at all. "Actually, great."

He nodded. "All the stuff they make works. Don't worry about the widows."

"Okay. If you say so."

"You trust me?" he asked, his voice a little softer.

"Of course I do," she said with confidence. She knew that Sawyer would feel terrible if she got bitten by a black widow. Well, bitten by anything, really.

"Come on." He grabbed her hand, as if it was the most natural thing, and started tugging her back toward the porch.

She was barefoot, which was never a good idea for her, and as they changed terrain from the grass onto Cora's front path, Juliet's right ankle wobbled and turned. Her knee buckled and she grabbed for Sawyer's arm. But before she even got her hand on his biceps, he'd slipped his arm around her waist, holding her up.

"Whoa."

He was staring down at her, his nose inches from hers. She was pressed against him now, his skin hot over all that hard muscle, and for the first time in her life, she was glad she'd wobbled.

"Sorry," she said, breathlessly.

"Don't be," he said, his voice husky.

He continued to hold her against him, looking into her eyes.

Juliet became very aware that her breasts were pressed against his side and there was no way he could miss the hard tips poking him. His big hand was splayed over her lower back and she felt every single one of his fingers burning through the thin cotton of her shirt.

She wanted to kiss him. She couldn't reach his lips unless he bent over. Or lifted her up. But she really wanted to put her lips on him somewhere. She actually wasn't picky.

She'd never met a guy like Sawyer. He was all man. The definition of alpha. He worked with his hands. He could cut wood and take apart a boat motor. But he also did the worst-case-scenario thing. He had a grandmother he obviously loved and an entire family that he saw every single day. He could French braid. He'd accepted the fact that she was going to wear a hard hat and put mosquito netting over her bed and he still seemed to find her attractive.

He was a lot of things, and she found every one of them hot.

She wanted him to know that. She wanted to *show* him how much he turned her on. She wanted to seduce him. She needed to get her mouth on him.

Juliet leaned in and put her lips against the first spot she could reach. His right pec. Well, more like the side of his pec, closer to his armpit. Okay, it was basically his armpit. Not directly *in* it. She was below any hair. But it was his armpit more than it was anything else. An armpit that smelled really good considering it was, well, an armpit.

Sawyer's muscles tensed, his arm tightened around her, he even stopped breathing. She knew because her lips were now against a part of him that moved when he was breathing in and out.

It wasn't moving now.

Well, this wasn't sexy. It was awkward as hell. This was what happened when she didn't What-If a situation. *What if I can't reach any sexy spots and end up kissing his armpit* would have been a good one to start with. As would have *what if you do end up kissing his armpit...then what?*

Since she honestly didn't know what to do next, Juliet just stayed right where she was, her lips against his lower armpit. She didn't move them. She just kept them resting there.

It took only about five seconds for that to get weird.

But she still hadn't moved after twelve.

What if you just give him a little nuzzle and pretend it's kind of a hug-thing?

What if running your whole face back and forth in his armpit is even weirder?

What if you say something sexy?

What if he thinks that means you have an armpit fetish and that's even weirder yet?

Finally, because she seemingly had no other options, she flicked out her tongue and licked him.

It might have been because he couldn't hold his breath any longer or because she'd freaking *licked him* just under his armpit and that was really only acceptable in maybe two situations—sex and being offered a million dollars to do it—but Sawyer did finally move.

His hand went to the back of her hair and he slid his fingers through it, to cup her head, then he tipped her head back.

Even the way he looked at her was intense.

Maybe she should have been grateful for the soft, lingering, slow kisses in the kitchen. Because in that moment, she wasn't sure she was ready for a full-on, take-over-everything-including-her-body-and-heart Sawyer.

That was absolutely the best way to describe how he was looking at her right now.

She had no time to *get* ready though. Sawyer's mouth took hers in a deep, hot kiss. He didn't say a word, gave her no real warning, just sealed his lips over hers and started kissing her as if it was his single goal in life to make her come with just his lips on hers.

It wasn't hard to believe that could happen. Heat exploded in her belly and shot through her, up and down her limbs, lingering at her nipples, then diving between her legs making her hot and wet and needy instantly.

Then he groaned. A deep, gravely, hungry sound and she felt her inner muscles tighten. His tongue slid along hers in a firm, carnal way that made her clit tingle, begging to be the focus of that same stroke. His hand tightened in her hair and he moved her fully to the front of his body so they could press closer.

He was huge and hard behind his fly when she felt him against her belly.

Finally, Sawyer lifted his head. He still had his hand in her hair, though, preventing her from looking away. Which meant staring into his hot, penetrating gaze. That look made everything in her melt.

He was breathing hard and that gave her a surge of triumph that surprised her. She liked having an effect on the big, gruff guy.

"What if," she said, her voice soft and husky, "we pretended that I didn't awkwardly kiss your...armpit? We could just focus on the part when our mouths met and we could pretend I was sophisticated and seductive about the whole thing."

He leaned in, nearly touching her nose with his. "*Yeah, but,*" he said, "then my desire to kiss and lick that same spot on you to see if it's an erogenous zone for you, too, won't make as much sense."

She wasn't sure if it was his clearly purposeful use of *yeah, but* or what he'd actually said—that spot was an erogenous zone on him? Good to know—but her nipples tightened almost painfully.

"Oh," was really all she could come up with in response.

He straightened and slowly pulled his fingers through her hair, letting her go. He was smiling at her with a combination of cockiness and wonder. As if he was completely surprised but very pleased by what had just happened.

Yeah, well, ditto.

He held out his hand. "Let's put you back to bed."

Oh, yes, please.

Once inside, instead of heading for the staircase, Sawyer went straight for the kitchen, however. Then onto Cora's screened-in back porch. He scanned the long wooden shelf that hung over the hooks full of jackets and the mat under them that was covered with shoes and boots. He reached for a spray bottle and turned it so Juliet could see the label.

It was a plain white sticker with scrawling handwriting that said, *Keep the Fuck Out.*

Juliet looked up at him. "The bug repellent?"

He smiled. "Yep."

She wasn't sure what was going on. They'd gone from making out to bug repellent. But they weren't discussing armpits, so that was something. Then he started for the stairs and she felt hopeful again.

That didn't last long.

"Get up on the bed."

She did so, eagerly.

Sawyer stretched to put the netting back up around the top of the bed. The sight of his muscles flexing and bunching along his shoulders and back was definitely captivating, and she had visions of putting her lips and tongue against the hard planes of the muscles that dove into his jeans and led to his very fine ass. But she resisted.

Then, however, he moved to her side of the bed, attaching the netting right above her. The stretch of his long torso made his jeans dip low and she couldn't tear her eyes from the tease of the denim sliding up and down over his lower abs.

She actually started to lean in, not thinking and not doing a single What-If—again— when his hands dropped to his side and he must have noticed her movement and read her intent. One of his hands went to the back of her hair and he took a handful, tugging her to a stop. "I *know* that's an erogenous zone," he told her gruffly.

Juliet looked up at him, very aware of the fact that she was on hands and knees on the bed, her mouth at belly-button level on him, his hand holding her hair in a very erotic way. "On both of us," she replied.

She leaned in again and his hand relaxed briefly in her hair.

Her lips brushed over the skin just above his waistband, and Juliet didn't think she'd ever heard as sexy a sound as the groan that came from Sawyer with that tiny touch.

"Jul—"

Then she heard the worst sound she'd ever heard in her life.

The front door to Cora's house opening and shutting.

Someone was home.

Juliet and Sawyer both froze.

No. *No.* It wasn't fair.

"No," she groaned.

Sawyer sighed. "Fuck."

Juliet dropped her chin to her chest and Sawyer let her hair go. "That damned bat." Then she looked up at him. "I'm sorry."

He lifted a brow. "What the hell for?"

"If I hadn't put that netting up—" She frowned, frustrated. "If I hadn't worried about—"

Sawyer bent and covered her mouth, kissing her for a long moment. It was sweet and made her ache with wanting. It was a strange desire though. It was heat and need, for sure, but there was also an ache in her chest like she'd never felt before.

When he lifted his head, he said, "It's okay."

It wasn't. It really wasn't. She wanted to be wrapped around him. Wanted him wrapped around her. Right now. All night long.

"It's so *not* okay." Juliet took a breath as he let her go and stepped back. "Most of the time I'm very happy with my choices to be extra careful, but every once in a while, they really get in the way of...being normal. And fun."

"I know what you mean."

He did. Spontaneous and fun were hard for him, too. At least now.

"But you've been spontaneous since I have. I've been careful since I was ten. You've only been careful for nine months."

"Yeah." He looked at her for a long moment. "And I'm starting to remember how to be fun, I think. Or at least to want to."

Thank God. She smiled.

But then Sawyer picked up the spray bottle of bug repellent. He sprayed the windowsill and along the baseboard under the window. Then he shot some into each corner—floor and ceiling—of the room. Finally, he came toward her again...and sprayed a circle on the floor around the bed.

He straightened and checked out the mosquito netting, tugging on it lightly to be sure it was secure and then spreading it out so it draped over the bed. With her inside. And him on the outside.

She sighed. Well, the bed would have been too creaky anyway.

Sawyer looked around. "That should do it. I think it's more than you need but better to repel *too* many bugs, right?"

She nodded. "So, this is kind of like a salt circle?"

He frowned. "A salt circle?"

"Have you ever seen the show *Supernatural*?"

"Can't say I have."

"Oh, well, they put salt circles around rooms, and people, to keep demons out."

He clearly wasn't sure what to say to that.

"You can't tell me that it's not *possible* that demons are disguised as black widow spiders," she said. "Seems very likely to me."

He chuckled. "I think you're overestimating the evilness of the black widows, actually."

That also seemed likely, she had to admit. She nodded. "Well, thanks for doing all of this to protect me even if it's more than I need."

He just looked at her for a few seconds, then he nodded. "Happy to do it."

She tipped her head. "Yeah?"

"Your plans make it so that if something does go wrong, it's still fixable," he said.

He didn't say it lightly. It seemed very serious to him. She also now knew him well enough to know that being something he could fix was really important.

"And you let me fix it when that happens," he added.

Right. That was really important to him.

She was a patient advocate, fighting to help others have fewer roadblocks and challenges when it came to getting the care they needed. She encouraged them to *ask* for what they needed and to flat-out demand it when asking didn't work. She saw a lot of people who needed a lot more help than she did and she was drawn to them because she knew how it felt to have people try to protect rather than help. Those were not always the same thing.

But she liked it when Sawyer took care of her.

Maybe it was because he did actually *help*. He French braided her hair when she couldn't, keeping it back and out of her way. But he hadn't told her she should put the power tools down. He got the bat out of her room—something she never would have been able to do on her own—and hung her mosquito netting back up. But he hadn't told her that was ridiculous, and he hadn't gotten frustrated that the netting had essentially ruined his plans for getting laid tonight. He'd kissed the hell out of her and then sprayed bug repellent around her bedroom.

That made her want to reach out for him and hug him.

Of course, she'd probably end up licking him again.

Not that that would be *terrible*. Because she would be very accurate about *where* her lips landed next time.

She liked him. She wanted him to be happy, to smile, to realize, the way her mom had, that worrying about the people he loved was different from being scared for them.

She was here for another week and a few days. As long as *she* stayed easy to take care of, maybe she could help Sawyer figure out how to let his family go out on those metaphorical bike rides they needed to go on. She could show him the difference between wrapping them up in bubble wrap and wrapping bandages around their bloody knees.

And she could, of course, get her mouth on more than his armpit.

Juliet laid back on the pillows behind her, totally relaxed, the epitome of comfort and ease, clearly not giving a single thought to mosquitoes or black widows or bats or—she suppressed a shudder before Sawyer could see it—and gave a contented sigh, then smiled. "I'm really glad you came over tonight," she said.

Sawyer cleared his throat and though his eyes didn't dip below the level of her chin, Juliet thought maybe he was suppressing something, too. Though hopefully not a shudder.

"Me, too."

"I'll see you tomorrow."

"You will."

He said it with promise and hesitated in the doorway just long enough to make Juliet sure that he did not want to leave. And that the next time she saw him, it would be...fun.

————

THE SUN WAS SHINING WHEN SAWYER STEPPED OUT ONTO HIS front porch the next morning. The air was fresh and clean and he took a big breath. The coffee was already brewing when he stepped into the front office of Boys of the Bayou—God bless the inventor of the coffeepot with a timer—and no one else was in yet. He'd always loved being the first one into the office in the morning. He loved just standing in the middle of it all and absorbing the feel of "mine" that came over him.

All in all, it was the perfect start to the day.

But his mood had nothing to do with the sun, the coffee, or the relative solitude. It had everything to do with the woman he was going to see in about twenty minutes. The gorgeous, sweet woman who had a little bit of a dirty streak in her, even as she was hanging mosquito netting over her bed. He should have kept her in the kitchen. That fucking bat wouldn't have been a problem then. But there was no way Cora's table would have been sturdy enough for what he wanted to do to Juliet Dawson.

He moved to the window, cup in one hand, the other tucked in his back pocket. He hadn't gotten laid last night. He'd had to go home and take care of things himself. But he was still in an amazingly good mood.

Juliet made him feel like wrapping her up in a big bear hug a lot of the time. At the same time, he wanted to bend her over the nearest sturdy surface. He hadn't felt that mix of things for a woman in...ever. She was funny yet earnest. Smart, yet easily intrigued. Most of all, she was good for him. He could feel it. He would have been physically attracted to her no matter when he'd met her, but knowing her *now*, knowing her story, too, made him *want* her in a way he'd never experienced before.

"Madison Evangeline Allain!"

Just like that, his peaceful start was shattered.

He turned as Tori came stomping into the office.

Sawyer took another sip, but noted the way his future sister-in-law swung around, as if Maddie might be hiding from her. Tori wasn't the bellowing, stomping type usually. In this family, the quieter ones were definitely noteworthy.

"Where is she?" Tori demanded.

Josh came through the door. "I told you she wouldn't be down here yet."

"She wasn't at Owen's," Tori said. "Is she at Cora's?" she asked, focusing on Sawyer.

"Not that I'm aware of," Sawyer said. "But I haven't been by this morning."

Which got him to thinking about their conversation about him climbing out Juliet's window.

"I'm right here," Maddie said, coming into the office with a to-go box from Ellic's. "Owen's out of eggs so I had to—"

"I got a call from Bailey Wilcox!" Tori exclaimed, cutting her off.

"Hey, Bennett just called," Kennedy said, coming through the door. "He said somebody at some government wildlife department is all riled up?"

"Bennett called you on your cell?" Maddie asked, looking at the office phone that sat silent on the front counter.

Kennedy opened her mouth, then shut it, then opened it again. "It was an emergency."

"An emergency that he didn't call the majority partner about?" Josh smirked. "Or was it really just an excuse to call you first thing in the morning?"

Kennedy shot Sawyer a quick look, then said, "Yeah, who doesn't need a big dose of Kennedy charm to start their day?"

Josh snorted.

"You don't realize how important it is because you get it in person automatically," Kennedy told him.

"Sure," Josh agreed with a nod.

Sawyer felt a niggle of suspicion. After last night's talk with Juliet about her mom, he had to ask. "Ken, did you tell Bennett that he should run stuff through you before calling me?"

His little sister shrugged. "I like to flirt with him. You said so yourself." But she wasn't meeting Sawyer's eyes.

Uh-huh. She was running interference. Covering up the bloody knees Bennett might be bringing in so they could heal a little before Sawyer found out. Dammit.

"Okay, what's going on?" He looked around the room.

"Maddie!" Owen called from just outside the door. "Look out. Tori's pissed at yo—"

The last word was cut off as the door bounced off the wall and Owen stepped over the threshold. "Oh, hey, Tori."

Tori crossed her arms. "Hey, Owen. How did you hear?"

"Leo."

"Ah."

"Pissed about what?" Sawyer asked, finally setting his coffee cup down and straightening fully.

"Is everything okay?"

Everyone looked over as Juliet peered around Owen.

Sawyer's heart thunked at the sight of her and he felt himself smile. Her eyes found him almost immediately and she smiled back.

"I saw everyone heading in here and heard Owen say Tori was upset," she said. "I know it's not my business but just wanted to see if there was anything I could do."

As she spoke, she slipped past Owen and into the room, crossing to where Sawyer stood and stopping next to him. She looked up at him.

She'd come in to make sure he was okay. Not because she thought anyone was upset with him but because she knew that these people worried him. And vice versa. Damn, he really liked her.

"Apparently Tori and Bennett are upset. Tori was just about to tell us why. *All* of us. *All* about it," Sawyer said. He wasn't going to let them protect him from whatever this was.

"Oh, okay, well, I'll be right outside then," Juliet said. "I was hoping you could French braid my hair for me today."

She wasn't trying to haul him out of here, wasn't trying to keep him from this like his family might prefer. But she was offering a nice bandage for after. Something that would make him feel good later. Because getting his hands on her would, absolutely, no matter what, make him feel better, no matter what this news was.

That was something huge Juliet had showed him—there could be good even after the bad. In spite of the scraped knees, strokes, splinters, and sharks... there could still be things to be happy about.

"I sure can." He reached for her, moving her in front of him and gathering her long silky hair in both hands, combing his fingers through it. "I'll do it while Tori talks."

Having her here, her hair trailing between his fingers, imagining how it would feel spread over his chest—and look spread over his pillow—would certainly not make whatever this "situation" was with Tori and Maddie *worse*.

He tugged gently on her hair, wondering if it reminded her of the way he'd done the night before when she'd been kneeling on the bed in front of him, her mouth hovering over his fly and then her lips against his lower abs.

He didn't hear a moan, which could be because she was in front of an audience, but he did notice her cross her arms. He grinned. She'd done that last night, too. But not before he saw her nipples responding. He could only assume—hope—that's what was going on now. *His* body was definitely responding to this.

It took him a few moments to look up from the brown, red, and gold strands running through his fingers. When he did, he realized that his family members were all staring at him and Juliet.

Sawyer grinned. And kept combing her hair. Did it look like she was standing in front of him, protecting him? Maybe she was a little. But little did they know she was probably instinctively standing there to remind him to listen and let them tell him about their bloody knees without worrying about his reaction.

Or maybe she just wanted to be close to him after last night, the way he wanted to be close to her. That was fine with him. He didn't know if she felt comfortable here in this conversation exactly, but he liked that she'd come in.

"So why is Baxter calling Kennedy at the crack of dawn?" he asked.

He started braiding Juliet's hair, slowly, letting his knuckles brush over her neck and shoulders. He noticed the goose bumps and made himself focus on Tori's answer instead of how much he wanted to taste Juliet's skin.

"Um..."

Sawyer looked up and saw Josh nudge Tori. She jumped.

"Oh. Um..." Then she frowned as she remembered what they were talking about. She looked at Maddie. "You told someone that Gus has *rabies*?"

"What?" Maddie looked away from Sawyer and Juliet.

"Bailey Wilcox is with the Louisiana Department of Wildlife and Fisheries," Tori said. "She called to check on a report that we have a river otter interacting with guests and that he might be rabid."

Sawyer's fingers paused in Juliet's hair. Tori looked on the verge of tears. Josh moved in and wrapped his arms around her from behind.

"I told her you were just kidding," Josh said to Maddie.

"It doesn't matter!" Tori said. "She's coming to check."

"You said that?" Sawyer asked Maddie. "Why?"

Was it his imagination or did Juliet move back slightly, closer to him?

He took a breath. He wanted them to talk to him. He couldn't overreact here.

Maddie looked dismayed. "It was a couple of days ago. Gus was showing off by the dock. Josh was telling some of the kids about him and this woman was hanging out and got in really close to him. To Josh," she clarified, looking around. "She'd been checking him out from the second she got there. She said she was thinking about skipping her tour with Owen to stay and learn more about otters from Josh." Maddie rolled her eyes.

Tori groaned. "You told her Gus was rabid to keep her away from Josh?"

Maddie shrugged. "Yeah. She sure didn't look like a wildlife expert."

"Isn't rabies really uncommon in otters?" Juliet asked.

Everyone looked over in surprise. Sawyer chuckled.

"You looked up mosquitos and ottersg but not black widows?"

She shuddered. "I looked *everything* up after you mentioned the black widows."

"Yes, rabies is *really* uncommon in river otters," Tori broke in. She scowled at Maddie. "It's ridiculous."

"I'm *sorry* I was trying to keep *your boyfriend* from being hit on!"

"Josh can take care of himself!" Tori exclaimed. "Gus can't." Her voice wobbled on the last two words.

Maddie looked properly chastised. "God, Tori, I'm sorry. I had no idea this would get back to anyone official. How did that even happen?"

"It wasn't the girl," Tori said, shaking her head and taking a deep breath. "Someone overheard."

Maddie crossed to her friend and pulled her into a hug. "I'm sorry. You are totally right. Josh can take care of himself and I need to keep my big mouth shut. I just reacted and didn't even think about Gus."

Tori squeezed her back. "I know. I'm sorry for yelling at you. I just..." She looked around the room. "I don't know what to do. They're going to come and check on Gus. And Bailey knows I'm here. She'll probably stop by my clinic and..." Tori cast a look in Sawyer's direction and pressed her lips together.

Sawyer felt his eyebrows go up. What the hell was that? Clearly she'd forgotten he was there. Or was, at least, hesitant to say whatever was next in front of him.

"And what?" he asked. He heard the tightness in his tone.

Juliet must have, too, because he felt her hand reach back and squeeze his thigh.

That actually made him breathe and soften his tone. "What's going on, Tori? You can tell me."

Huh, Juliet was reigning him in. Interesting.

Tori looked over her shoulder to Josh, who gave her a slight nod. Maddie moved over a step but stayed by Tori's side. Owen moved in closer to the little cluster as well.

Sawyer almost rolled his eyes at the sign of solidarity. They didn't need to do that.

But, then he admitted that maybe they did. He didn't know what Tori was about to tell him but if it was something that was less than fully safe and sound, they had good reason to think he might yell first and listen later.

"We might need to...reallocate...a few...things...from my clinic to other places while Bailey and anyone else come out to nose around the wildlife in the area," Tori said carefully.

Juliet squeezed his thigh again and Sawyer realized he'd been pulling a little hard on her hair. He loosened his grip and continued braiding.

"What does that mean?" he asked, his eyes on Juliet's hair instead of on his family. In case he was scowling. Which he probably was.

"Just tell him," Josh said.

Tori sighed. "I have a bald eagle in the barn."

Sawyer looked up. "What?"

"Broken wing. I'm just nursing her back to health and will let her go, obviously," Tori said.

Sawyer paused in the braiding again. The silky feel of Juliet's hair in his hands kept him breathing steadily, though, and he asked calmly, "What else?"

Tori chewed on the inside of her cheek for a moment. Finally she said, "A gray wolf. And her pups."

Sawyer bit his tongue. Literally. Bald eagles and gray wolves were on the threatened species list. He had to assume it wasn't just A-Okay with government officials for private citizens to keep them in their homes. Or their vet clinics.

"They're a vulnerable population," Tori said, before he

could comment. "When she chose our back shed as a place to give birth, we decided to let her stay. And not tell anyone."

"Well, you didn't *put* her there," Sawyer reasoned. "Surely they wouldn't have a problem with her being there."

Tori shrugged. "It could be complicated. They'd probably want to rehome her. She's a wolf after all and she's kind of close to town."

She was *in* town. Technically. Tori and Josh lived on the edge of town, but they were still walking distance from Ellie's and the boat docks and lots of other places with lots of people.

"Is rehoming her a bad idea?"

"The pups are still small and mom has an infected foot," Tori said. "It would probably be better if they could stay put for now."

"Is she a threat?" Sawyer asked.

"Um..." Tori looked like she was trying to come up with a good answer.

"Tori," he said firmly.

She sighed. "I mean, she's a *wolf*. It's not impossible to think that pets or chickens or stuff like that could be at risk. But I'm keeping her fed and safe so she won't feel threatened so she won't act out in self-defense or hunger. I think if we can keep things stable until the pups are a little older then *we* can rehome her just fine."

Sawyer went back to braiding, finally finishing it and tying it with the elastic band that Juliet handed to him over her shoulder wordlessly.

He let her hair go, but he didn't step back. He liked being close to her. The lilac scent that surrounded her fit now. She was sweet and comforting and fresh and made him feel lighter. He liked how he felt when she was close. She also didn't move away from him. He was still in arm's reach if she needed to reach back and squeeze him.

Sawyer actually smiled thinking about that. He liked that she could read him.

"So you don't want Bailey what's-her-name down here poking around about Gus because she might find out about your other animal projects."

Tori nodded. "I know you probably don't approve of all of that."

"Messing with endangered species that could get you into trouble with wildlife protection agencies...or that could take one of your fingers off. Or worse," Sawyer said. "No. But I trust that you're doing it for a good reason and that you're being as careful as you can." It struck him as he said it that this was probably a little like how Juliet's mom must have felt. He'd have to figure out what to do to be ready to help Tori with this.

Tori looked at him with surprise but gratitude and obvious affection that punched him in the gut. "Thanks, Sawyer."

"I'll always have your back," he told her. "All of your backs."

"So you'll be okay with whatever plan I come up with for Gus?" Tori asked.

Sawyer felt trepidation slide down his spine, but then he caught a whiff of lilacs and he heard himself say, "Yes. Whatever you think will work."

"I'll need to capture him," Tori said, almost sadly. "I don't want to do that. I don't want to scare him and I don't want to keep him in a cage, but hopefully it will just be temporary."

"If Bailey can't find him, she can't confirm he doesn't have rabies," Maddie pointed out.

"But if she does find him, I don't even know if she'll bother to confirm it," Tori said. "He's a river otter. Not endangered. She might just want to get rid of any potential risk."

"Oh." Maddie looked downright horrified at that. "My God, I'm so sorry."

Owen wrapped an arm around her and pulled her up

against his side. "We'll fix it," he told her. "It might not be perfect, but we'll figure it out."

And that was the bottom line, Sawyer realized. It didn't *have* to be perfect to work and to fix it.

"How will you capture Gus?" Sawyer asked.

"I haven't thought it all out," Tori said. "But he trusts me, so I can get him to come up to me, I'm sure." She looked sad. "I hate using the fact that he likes me to get him into a cage."

"It's to save him, Tor," Josh told her, running a hand up and down her back, comforting her.

"He won't understand that," she said.

"It doesn't matter," Josh insisted. "You're doing it for the right reasons, that's what matters."

Sawyer felt his gut tighten again. He realized listening to them, and watching them, that Juliet had been right. None of them blamed him for how he reacted to the dangers that confronted them. Even the perceived ones that weren't all that dangerous at all. They understood and they tolerated it. They even protected him in their own way.

Almost as if she could sense his emotions, Juliet reached back again, but instead of squeezing his thigh, she hooked her pinky finger around his.

Desire that was so much more than just physical swept through him, and it took everything in him to not wrap his arms around her and pull her in against his body.

"I'll have to do it tonight," Tori was saying as Sawyer tuned back in to something other than his fierce craving for the woman in front of him.

"After dark," Tori went on. "I can't risk someone seeing me." She chewed on her bottom lip, clearly lost in thought.

Sawyer did *not* like that idea at all. Tori would have to get down on the banks under the far dock to get near where Gus hung out. Down where there could be cottonmouths and God knew what else. Just as he'd told Juliet the first day. In the dark it would be even more dangerous. She'd need to watch where she stepped, and it could be hard to judge the water depth even in the light. Tori, while definitely more of a tomboy than Juliet, was not a bayou girl. She'd grown up on a farm in Iowa. She was no expert around the murky waters of the swamp.

But he forced himself to breathe in and out and swallow his protests. He became aware that his finger was curled tightly around Juliet's, but she wasn't trying to get free or asking him to loosen his hold. In fact, when he did start to relax, she trapped his finger with hers, squeezing.

"We can build a whole enclosure thing for him. Even get one of those little plastic swimming pools for him," Owen said. "We'll put it behind Leo's trailer. No one will think anything's goin' on over there. The damned thing looks abandoned anyway."

Sawyer couldn't disagree. Their grandpa had moved out of the house he'd shared with Ellie into a double-wide about a hundred yards away when they'd split up. He didn't bother with things like painting it or fixing the roof, claiming that it felt a lot like camping and he loved being able to look up at the stars through his living room roof. The truth—that was suspected by everyone including his ex-wife—was that he didn't fix the place up because it meant he got to sleep at Ellie's when it got stormy. Initially, he'd slept on the couch. Now, everyone was pretty sure he was back in the bedroom. And not just when it was raining. But no one asked specifically because Ellie and Leo were both more than willing to share far more information than anyone in the family really needed or wanted to have.

"Hell, we can set the eagle and wolves up in the trailer, too," Josh said. "Make it into a mini preserve. No one will go looking and it will give Leo a great excuse to stay with Ellie."

That got a grin out of Tori. "Why don't they just tell us they're back together?"

"And be boring and traditional?" Owen asked with a laugh. "Just not their style."

Sawyer didn't laugh with them. Instead, he was biting back words. Lots of words. Words about how making Leo's old trailer into a wildlife preserve for potentially dangerous and mostly endangered animals—that could get them fined or arrested or both if discovered—was a terrible idea. Words about how if the cops showed up to arrest Tori, he knew Leo would tell them it was his trailer and the animals were all his and he'd go to jail for it and how ridiculous that was. Words about how Sawyer knew the Boys of the Bayou would pay whatever fines there were but how stupid that would be when they really could use the money for so many other things. But he didn't. Gus was important to Tori. And hell, Gus shouldn't suffer because Maddie had tried to defend Josh. Sure, she should have thought it through and not overreacted, but that was how Maddie did things...passionately. And Sawyer wouldn't change that about her, even if it did—and always would—make his life a little more chaotic.

Tori shouldn't have an eagle and a wolf secretly under her care, either, but Tori's heart for animals was one of the things they all loved most about her.

He wouldn't change either of these women. He didn't want either of them to be more "careful" if that meant being less of who they were. So that meant dealing with the consequences of the things they did and said. Bandaging it all up later.

They were going to move a wolf, an otter, and a bald eagle into their grandfather's trailer, risking snake bites, jail time for Leo, and debt and bad news coverage for the business. And Sawyer wasn't going to say one damned word.

He focused on Juliet's finger. Then thought of all the other places he'd like to have her fingers. Then shifted, slid all of his fingers between hers, linking their hands together, and said, "Okay, so Juliet and I are going to go work on the dock."

He started for the door.

There was total silence other than the sound of Juliet's boots on the wood floor as she tripped along behind him, clearly as surprised as the rest of them.

"You are?" Owen finally said. "That's it?"

Sawyer stopped and looked down at Juliet. She was watching him with surprise and satisfaction. That was all he needed to see to know he'd made the right call. He looked up at his family. "Yeah, that's it."

"You don't want to talk us out of this?" Maddie asked.

"I..." He took a deep breath. "Of course I do," he told them honestly. "But I'm not going to."

"You're not?" Tori looked stunned. "You're not even going to run down all the things we should be sure to think about and plan out?"

He gave her a sincere smile. She was expecting a bunch of What-Ifs. She and Maddie and Josh and Owen—and hell, Leo and Ellie and everyone else—might sometimes make his life a little more adrenaline filled than he'd like, but he would do anything for any of them. Tori and Maddie had come into their lives more recently and brought a hell of a lot more good than bad.

"Let me know if you need a bandage for any bloody knees," he said. Of course, that was totally for Juliet's sake. And he was rewarded with a squeeze to his hand.

"Um...okay," Tori said slowly.

"And call me if you need help building anything at Leo's or carrying stuff over there," he said. "Or bail money. Or an alibi. Or...anything."

Tori gave him a big smile, her eyes bright, almost as if they were watery. "I will."

He gave her a little nod and then headed out the door with Juliet in tow.

7

THEY MADE IT A FEW STEPS UP THE WOODEN PLANKS THAT LED TO the sidewalk when Juliet pulled him to a stop. "Hey."

He turned to face her but didn't let go of her hand.

"That was great," she told him with a big smile. "You did good."

"I'm glad you think so."

"Yeah?"

"Because you have a big job now," he told her. He gave her a little tug, making her take a step closer.

"Oh?" she asked, her voice softer. "What's that?"

"Distracting me."

"Distracting you from?"

"Whatever they're all getting into," he said, inclining his head toward the office.

"You don't want to stay and hear it yourself?"

"No. I think it's best if I just trust that they've got it covered."

She smiled. "Remind yourself that they took that safety class and bought all the safety gear for the bike ride."

He nodded. "Something like that. And hope that they'll tell me about the fall if there is one."

Juliet squeezed his hand again. "I think they will."

"And so while they're off on their 'bike ride,' I need something to preoccupy me."

She tipped her head. "Huh," she said softly.

"What?"

"I never really thought about it, but I'll bet my mom tried to distract herself while I was out on those bike rides, too."

"I'm sure she did," he told her. He was absolutely certain. You didn't just forget that someone you loved was off taking a big risk.

"She started doing stained glass artwork," Juliet said, looking past his shoulder as if lost in thought for a moment. "Around that same time. I never really thought about why." Her gaze focused back on him. "I'm happy to help you however I can."

Sawyer wondered if she had any idea how sexy her smile was just then. He wanted her. The only question left was what *exactly* he wanted her for. Sex? Abso-fucking-lutely. But there was more. Like her pinky hooked around his. For starters.

"Do you want to meet Gus?"

"The probably-not-rabid but definitely-wild river otter?"

Sawyer grinned. "Yep."

"I'm good. Also, no on the wolves, too, before you even ask."

He laughed. "Gus is pretty cute."

"And he's well-loved and protected by Tori. He doesn't need me." She leaned closer. "Besides, *you're* pretty cute. I'd rather hang out with you."

Sawyer gave a little snort of surprise. He'd never been called cute, not even as a kid. Precocious, yes. Cute, no.

And more, maybe Gus didn't need Juliet. But maybe Sawyer did.

"Then let's hang out," he said. He had no intention of *not* being around her today.

"Okay."

They grinned at each other, then turned together and started across the grass toward the building area.

"You don't have to help me with the dock though," Juliet said.

Sawyer stopped next to the closest stack of wood. "You think I'm just gonna sit here and watch you work?"

He would. Happily. Watching Juliet do just about anything was a pleasure. But no way was he going to have her pounding nails and putting together his dock while he sat in a lawn chair and drank lemonade.

She shrugged. "Show your family you remember how to relax and kick back."

He stepped close and reached up to run a finger down the side of her face. He knew it was an intimate, probably unexpected gesture, but the fact that she didn't seem surprised pleased him. "I think they're seeing some important changes in me," he said honestly. He dropped his hand, trusting that she knew he meant they saw how he was reacting to *her*. "Besides, do you have any idea how much shit I'd get if I sat around while you worked?"

She laughed. "Well, okay. But mostly because Chase is helping Cora with some stuff this morning and then I overheard Ellie and Leo say something about taking him out fishing 'the right way' and I need a second pair of hands to get the boards onto the frame today."

Sawyer grinned. "The right way means with actual fishing poles."

"Mitch hasn't been taking fishing poles when he's taken Chase fishing?" Juliet asked, the corner of her mouth twitching.

"I'm guessing 'fishing' with Mitch has been more screwing around on the boats and a lot of bullshitting. Maybe some flirting with girls at the other docks. Probably not a lot of actual fish catching."

Juliet laughed. "Chase has been having a really good time. I hope he's been helpful, too."

Before, he'd been annoyed that Chase had gone off and left Juliet behind to work. Now he was fine with it. Partly because Chase being with his family was actually making Juliet even happier than when the kid was building the dock. And partly—okay, mostly—because now Sawyer got her to himself.

"Ellie and Cora have made sure he's stayed busy," Sawyer assured her. He dropped his voice a little. "Mixing business with pleasure is somethin' we know a lot about down here."

Juliet grinned up at him. "Even you?"

"Oh yeah. Until I forgot." Unable to help himself he leaned over, putting his lips nearly on hers. "Thanks for remindin' me."

"Happy to help," she said softly.

When he kissed her, he did so without hands, or even tongue. But he still felt it to his bones. This woman rocked him. In ways that he hadn't been before and in ways he wasn't sure he'd recover from.

And he was fine with that.

When he lifted his head, they looked at each other for a long moment.

"Yeah, this distracting thing is going very well," he finally told her.

"What is it I'm distracting you from again?" she asked.

"Don't remember."

"Perfect."

One more goofy grin and then they actually managed to move apart.

Juliet reached for her safety vest and Sawyer smiled and shook his head. That seemed second nature to her now. He didn't think she was actually worried about being run into or over, but the vest made her feel better. No, actually, it made her feel like she was reassuring everyone *else* so they'd leave her the hell alone. He lifted a board up onto a sawhorse, thinking about what he knew about her now. He loved it all.

She was strong and smart and self-deprecating and brave. She could think of the craziest What-Ifs there were, but she didn't let those stop her from doing the things she wanted to do and felt she needed to do. She just used them to help her prepare. She didn't expect people to make exceptions for her. She researched and planned and then did her thing.

Caleb needed to meet her.

Sawyer measured the board in front of him and cut through it as he thought about his friend. Caleb Moreau was a firefighter and had been raising his niece Shay since his sister's death two years ago. Recently he'd found out that Shay had sustained a brain injury in the car accident that had killed her parents. The injury caused some weakness and coordination issues along with some learning struggles. Caleb had Lexi, the love of his life and Shay's favorite person, helping him navigate all the new information and therapies Shay's diagnosis had brought into his life, but it could be good for him to see a strong, successful woman like Juliet obviously living a full life and managing all of her challenges.

He looked up at the woman he was more and more intrigued with every moment.

She was carefully measuring every cut five times—and that wasn't a random number he'd thought up—she literally measured five times before every cut.

He straightened to watch.

There really might be such a thing as too careful. That was the kind of thing that could get annoying, actually. If anyone else was doing it. He simply felt amused and slightly baffled by Juliet. That might have something to do with the fact that he really did love her big brown eyes. And how she filled that safety vest out. But it also could have been that she didn't seem *worried*. She didn't seem stressed or under pressure. Not about any of it, now that he thought about it. She'd put mosquito netting up over her bed, but it seemed practical when she did it, not overreactive. She hadn't made a big deal about it. She hadn't freaked out about the bat. She'd given a little shriek when he'd flown away, but she'd seemed way more annoyed about him ruining the sexy mood than *worried*.

The woman had decided to spend time on the bayou, so she'd looked up what it was like to live down here. She'd missed a few things, but when she'd found the mosquito stats she hadn't run back to Virginia. She'd bought mosquito netting. And hung the damned thing herself, the first time anyway. He was sure she would have figured out how to get the bat out of her room if he hadn't been there, too.

She might not be a bayou girl. She might seem like the last person who could live down here. The lifestyle here was laid-back and take-it-as-it-comes. Perfectionists and planners weren't really nurtured here. There was simply too much that was unpredictable about living on the bayou, or honestly, life in general. But she'd handle whatever came up. He really liked that.

And in the middle of all of this wild-and-weird stuff she was encountering down here, she was reaching out and linking her pinky with his, helping him handle his stuff, too.

Fuck, he wanted her.

He might have grabbed the back of her pants and kept her from going over the edge of the dock that first day, but he felt like he'd been the one dangling over the edge off the dock—metaphorically—for the past few months and she was now the one with the firm grip on *him*.

She glanced up at him as he set down his saw. He took a step toward her, reached for the bottle of sunscreen she had resting on top of a stack of wood to his right, and then reached for the bottom of his shirt, stripped it up his body and over his head. He squirted a little lotion into his palm and began rubbing it over his lower abs.

His neck, back, and shoulders were a lot more at risk of sunburn than his abs, but that wasn't really the point here.

Juliet started to set her saw down as well but missed the edge of the board where she was trying to put it. Because her eyes were riveted on his hand. Exactly as he'd intended. The saw tipped and fell to the grass. She jumped to the side so that it would miss her toe and in doing so, she knocked into the sawhorse holding the board she'd been working on. The board flew up, just the way she'd said it could the first day he wouldn't have believed it if he hadn't seen it himself—along with the metal ruler she'd been using to measure. The ruler glanced off her safety goggles making her flinch, then freeze.

It all happened within seconds, of course, but it was quite a chain of events. And he'd be a liar if he said that he didn't feel a little smug about causing it. He liked having an effect on her. She sure as hell had one on him.

Sawyer watched her squeeze her eyes shut and take a deep breath, then she set down the pencil she was holding, picked up the board that had fallen, set the saw on top of it. And returned to measuring as if nothing had happened.

Sawyer grinned and moved around the end of the board she was marking and then up close to her. Close enough she could easily smell the sunscreen.

"What are you doing?" she asked, without looking up. But she had stopped measuring. And maybe breathing.

"Remembering how to be the old Sawyer."

"Oh." She looked up at him. Kind of.

She looked at his pecs anyway. And his shoulders. And abs. And arms. And back to his pecs. And down at his abs again.

"And what does that mean exactly?" she asked.

"It means getting some sun, getting a little sweaty, flirting with a gorgeous woman I want badly. And having some fun."

ERIN NICHOLAS

He paused. Then held out the bottle of sunscreen. "Help me put this on?"

Juliet wet her lips and her eyes finally made it back to meet his. "Smear lotion all over your naked chest and back with my bare hands?"

Heat arced through him. "Yeah."

"That does sound like fun."

He gave her a slow smile. "I'm happy to run my hands over your bare body in return."

She held up her arms. "Long sleeves."

"We can fix that." God, he wanted to fix that.

"I think I need to be very careful to keep all of my safety stuff on when you're around, as evidenced by the fact that I literally could have put a metal ruler in my eye a minute ago without the safety goggles."

"I might need to take sharp objects away," he agreed. Then he popped the top of the lotion bottle. Because he needed her hands on him. Now.

She pulled her work gloves off, turned her hands palm up, cupping them slightly, and held them out.

Sawyer squeezed lotion into them, then watched as she rubbed her hands together, her eyes again running over his torso.

"You okay?"

"Just trying to decide where to start."

He reached out and wrapped his fingers around her wrists, tugging her forward. She tripped over the board on the grass and her hands ended up splayed on his chest.

"Right here," he told her gruffly.

She started rubbing, spreading the lotion over his skin, making slow, torturous circles over his chest. She covered his pecs, her palms brushing over his nipples, sending bursts of heat through him. She stroked up to his shoulders and up the sides of his neck.

Her touch made everything in him tighten, while at the same time making him feel like he was able to exhale for the first time in months. This felt so good, so fucking normal and right, and was pleasure on a level he had nearly forgotten.

Juliet held a hand out for more lotion. Not because his skin needed more protection, but clearly because she was enjoying the touching as much as he was. He squirted more into her palm and she ran her hands over his ribs and down his sides and across his abs. Twice. Then three times. Then again. Just as he was about to grab her hand and urge it lower, she slid around him, trailing her fingers around to his back, then took the bottle from him. He felt the coolness of the lotion hitting the skin between his shoulder blades. She spread it up and down his back, on both sides of his spine, lingering over the area above his waistband. Her hands circled until, he assumed, the lotion was rubbed in.

Finally, she stepped back. "That really *was* fun."

He quickly turned, grabbing her hand before she could get away. "Let's keep doing it."

She dropped the bottle of lotion as he ran his hands up her arms to cup her face. She let him tip her head back and she spread her fingers over his ribs, running them up and down like before.

Heat arrowed to his cock and he pressed close.

"We're never going to finish this dock."

"I don't care about the dock."

"You do."

"Not as much as I care about getting you naked."

She smiled. "You cared about it more than anything two weeks ago."

"That's before you reminded me that I kind of liked the old Sawyer."

"The old Sawyer does seem like a pretty great guy." She ran

her hands up and down his sides. "But I happen to like this one, too."

"I'm really glad." He lowered his mouth to hers, taking her lips in a slow, deep kiss.

She arched into him, her fingers curling into his sides, but the lotion made it too slippery for her to really get any grip. Instead, she dropped her hands to his waistband, hooking her thumbs in his belt loops and turned him, backing him up against the stack of wooden slats behind him.

He almost grinned. He liked the show of dominance. He was so much bigger than she was that he could easily lift her and put her wherever he wanted her. But he liked having her show him that she wanted this, too. Of course, he couldn't grin. His mouth was far too busy with other things.

Sawyer pressed his thumb against her chin slightly, encouraging her to open, and she did with a sweet, hot sigh. He swept his tongue along hers, tasting her deeply.

He didn't care that they were outside, he didn't care that it was very likely most, if not all, of his family was watching, he didn't care that the dock might not get done or that he'd just knocked her hard hat off. Even more, *she* didn't seem to care that he'd just knocked her hard hat off.

Juliet moaned as he cupped the back of her head and pressed into him, trying to get closer. She stepped in and suddenly jerked, her mouth ripped away from his, her body falling. Instinctively, he grabbed her, hauling her up against him.

Her big brown eyes blinked up at him.

"What happened?"

She grimaced. "Stepped on the lotion bottle with my wobbly ankle and it rolled."

He gave a soft chuckle. "Even when we're trying to be safe, stuff happens."

She didn't smile. She pulled back slightly and he let her go.

She took a deep breath. "Yeah," she finally agreed. "That's the thing."

He frowned. "What's the thing?"

"That even when I do everything right to be safe and avoid problems, stuff still happens."

"That was *my* lotion bottle, not yours."

She shrugged. "I wear hips waders and a life jacket so I'm safe on the dock and then almost fall off that dock and break my neck."

Sawyer shook his head. "Come on."

"You said that yourself."

"I was—" He bit off what he was going to say. But not soon enough.

Juliet lifted a brow. "Overreacting?"

"No. I was..." He blew out a breath.

"You either agree it was an overreaction, or you agree I could have pitched over the edge of the dock and ended up paralyzed."

"*Could have*," he agreed. "But you didn't. I caught you."

"I put up a mosquito net and caught a bat."

"I took care of the bat."

She hesitated, then nodded. "Yeah, you took care of all of it."

"And I caught you just now." He lifted a hand to her cheek.

"Yeah, and I'm decked out head to toe—hard hat to steel-toed boots—to work around wood, and then I try to make out with you for ten seconds, and the *one* area I don't have protected ends up hurt."

She held up her hand, palm toward him. There was a big sliver of wood embedded in the tip of her middle finger. She must have grabbed the wood behind him when she'd slipped.

"I know it's stupid. It's just a little sliver. It's not a big deal." She took a breath. "But dammit...I just took my gloves off for five minutes...to put sunscreen on you so you wouldn't burn."

Her bottom lip actually wobbled with that and with his hand on her face, Sawyer dragged his thumb over that lip. "Okay, first of all, let's just both be honest that the sunscreen was not about being safe," he said, looking into her eyes. "That was pure and simple foreplay."

Her throat worked as she swallowed hard.

"Second of all, I can take care of this sliver, too," he told her. "You're not failing at being safe, Juliet." Somehow he knew that's what this was about. He'd felt the same fucking way. It was frustrating as hell to work to do the right thing, be safe, keep others safe, and have shit still happen but...that was life.

And until this gorgeous, slightly klutzy, quirky, amazing woman had walked onto his dock, he'd been fighting it. Just like she was. Sure, she had her stuff together, she'd accepted her situation and was more than making the best of it. She was strong and confident and capable. But of course, there were moments when it was overwhelming and frustrating. She was human.

And he was falling for her.

"Okay," she said after a moment.

Yeah, it was all okay. And taking care of the sliver meant he needed to take her into the office. The interior office. That had a door. With a lock on it.

He took her hand—the non-injured one—kicked the bottle of sunscreen out of the way and started across the grass.

They headed around the side of the building. They could get to the interior office through the front office where the tourists were signed in and paid for their tours, but that would only delay him getting Juliet alone.

He really needed to get her alone.

They rounded the side of the building and Sawyer opened the door that led into the office. It had once been an office anyway. It was where Sawyer's and Tommy's grandfathers had sat at their desks and made plans for the business...

and drank a lot of "bayou whiskey," aka moonshine. The desks were still there. So were the chairs. The filing cabinets, too. It was where Sawyer and Tommy had sat when they'd first taken over the business, feeling important and grown-up, and in over their heads. But they'd sat in their grandfathers' creaking old chairs, lifted up mason jars of moonshine, and determined to grow the family business no matter what it took.

This was where he'd assumed their grandsons would sit someday doing the same thing.

But as Sawyer ushered Juliet into the room, the sadness was less acute than it had been the last time he'd stepped into the office.

He'd largely avoided the office over the past several months. It had never been a place to get actual paperwork done. That was clear by the stacks of papers, folders and invoices covered in a fine layer of dust that sat on top of the two desks, the seats of three chairs, and the tops of the two file cabinets. It had been a place of conversations. Plans. Arguments. Celebrations. Mourning.

They'd all toasted their first month in the black in here. They'd fought about their first six months in the red in here, too. It was where they'd celebrated adding Josh and Owen as partners.

It was also where Sawyer had gotten drunk after Tommy had died.

Five nights in a row.

This room was the heart of the Boys of the Bayou.

It was the place that grounded them. Reminded them of the history here and what really mattered beyond the accounting ledgers and merchandise orders and online reviews and tour schedules. This room reminded them that the business was about their roots and the future at the same time.

Stepping into the room with Juliet felt stupidly hopeful to

him. Maybe she could make the office feel good again. Like she had so many other things.

Sawyer shook his head as he closed the door behind them. He hadn't realized what a huge fucking sap he'd become since Tommy's death.

Juliet looked around, scanning the room as she turned to face him, not saying a word, clearly waiting for him to say or do whatever came next.

He crossed to one of the file cabinets and pulled the third drawer open. He grabbed the white metal box from within, then shut the drawer and opened the one under it. He took the glass jar from that one and pushed it shut. He crossed to the desk, pushed a stack of papers out of the way and said, "Come here."

"What are you doing?" But she started toward him.

"Showing you that you don't always have to be the one prepared for anything and everything." He held up the box. "You don't always have to be the one with the first aid kit ready to go."

Her eyes widened slightly, then she smiled. "I've got one right outside."

"I'm sure you do." That didn't surprise him a bit.

"It might be better stocked." She pushed herself up to sit on the desk in the spot he'd cleared.

"Probably is," he agreed. That was almost a certainty. "But mine comes with something yours doesn't have."

"What's that?"

"Kisses to make it all better."

A little shiver went through her and he grinned.

"Yours is better," she agreed and held her hand up.

He took it, turning it so he could see the splinter more easily. It was long and stuck

in at an angle, but the end of it wasn't embedded under the

skin, so it would be easy to remove. "You willing to let me do this the bayou way?" he asked.

She lifted a brow. "There's a bayou way for removing slivers?"

"There's a bayou way of doin' most everything."

She nodded. "I'm willing."

He grinned and lifted the jar. "First, disinfectant."

"Homemade by Cora and Ellie?" she asked.

"Homemade by Mitch with Kenny's recipe."

"Who's Kenny?"

"Maddie and Tommy's grandpa. One of the founders of the business. He was best known for being the best fishing and hunting guide around here, but secondly for his moonshine."

"This is moonshine?" she asked, eyes widening.

He chuckled. "Yep." He opened the jar, then took her hand again, and poured a little of the liquid out over the wound, the excess dribbling to his hand cupped under hers. He lifted his hand and licked the moonshine off. Then he tipped the jar back for a drink, grinning at her look of curiosity. He held it out. "Want a taste?"

"I don't know."

"Here, see what you think." He leaned in and kissed her, sliding his tongue over her bottom lip, then stroking along her tongue. He lifted his head a moment later. "Do you want more?"

"I do," she said softly. "More of *that.*"

"Let's get your hand taken care of," he told her. "Then I'll give you anything you want." He meant that with everything in him. And he hoped she'd ask for *a lot.*

Her pupils were dilated when he looked down at her. God, she was beautiful.

He lifted her hand and looked at her finger again. Then lifted it to his mouth, drew it in and sucked gently. It would soften the skin and draw the splinter out a bit. Juliet pulled in a quick breath and squeezed her knees together. Yeah, he'd been hoping it would make her hot and tingly, too. It tasted like the moonshine, of course, but he could definitely taste Juliet underneath the potent alcohol and he wanted more.

He let her finger go and blew on it gently to dry it, then reached into the first aid kit. He pulled out a roll of duct tape. He pulled off a strip, lifting it up to tear it off with his teeth.

"Duct tape?" she asked. "I was expecting a needle."

"This should work. If not, we'll do what we need to."

He lifted the piece of tape and pressed it against the splinter, wrapped his hand around it gently, warming the tape a little, then started to peel it back slowly. The tape pulled the splinter out as it came away from her skin.

"I love duct tape," she said. "I never go anywhere without some."

"See, you have more in common with us than you thought."

When the splinter was about a third of the way out, he felt more resistance and he reached for the tweezers in the kit, pulling the rest of it out. Then he dabbed ointment on the area, wrapped a bandage around it, then lifted it to his lips for a kiss.

His eyes were on her face the whole time and he saw her lips part as he kissed her finger.

"That was pretty smooth," she said.

He nodded. "No problem at all."

"And now it's time for anything I want?"

Sawyer pulled a breath in through his nose. He nodded. "Anything."

She ran a palm over his chest, watching her hand as she did it. Then she lifted her eyes to his. "You said I didn't always have to be the one that was fully prepared for everything."

"Right."

"Does that mean that you've got a condom in your pocket, Sawyer?" she asked, her voice soft and husky.

He ran his hand up the side of her neck to the back of her hair as heat and want tightened his body. "Yes, Juliet, it does."

"Awesome," she breathed.

"You need to What-If anything? The door? My family and the tourists outside? The ridiculously thick layer of dust in here?"

She didn't even give him a smile. She shook her head. "The only thing I can focus on is what if I have to walk out of here without you touching me."

There was no way in hell that was going to happen.

Sawyer bent to kiss her, but Juliet somehow arched her back, lifting to meet him partway. Their mouths met in a hot, wet clash of desire and enthusiasm. Lips touched, tongues stroked, hands roamed.

Sawyer grasped her hair in his hand, tipping her head back so he could truly plunder her mouth. Her hands stroked over his chest, her fingers digging in, the feel of her nails stinging slightly and making his cock ache. She lifted her legs, crossing her ankles at the back of his thighs and he pressed forward. But his height and the height of the desk made the fit not-quite perfect. Frustrated, he pulled away, looking down at her, breathing hard.

She looked dazed, her lips pink from the pressure of his mouth, her breathing also fast.

He glanced around and saw one of the tall stools like the one Kennedy used behind the front desk in the main office. Without hesitation, he scooped Juliet up with his hands under her ass and carried her across the office, depositing her on the stool. It swiveled slightly, but he clamped his hands on her hips and she again wrapped her legs around him. Pressed together like that, the stool was going nowhere. Her arms were around his neck again, her body arching against him, as they went back to the hot, deep kisses.

Sawyer pressed his cock into the soft notch between her

thighs and they both groaned. His hands moved to her ass, pulling her against him more tightly. She circled her pelvis, rubbing against his cock and Sawyer knew this was going to go absolutely as far as she let it.

He hadn't wanted sex in months. He'd had absolutely no appetite for it. He hadn't been good company, he hadn't been able to work up any energy or desire for wanting to give someone pleasure or for taking any for himself. That had all changed in a flash. Because of Juliet Dawson. He not only wanted to lose himself in her, to claim every ounce of pleasure, to just fucking indulge in every way, he also wanted to give her the same. He wanted her to feel pure fulfillment. From him. He wanted her to give up some of the worry and attentiveness that she carried around with her in everything she did. For him. He wanted her to let go, completely, and let him catch her. Yeah, it was a little caveman, but the woman took care of herself all the damned time and she didn't *need* him to take care of her. He wanted her to *want* him to take care of her.

He gathered her hair back and put his mouth against her ear. "This is all up to you," he told her roughly. "Whatever you want. However you want it."

"I want it all, Sawyer," she told him, breathlessly.

"You're sure?"

"Completely."

And the thing about a woman like Juliet who was always prepared for everything, he didn't feel like he had to ask twice. After last night she had, no doubt, gone over the What-Ifs of the next time they found themselves alone together. This might seem pretty spontaneous at the moment, but he knew that at least on some level, she was ready for him.

Thank God.

"Take your..." He paused and grinned down at her.

"What?"

"I was going to say 'take your clothes off.' But I need to add 'and your safety jacket. And your steel-toed boots. And your... whatever else you've got between me and your gorgeous naked body.'"

An obvious little shiver went through her even as she grinned at him and uncrossed her feet from behind him. She slipped the safety vest off and tossed it to the floor. That damned thing. It was a fucking turn-on and he was very ready to accept it at this point. She bent to untie her boots, but he knocked her hands away.

"Never mind, I'll do this. Get your shirt off."

Her tits had been taunting him since day one. It was time to get them bare and in his hands. And mouth.

She gave him a knowing smile that was full of sex and mischief. Her fingers went to the buttons on her shirt and she started undoing them as Sawyer yanked the shoestrings loose from her boots and tugged the heavy things off her tiny feet, dropping them with dull thuds on the floor. How was she walking around in those things? He pulled her socks down and discarded them as well. Then reached for the button on the front of her jeans. She wasn't even done with the buttons on her shirt yet.

"Juliet," he said, low and firm. "I need your pretty tits in my hands. Right now."

Her smile died and she sucked in a quick breath. Her fingers also sped up. He bit back a smile and flicked open the button on her jeans.

By the time he had her unzipped, she'd tossed the shirt on top of her socks. Then she slipped the fitted white tank over her head and reached behind her for the hooks on the plain beige satin bra. A moment later, it was also on the floor. He assumed. He didn't look to see where it landed. His full attention was on the most beautiful pair of breasts he'd ever seen in his entire life. They were full, with large, dark pink nipples that he could practically feel against his tongue, and all he could think about

ERIN NICHOLAS

was how much he was going to enjoy watching them swing when she rode him. Or when he fucked her from behind. He wanted to do it all right now. Over and over again. Every position. Every surface. Until neither of them could so much as roll over for an hour after.

"Sawyer," she said, lifting her hands to her breasts, lifting them and squeezing, as if trying to ease a pain.

"What do you need, Juliet?" he asked, almost not recognizing his voice, gravely with desire.

"Touch me."

8

"Fuck." He reached out, almost reverently. He settled his hands on her waist, stroking up and down, watching goose bumps chase each other up her body and tighten her nipples even further.

She moved her hand as he moved to cup one breast, memorizing the weight, the heat and silkiness of her skin, the way she sighed, almost as if in relief, as he did it. Then he looked into her eyes as he stroked his thumb over the nipple.

She moaned and arched closer. He rubbed over the tip harder, then circled it with just the edge of his thumb nail, making it tighten and her thighs tense as if wanting to squeeze her knees together. He wedged a hand between them, keeping them apart. He stepped forward, putting himself firmly between her thighs. "You aching for something, Juliet?"

"Yes. God, yes."

"Well, the only thing that's going to relieve that is my fingers and cock right now."

He hadn't planned on talking dirty to her, but it just came out. And she didn't seem to mind.

She wet her lips. "Please."

That was exactly the right answer. "I like you begging."

Was he a little dominant during sex? No. He was *very* dominant during sex.

He didn't mind a woman telling him exactly what she wanted and needed. He didn't mind demands at all. But he made them, too, and he very much liked a woman who could keep up with that.

Damn, he hadn't felt any of this in far too long. He'd been a demanding asshole in the past few months, for sure, but not in any way that would result in anyone's *pleasure.*

"Take your pants off. Take everything off," he told her, backing up just enough to undo his jeans and shove them to the floor and kick them away.

She did, but it seemed almost automatic because her eyes were glued to his cock. Which was pressing insistently against the front of his boxers, wanting her attention badly.

Juliet licked her lips as she kicked her pants off of her feet and her thumbs hooked in the top of her panties. She started to push them down, wiggling on the stool seat as she did it.

Sawyer couldn't take it anymore. He should take this slow probably. But damn, it felt like they'd been engaged in foreplay since that first day on the dock when he'd felt the skin of her lower back against his hand. After he'd saved her from pitching over the edge. When she'd hugged him.

Hell, he should have known then that she was going to be special. That she was going to heal him. That he was going to need her in a way that was foreign and so fucking good at the same time.

He stepped in and grabbed the front of her panties, pulling them down her legs and over her feet, tossing them over his shoulder.

"Fuck, you're gorgeous," he told her sincerely, running a big hand from her knee over the top of her thigh. He needed to touch her. He just couldn't *touch her* yet. Because he wasn't going to be stopping once he started. But his hand was huge splayed over her thigh, and his thumb came very close to the hot center where he *needed* to be.

She parted her thighs and Sawyer's mouth went dry. Then she reached for the waistband of his boxers. She tucked her fingers in the top and ran her knuckles back and forth over his lower abs, her fingertips grazing his head.

"Juliet," he said on a near-groan. "Fuck."

She ran her hand up over his abs to his chest in a slow motion, almost as if she was spreading imaginary sunscreen on him again. "I love your body. You're so big and hard and *hot.* Even when you're not out in the sun. You're just so...much."

"It's all yours." He took her hand and pressed it against his cock. "You're making me feel again, Juliet. And I want it all. I want to fucking revel in it."

She looked up, her fingers curling around him. She met his eyes. "Yes. Revel in it with me."

She tugged on the front of his boxers and he used one hand to help shove them to the floor, kicking them away. He was throbbing, harder than he'd ever been, his cock rising against his belly. He wrapped a fist around it, giving it a squeeze, trying to relieve some of the ache.

"I want you so much," she said softly, reaching to wrap her hand around his.

He gladly moved his own hand out of the way. "Juliet," he said raggedly.

She looked up at him. "Kiss me, Sawyer."

He did. He cupped her face and took her mouth, fucking her with his tongue the way he wanted to take the rest of her body. Her hand tightened around him, squeezing and stroking, her other hand running up over his abs to his chest, and then to the back of his neck. She curled her fingers, hanging on tight. He shifted, one hand teasing a nipple, the other running up her thigh, his thumb grazing her clit.

Juliet moaned and Sawyer pressed harder. She was already slick, and the way she wanted him almost brought him to his knees. She was amazing. She was sweet. She was kind and caring, quirky and wounded, brave and strong, but she was also hot and sassy and knew what she wanted. And she wanted it from him.

"I wish I'd thrown you over my shoulder and taken you to my house," he said, his breathing erratic against her mouth. "I want to bury my face in your pussy and taste you when you come for me the first time. Need more space. Need a place where I can spread you out."

Her grip on his cock tightened and she moaned. "Later. For sure. Please."

He chuckled roughly. "I love the begging, but I think all you have to do is crook your finger and I'm there."

She eyed the desk behind him.

He shook his head. "Dusty."

"Don't care."

He quirked an eyebrow. "There are just some places you shouldn't use disinfectant wipes, Juliet."

She laughed and groaned. "You're making me not care about any of that."

"I take that as the highest compliment," he told her, actually meaning it. That was what getting Juliet Dawson to let go looked like. "But, it's also too short," he said. "I'm going to spend a lot of time between these pretty thighs and I don't want to risk a neck or back injury by leaning over for too long." He gave her a little wink and she laughed again.

"So licking this sweet pussy until you scream my name *is* going to happen, but not in here." He turned his hand so he could slide a finger into her wet heat. "But that doesn't mean I'm not going to hear you crying my name and coming hard."

Juliet spread her legs, encouraging him with a *"yes, Sawyer."* He added a second finger, sliding in and out, rubbing over her G-spot and pressing against her clit at the same time.

She bucked against his hand, her fingers tightening on his cock and his neck, holding him close, or holding on.

Sawyer lifted a hand to one breast, taking the nipple between his thumb and finger, tugging and squeezing, then leaned to suck it into his mouth as he finger fucked her. She couldn't move much on the stool without sliding off, so she was left to just hang on and take it. But she took it all like a champ. Her hands dropped to the seat and she gripped the edges, letting him suck and lick and stroke and rub as she arched against his hand, pressing hard into his fingers. She gasped his name and gave him lots of "Oh yes" and "Right there" and "Oh, Sawyer" encouragement, until she clamped down on him hard, her body tensing, as an orgasm rolled over her. Sawyer felt her muscles milking his fingers and the sweet heat of her climax but kept his fingers moving. She was so fucking gorgeous. Her nipples were tight, her mouth open in a sexy "o," her head thrown back, her body offered up to him. He didn't move as she continued to circle against his hand, but as soon as those movements slowed, he leaned to grab the condom from his jeans' pocket. He rolled it on quickly. "You ready for me, Juliet?" he asked, straightening.

"I've been ready for you. For so long," she told him, almost buckling his knees.

"Come here."

He didn't know if she could balance on the stool any longer, and there was about to be a lot more force trying to knock her off of it. He slid her forward. When her feet touched the floor, he turned her, bending her so she braced her hands on the seat of the stool.

She shivered. "Oh God."

"You okay?"

"So okay." Her voice was breathless.

He ran a hand down her smooth back and over her gorgeous ass. The first part of her he'd seen when he'd found her on the dock. It felt like a year ago and like it had just been yesterday. He rubbed his palm over her left cheek. He'd never wanted a woman like this. The need for her tightened his gut to an almost unbearable point, yet he could take a year to just touch her, study her skin, her nipples, the way her hip curved into her ass and ran up to her lower back.

She looked at him over her shoulder. "Need you, Sawyer," she told him, her voice husky.

He took the French braid he'd created in one hand as he leaned over, putting his mouth against her ear and running a hand up the back of her thigh to the wet heat between her legs. He slid a finger deep. "I thought I just gave you what you needed."

She gasped but shook her head. "I need more. I need *you*."

"What exactly do you need, Juliet?" he asked, tightening his grip on her hair and teasing her clit with his other hand.

"Your...cock."

God that was hot. "You need me to fill you up? Stretch you out? Go deeper and harder?" he asked, emphasizing his words with thrusts of his fingers.

"Yes. Oh, please."

"Foot up." He waited until she'd moved to rest one of her feet on the rung at the bottom of the stool. It spread her wider and he slid another finger into her, relishing how wet she was and the way she pressed against him.

"Play with your nipples," he told her. He was just messing with her a little now, making it dirtier, ratcheting their need higher.

She lifted a hand to squeeze and pinch. She apparently liked it a little rough. Noted.

"Now reach back and stroke me."

She did, immediately, wrapping her hand around his cock and stroking up and down over the condom.

"Now point me home," he told her, moving his hand so that he was still circling her clit, but her pussy was empty, needing him.

She gave a little moan but instantly positioned him at her entrance, even pressing back in encouragement, taking his tip between her folds.

Heaven. Even that first half inch was freaking heaven.

Sawyer pulled a sharp breath in through his nose and moved both hands to her hips. He was going to need to hold her steady for this.

"Hold on, babe," he told her gruffly.

She grabbed the seat of the stool with both hands and he bent his knees, then slid home. Slow but sure. She was tight and hot and gripped him like she was never going to let him go.

He saw her knuckles turn white as she gripped the seat. "Oh. Wow. Sawyer," she said in little gasps.

"You feel...fuck," he said, not even having words. "You're amazing, Juliet. Please tell me you're good because I've gotta move."

"*Please* move," she said, her voice tight, pressing back against him. "Please."

"Fuck yes." He pulled out and thrust again. Her velvety heat was unbelievable. He'd never felt anything like it. "God, I never want to leave this spot."

She gave a husky laugh. "No one's going to ask you to, I promise."

He pulled out slowly again, then pressed in, sliding deep. They both groaned. "The next time I take you from behind, it's gonna be with a mirror though," he told her. "I want to see your tits bouncing."

Her pussy clenched around him at that and he loved knowing that she loved the dirty talk. He wasn't sure he'd be able to keep it in. Her body was every wet dream he'd ever had. He wanted to do all kinds of dirty stuff to her. He wanted to come on those tits. He wanted to fuck her in every room in his house, in every position. He wanted to worry about the windows being open and Cora hearing her screams of pleasure. He wanted to put nipple clamps on her. Her nipples were fucking made for that.

Those thoughts, along with the needy sounds Juliet was making and the hot-as-hell glove of her pussy, made him thrust harder and when he did, she gave him a heartfelt *yes* that had him doing it again. And again. Deeper. Faster. Until he was fucking her hard and they were both climbing toward orgasms.

He started to reach for her clit to be sure she was with him, but just as he brushed over the sweet spot, she clamped down hard and cried out his name, her head falling forward as her body shuddered with her climax. He gripped her hips and thrust for several strokes before he shouted, "Juliet!" and came, the orgasm ripping through him.

———

SAWYER'S GRIP ON HER WAS POSSESSIVE AND HOT AND SHE ALMOST didn't want to disturb it. She loved the way he held her hard against his body, him still buried deep, as their breathing slowed and her skin started to cool slightly.

Holy crap. She'd never had an orgasm like that. Like either of the ones Sawyer had given her. She had orgasms and that was great. Self-induced and even with partners. But what Sawyer Landry had just done to her body defied anything she'd ever felt before.

That was a product, she knew, of their bonding over other things along with their chemistry. It was about the return of this flirtatious, fun-loving Sawyer that she'd thought was possibly just a myth and was delighted to find was not. It was also because she was further delighted to think that she was playing a part in him rediscovering this side.

He related to her mom, maybe, but Sawyer had been missing out on some "bike rides," too.

Eventually he shifted behind her and she glanced over her shoulder. He met her eyes, and rubbed a hand, almost affectionately, over her ass as he slipped out of her. He was still big, even freshly spent, Juliet marveled.

She wanted him again. That was unprecedented.

"Damn, girl," he said, his tone sincere, even with the half smile tugging up one corner of his mouth.

"I have to say that I really approve of how y'all take care of splinters down here," she said. Giving him a little fake accent. "Doesn't hurt a bit."

He chuckled and caught her bandaged hand, turning her to face him.

Of course he was completely unabashed about being naked and what they'd just done. That was exactly the way she would have expected Sawyer and all the Landrys, really, to approach sex. With enthusiasm and not a touch of shyness. They approached most things with enthusiasm and there wasn't much shyness around here about anything.

He lifted her finger to his mouth and gave it a kiss. "Well, now you know I'm your guy for any aches and pains you've got."

"Yeah," she said, softly, feeling warmth bubble up in her chest. "But I already knew that."

Something flickered in his eyes. Something that looked like heat but also satisfaction and almost possessiveness.

Sawyer had been taking care of her since the second they'd met. And she kept giving him reasons. He'd distracted her from that thinking with the hot kisses and his big hands and everything else, but when she'd slipped on the bottle and gotten the splinter, it had all come roaring up into her consciousness.

Yes, Sawyer was protective. Yes, he'd be there to take care of things. And she liked when he did. Which was why her being here temporarily was a good thing. He didn't need more people to worry about and protect. He didn't deserve that. Just when he was getting over the loss of one person he hadn't been able to protect and save, he didn't need someone who was *always* going to need that.

This was her reality. She was always going to be a little unsteady, always going to need to be overly prepared, always going to have to What-If every damned thing. If she stuck around, Sawyer was going to be catching her and picking her up and fixing things constantly.

It made her a little sad thinking about that. But this man was wired to be the guy who never quit trying to save everyone and everything, and he lived in a place and had a lifestyle that would always physically challenge her.

She would exhaust him emotionally because she'd never be completely fine. And while *she* was okay with that, she wasn't sure Sawyer would be.

They cleaned up and got dressed and Sawyer put all of the first aid supplies away all without speaking but as she started toward the door, he caught her wrist and pulled her around. He cupped her face and kissed her deeply.

When he finally let her go, long seconds later, he ran his thumbs over her lips. "We'll go work on the dock a little more, but I want you again later. And then again later after that."

She couldn't do anything but nod. She wanted him again, too. She was only here for a few more days and she was going to take whatever she could get from this man.

He kissed her hard and quick and then let her go. He bent and grabbed her safety vest from the floor and held it out. Juliet let him help her into it, buckling it for her and straightening it, before taking her hand.

They got out to the building area just in time to see Chase

boarding a boat with Leo and Ellie. They all waved with huge grins on their faces, and Juliet felt an overwhelming number of emotions looking at her brother with the Landry matriarch and patriarch.

He was happy. He was relaxed and happy and feeling adventurous and, more than anything, accepted. The Landrys and all of their friends and acquaintances had not just welcomed her and Chase with open arms, they'd reached out and pulled them into those open arms. Chase was a friendly guy, he got along with people, he liked to have fun. But he was used to being on his turf, knowing his way around, feeling confident in what he was doing. Everything about the bayou was as new to him as it was to her. And he was reveling in it.

Her heart swelled. She loved it here. It was stupid. This place was everything that was a challenge for her—physically demanding with risks to someone who had less than one hundred percent strength and coordination as well as a completely new culture with foods and customs and even music that was foreign to her. But she loved it. And she loved these people.

Her gaze landed on the man who was now bending and stacking boards, muscles rippling, skin glistening, his big, hard body taking care of everything. Her body heated just watching him. They'd just had sex. *Good* sex. And she wanted him all over again.

Juliet blew out a breath. It wasn't about his muscles or the big hands or the other big parts of him...no, that wasn't true. It *was* about one big part of him. His heart. Also, his big hurt and his big family and his big ability to see her and understand her and to want her and to want to take care of her.

She almost groaned out loud.

She was falling for him.

That had definitely not been one of the What-Ifs for this trip.

WAS IT A SIGN OF BEING IN LOVE IF A WOMAN COULD TURN YOU ON while eating shrimp?

Sawyer sat lounging in his chair, his arm draped over the back of Juliet's, watching her as she ate and talked to her brother. Chase was telling Juliet about Leo's old hunting cabin and how Ellie had taught him to clean fish two days ago. Juliet seemed to think the idea of Chase Dawson covered in fish guts was hilarious. Sawyer would concur. But Chase was grinning about the whole thing.

Sawyer knew his grandmother. He was certain that she'd had some plan around the fish cleaning. It was more than teaching Chase a life skill—particularly one that the guy would in all likelihood never use. Sawyer was sure she'd told Chase some old stories and somehow worked in some advice as they'd done the cleaning. Sawyer wasn't sure what metaphor she'd used, but he was certain Chase would remember it.

The thing about Ellie's life lessons and metaphors was the way they were delivered. Always in a unique way, and with a tone of voice that said I love you but I know you're going to do some dumbass things.

Sawyer loved that his grandparents had made Chase feel like an adopted grandson. It was clear that he was enjoying being a part of the Landry family and that it made Juliet feel good, too.

"Hey, Sawyer?"

He looked up to find Tori and Josh standing by the table. Josh had one hand on Tori's lower back. The other was wrapped in white gauze up to his elbow.

Sawyer felt his body tense, but then felt Juliet's hand on his thigh. He took a deep breath. "Hey," he said, casually. Or as casually as he could when his brother was clearly bandaged up for some reason.

Josh gave him a wary look, like he didn't totally trust that tone. "So we got a thing set up down there to trap Gus."

Tori took a deep breath. Josh glanced at her. "It's just a cage that will lure him in and then shut behind him. Won't hurt him at all. Then I'll go get it in the morning and take it up to Leo's. Tori will let him out in the new pen we put together with stuff for him climb on and the pool to swim in and stuff. Since she's not the one collecting the cage, he won't associate her with trapping him. He'll think of her as his savior."

It was clear Josh was saying all of this for Tori's benefit rather than for Sawyer's.

"Sounds good," Sawyer said. It did. It wasn't perfect, but if it kept Gus safe and made Tori feel better, then it was good.

"Yeah, it will be fine," Tori said, as if talking herself into it. "But—" She glanced at Josh. "We thought we should tell you that Josh accidentally stuck his hand in a fire ant mound."

Jesus. Of course he had. The little bastards were another common menace around here. Sawyer grimaced. Why the hell *did* they all live down here? There were more things that wanted to harm and kill them than in a lot of places in the country. They could all move to... Montana. There were bears and stuff there, but from what he understood, the bears really preferred to just be left alone.

"You okay?" Sawyer asked his brother.

Josh shrugged. "Think so. Been a while since I got stung. Forgot how much these fucking hurt. But Tori got them off of me quick and we put Ellie's cream on it."

Sawyer actually felt himself smiling. Ellie and Cora had a cream, salve, elixir, or powder for everything. And most of it even worked. He looked at Tori. "You knew what to do about fire ants, farm girl?"

She lifted an eyebrow. "We have fire ants in Iowa," she said. "Josh warned me there might be some down there."

Sawyer nodded. That made sense. He wasn't the only one

around here who knew the dangers and knew how to handle them. He was just the one that wanted to keep everyone wrapped in bubble wrap and never near any of those dangers. Which would mean none of these people that he loved, who loved what they all did for a living and loved the bayou and the river otters and other things about it, would be living any kind of life. They'd be sitting inside doing...nothing.

"Sounds like you guys handled it well," he said.

They both looked mildly surprised for a moment, but then they both smiled.

"Well, I didn't want to get too close or touch the cage or the plants around there much because I didn't want Gus to smell me on everything. But that meant I was standing back, holding the lantern, and wasn't right there, so it took a few seconds for me to get to Josh to get them rubbed off."

"It's fine," Josh assured her. "I'm okay."

She nodded, still looking a little upset. "It's because of me that you got bit though," she said. "I know I should relax about Gus and everything."

"No. You're right to want to protect him. We'll do whatever we have to."

If Josh and Tori were surprised that that answer came from Sawyer—and they clearly were, because they both stared at him—then Sawyer was even more surprised.

However, the way Juliet squeezed his thigh told him that even if she was surprised, she was also proud of him.

"And if Ellie's cream doesn't work quick, try cucumber slices on the bites," Sawyer said.

"Yeah?" Josh asked. "How do you know that?"

Sawyer leaned in and lowered his voice. "Mom. But she never wants Ellie to know that she's giving out information AEA."

"AEA?" Tori asked, clearly amused.

"Against Ellie's Advice," Sawyer told her. "But the cucumbers work."

"Hey, Tori," Josh said, pulling her close and kissing her temple. "Want to go home and apply cucumbers to my sore spots?"

She blushed. "Sure. But you didn't get bitten anywhere but your arm."

"No," he agreed. Then gave her a slow grin full of mischief. "Not yet."

Tori's cheeks turned pink but she nodded. "Good point."

Sawyer laughed. God, he loved the two of them together.

Of course Tori cared if Josh was at risk for injury. He had to quit thinking that he was the only one aware of the risks and consequences. He had to trust that they all wanted to take care of each other as much as he wanted to take care of them. He also had to trust that if things went sideways, there were a whole bunch of people ready to help out.

"See you guys later," Josh said, turning Tori toward the door.

"Let us know if you need anything," Sawyer said.

He felt Juliet squeeze his leg again and he realized he'd said *us*. As in him and her. Josh and Tori could come to *them* if they needed anything. If she hadn't been sitting there with him, he wasn't sure how he would have responded to Josh's bandages. Maybe not badly. Fire ant bites were just a thing that happened down here. But would he have said something shitty about how Josh should have known better and why hadn't he looked around and this is what happened when people messed around down there in the dark? Yeah, he would have. When Josh was down there in the dark because he was trying to make Tori happy and he was keeping *her* from being bitten by fire ants. When Tori was willing to go down there because she was trying to save Gus from animal control. When Maddie had gotten animal control involved accidentally because she'd been trying to save Josh from an overly flirtatious tourist.

They were all looking out for one another and it was a mess of blunders, but it was their mess and they were trying to fix it and what he should have said was "I've got your back and just let me know what you need and I hope those fire ant bites don't hurt too much." That was the supportive, non-asshole thing to say. And because of Juliet, that was essentially what he'd said.

That felt really fucking good.

He needed her around for all of the things he needed to face that he'd been handling with a severe lack of finesse and appreciation for the amazing, imperfect, full of love and passion people that he had in his life.

Suddenly Juliet leaned over and pressed her lips to his cheek. "That was really good," she whispered.

She'd just kissed him. In public. In front of her brother. On the cheek, but still. He glanced at Chase to find him smiling as he dragged a French fry through the Cajun mayo on his plate.

Juliet started to lean back, but Sawyer lifted his hand to the back of her neck, holding her in place and turned his head to seal his lips over hers. She stiffened in surprise for a second, but quickly sighed and melted into him, letting him urge her mouth open and kiss her deeply for nearly ten seconds.

He let her go, but not before he met her eyes with a look that he was sure clearly said, "I'm getting you naked as soon as I possibly can."

He needed her. In a way that felt primal and raw and should have been terrifying but felt so fucking right he almost couldn't breathe.

She settled back on her seat with a little sigh that he saw more than heard and then picked up her iced tea—unsweetened of course—and took a long draw, as if she needed to cool off.

An idea occurred to him as he watched Chase bite into a

fried alligator nugget, and he reached into his back pocket to pull his phone out.

What do you think about coming down for a swamp tour soon? Sawyer sent the text to his friend Gabe Trahan and waited, his heart pounding more than it should have been.

He'd not only done so many swamp tours he was in triple digits, he'd taken Gabe and his kids out on the boats a dozen times. Gabe's daughter, Stella, was an alligator freak and loved everything about the bayou. She was only nine, but she'd even proposed to Sawyer at one point thinking that if they were married, she'd get to work at Boys of the Bayou and drive the swamp boat tours herself. Of course, she'd broken things off with him when she found out that he'd hunted alligators, too. He'd been pretty confident that he'd be able to win her back over. There was a nest of snapping turtle eggs he'd intended to show her and some new baby alligators down around the east bend. And Gus. The river otter had moved in just a week or so before Tommy's accident, so Stella hadn't met him yet.

Sawyer frowned. Wait, that might not be true. Owen might have introduced them.

It was especially stupid to feel jealous about *that*, but Sawyer realized that his fear about facing Stella with his scar had probably kept him from seeing her eyes light up over the river otter and had kept Sawyer from her brother Cooper's litany of river otter facts that he no doubt would have pulled out of his head or immediately off of his mom's phone.

Dammit. He really didn't want to avoid Stella and Cooper anymore. Or Gabe, Logan, or Caleb for that matter.

He just hadn't wanted to scare the kids. If the scar didn't scare them, the story about how he'd gotten it would. Stella would be morbidly fascinated with the story about a shark in the bayou, but her brother Cooper would have been completely freaked out. The kid worried about everything.

Sawyer grinned thinking about the kids that he was incredibly fond of. They had a little sister now, too, not to mention cousins and friends, like Caleb's little girl Shay, who would all come down for the day. It would be great. He'd missed them.

That would be great. You serious? Was Gabe's reply a minute later.

Definitely. You want to bring Logan and his girls, too?

Absolutely.

Gabe's brother Logan was also his business partner and they were two of Sawyer's best friends. They owned and operated one of the most popular bars in the French Quarter in New Orleans, and before his accident and Tommy's death, Sawyer had been a regular.

Next weekend, Sawyer said. *Tour's on the house.*

No need for that. But it's really good to hear from you, man, Gabe texted a moment later. *Glad to have you back. Stella is going to be thrilled.*

Sawyer smiled. He had good friends. He'd seen the guys since Tommy's accident. They'd come down to hang out, without their kids. They'd called and texted, trying to pull him out of his funk. He knew that Josh and Owen had shared their concern about his mental and emotional state with the New Orleans guys and that Gabe, Logan, and Caleb had been worried, too. But the first time Gabe had scheduled a trip to Autre with his kids after the accident, Sawyer had insisted Owen take them out. The second time, he'd made Kennedy cancel them.

Stella and Cooper weren't just some random tourist kids. They were his friend's kids. More, he cared about Stella and Coop, too. He'd known them for about three years now and had watched them grow up. Watching Gabe and his wife Addison bring their kids together and make a family had been awesome. Watching Stella and Cooper grow closer together and have each others' backs even while teasing and arguing at times had reminded him of himself and Josh and Owen and Tommy.

He also knew that taking them out on the bayou would be even harder than taking the random tourist kids. He couldn't stomach the idea of something happening to them. Or worse, scaring them off.

That was actually the bottom line, he realized.

He didn't want Stella to fear the bayou she loved so much.

Like he did now.

He didn't want her to know the story of what had happened to his face. And she would ask. For sure. He knew Owen and Gabe had told her he was sick last time because she'd sent him a homemade get-well card. This time, when he saw her, she'd notice the scar and she'd ask. He didn't want to lie to her. He also didn't want her to see his true emotions about it all. She was his biggest admirer. He knew that if he showed her even a hint of fear about the bayou, it would make her fearful, too. But if he *didn't* use this to show her how dangerous the bayou could be, she would continue to love everything about the bayou and the animals there and would possibly not take the necessary precautions.

Which was where Juliet came in.

He needed her to go on this tour with him. He needed her to be there to make him breathe deep through it all. And he needed her to be the one in charge of the safety precautions. She'd wear her life jacket and sit still and keep her hands inside the boat for sure, and he knew that she'd instruct the kids to do the same. He could be the bayou-loving-but-careful guy the kids had always known, while Juliet made sure that everyone stayed safe and secure and that they had a plan B for anything that went wrong.

He could do this if Juliet was there. She'd keep him calm. She'd remind him that whatever happened, they'd handle it.

This have anything to do with the hot brunette I heard has been hanging around down there? Gabe asked a moment later.

Sawyer snorted as he read the message. Clearly Owen and

Josh had been up to Trahan's Tavern since Juliet had been to town.

Yeah, it does, he said honestly. Hell, Gabe had fallen hard and fast for Addison. He could hardly give Sawyer shit for the same thing.

And had he fallen hard and fast for Juliet?

Oh, fuck yeah.

Glad to hear it, Gabe told him.

Sawyer grinned. *Can't wait to see you all*, he told Gabe honestly. *Thanks for being patient with me.*

Hey, we've all had our stuff, Gabe replied.

Yeah, everyone had their stuff to deal with. So why had it taken Juliet Dawson's arrival to pull Sawyer out of his dark place? He didn't know, but he was grateful that Chase had plowed the airboat into the Boys of the Bayou dock.

That was crazy, but true. The thing that had been Sawyer's biggest headache just a little over a week ago had turned into the best thing to happen to him.

Grinning, Sawyer slid his phone back into his pocket and watched as Juliet wiped her mouth and then scooted her chair back and excused herself to the restroom. Chase stretched.

"I think I'm headin' to bed," he said.

Sawyer nodded. He assumed this was Chase's way of giving him and Juliet some time alone. Not that anyone was ever really *alone* in Ellie's. "Big day."

"Yeah. Seriously." Chase gave him a grin. "Your grandparents are the best."

Sawyer couldn't disagree. "I'm a lucky son of a bitch."

"Leo wants to teach me to shoot tomorrow."

Sawyer had figured that was coming. Leo was going to take Chase out to the woods and line up tin cans on the tree stumps, just as he'd done when the boys were small. "He likes you."

Chase's face brightened. "Yeah? I mean, it's kind of pathetic that I'm twenty-two and don't know a lot of this stuff, isn't it?"

Sawyer shrugged. "How would you know this stuff? Someone has to teach you. And I promise you, Leo doesn't know anything about yachts and Bentleys and fancy food and wine and shit." Truth was, Sawyer didn't really know what stuff Chase knew about.

Chase snorted. "Guessing what Leo knows could translate to all of that. He could take apart a boat engine no matter what kind of boat. Same with the car. And the food down here is way more interesting than anything I've ever eaten. And the wine? It's like grape juice compared to the stuff Leo drinks."

"Maybe," Sawyer agreed. "But Leo would be as out of place in your world as you first felt down here."

Chase sobered slightly and shook his head. "Honestly, I only felt out of place for about five minutes," he said. "Your family is awesome."

Sawyer nodded.

"And Leo wouldn't feel out of place," Chase said, his voice getting a little deeper. "Because he wouldn't care what those people thought of him. He only cares what people who matter think of him."

Sawyer smiled. That was very true. Leo knew who he was and he didn't apologize for it. He seemed like a crochety old guy who didn't care who he offended, but he loved people. He'd never judge someone for having money or not having money, or for not knowing how to bait a hook or shoot a gun or repair an engine. But he'd definitely judge someone for being an asshole. Cruel, thoughtless, selfish, hateful—those things Leo Dawson would judge and call out. But if you were just a rich dumbass who didn't know any better? He'd take you under his wing and teach you to be a rich good guy. Who could bait a hook and shoot a gun and repair an engine.

"And that's why I'm not giving you a lecture about being good to my sister," Chase said, pushing back from the table.

Sawyer lifted a brow, waiting for the younger guy to go on.

"You know about people who matter. You know about what's important," Chase said, stretching to his feet. "You've been taught that all your life."

Sawyer felt like there was a tight band around his chest. He did know about those things. He'd been trying to protect those things with everything in him. Holding on tight to them. And nearly squeezing the life out of them.

But no more. He was going to let them live, and he was going to be there to help when things went wrong and be grateful when they went right.

"Which means that you already know that Juliet is a person who matters and that making someone like her happy is definitely something that could be very important."

Sawyer cleared his throat. Damn, this was suddenly really serious. From the dumbass frat boy who'd stolen his boat and smashed his dock.

"I'm glad you realize that your sister matters," Sawyer said.

"Juliet is special," Chase said with a nod. "And you all are exactly the type of people to see that and make sure it doesn't get lost."

"You sure about that?" They were. They would not only see what made her special, but they'd draw it out of her and help her make it even bigger. Tori and Maddie had both blossomed here. Even Bennett, in his short, sporadic visits to Autre, had become more comfortable in being a part of things here and how he fit in.

But Sawyer wanted to see what Chase really saw about his family. He felt his heart try to pound against that tight band around his ribs.

"I am. Because you gave *me* a second chance to be who I can be, and I'm nothing compared to Juliet," Chase said. He reached for his tea glass, took one last swallow and set it back down. Then he gave Sawyer a grin. "And if you fuck it up, Leo will make you feel way worse about it than I ever could."

Then he sauntered toward the front door, stopping to talk and laugh with nearly everyone on his way out as if he'd been a part of this town and this family for years rather than a week.

Sawyer shook his head. That was...something.

"Chase went back to Cora's?" Juliet asked, sliding back into her seat a moment later.

Sawyer turned to face her. He nodded. "Yeah."

She picked up her glass and took a swallow. He watched as a drop of condensation fell from the plastic to the upper curve of her breast, exposed about the neckline of her dress

"I need you to do something," he said suddenly.

She looked curious. "Okay."

"Come with me." He got up and held out his hand.

She set her glass down and got to her feet, sliding her fingers between his. Just like that. No questions. No hesitation. Just willing to follow him wherever.

He led her out through the kitchen, knowing that their exit through the front would be like Chase's with multiple stops and conversation. He didn't want anything slowing them down.

Without a word, he started across the dirt parking lot, then the grass that stretched between Ellie's lot and her house next door. They cut through the darkened yard, past Leo's trailer, across the alley that ran between her house and Cora's, then through Cora's yard, right past the back door that would have led them up to Juliet's bedroom. They weren't going to Juliet's bedroom.

They were going to his.

He led her through his side yard and around to the back, up the few steps to his back porch. If Juliet hadn't realized what was going on two backyards ago, she certainly understood by the time he pulled the screen door open and stepped back to let her in.

She didn't even pause for a second. She stepped up into the porch and headed for the kitchen door.

He stepped inside behind her, nearly on top of her.

She turned. "What is it that you needed me to do?" she asked, breathless.

"I need you to take your panties off."

Juliet grabbed the counter to her right, bent, unhooked her sandals, and kicked them off, then reached up under the skirt of her sundress and pulled a pair of cherry red panties down her legs. She held them up. "Okay."

He really wanted to fuck her on his bed this time. The office had been hot. He loved that he'd think of her every time he walked into that room from now on. He couldn't have waited another second to have her. But this time, he could wait until they'd climbed fourteen stairs.

Probably.

"Drop them," he told her. That way if anyone decided to come over to borrow something, they'd see them laying on his kitchen floor—the kitchen was always the first stop whenever anyone went to anyone else's house in this family—and they'd know they were not welcome beyond the threshold that separated the kitchen from the front hallway.

Juliet tossed them down on top of her shoes.

Yeah, they needed to get upstairs. Right now.

Sawyer bent, put a shoulder into her stomach, and lifted her over his shoulder.

His hand splayed over her ass as she giggled.

"I'd gladly climb the stairs to your room," she told him as he headed for the staircase.

"I'd gladly carry you with your gorgeous ass in my hand everywhere we go," Sawyer told her, also feeling the strange urge to giggle. That was, of course, never going to happen. But he understood the feeling of being unable to contain the pure joy of the moment.

She wiggled that gorgeous ass against his hand and he squeezed. He was minutes away from having her spread out on his bed, wiggling, panting, moaning, begging, all his for the rest of the night. If either of them thought that they needed to be concerned about her sneaking back into Cora's tonight, they were lying to themselves. Everyone knew what was going on and if Juliet *wasn't* in his bed tonight, they would all think something was seriously wrong. They might even think they should get more directly involved in getting Sawyer and Juliet together.

Neither of them wanted to face *that* intervention. He didn't even want to think about how that might look. He knew it would happen at Ellie's. There would be cheesy grits. And the truth about Juliet's dislike for sweet tea would come to light.

He really did need to keep her here all night. It was best for everyone.

He ran a hand up the back of her thigh under the edge of her skirt, to the smooth, naked curve of her butt as he climbed the stairs. She squeezed her thighs together, but as he moved higher, brushing his thumb over the slit between her legs, she relaxed with a little moan.

"Damn, girl, seems you like being wet more than you're letting on," he teased, turned on and humbled by the fact that she was already slick for him.

"It's you that makes me this way," she said. "This kind of wet doesn't scare me."

He ran his thumb up and down again, pressing in, needing to feel the sweet heat. It scared *him* a little. This woman was making him want and need things he hadn't wanted or needed in a long, long time.

She gasped as he thumbed her clit and then sank his thumb into her pussy. He had a good grip on her or she might have slid right off his shoulder to the floor.

"Sawyer," she said, with a breathless moan that made him ache. His cock. And his heart.

Sawyer took a deep breath just outside his bedroom door.

He'd never had a woman here. If he messed around with tourists, it was always in their hotel room. Made leaving easier. There had been a couple of quickies in New Orleans back rooms. Once he'd had a hot encounter during Mardi Gras that involved an outdoor brick wall and a Mardi Gras mask. Back when he'd messed around with local girls—something all of the Landry boys had realized was really more trouble than it was worth and had given up a long time ago—it had been in backseats or truck beds. But he'd never brought a woman *home*.

Tonight he couldn't imagine being with Juliet anywhere else.

———

SHE'D LIED TO HIM.

As Sawyer deposited her on the floor next to his bed, Juliet realized she was most definitely scared. But this wasn't the same scared as she got by water. This was all about the pounding in her chest and the butterflies in her stomach and her mind screaming, *This guy is everything! Keep him forever!*

He'd freaking put mosquito netting up over his bed.

Her eyes filled with tears and she had to blink rapidly.

She was falling in love with him already and they'd already had sex and it had been amazing, but she was afraid that had been nothing like what was about to come. Because he'd put mosquito netting up over his bed.

And she was not falling in love with him.

She was already there.

He stared down at her. "This is going to get dirty."

She nodded as her breath caught in her throat and her core clenched. "Good."

He smiled and brushed her hair back from her face. "But I want you to know, that I think you are the sweetest, most amazing, sexiest, strongest, bravest, funniest person I've ever met."

Juliet felt both eyebrows rise. "Well...wow." This guy was unlike any she'd ever met. She'd been at her most eccentric with him, and he thought she was strong and brave and amazing. Hell, he encouraged her eccentricity with the What-Ifs and the safety vest and the mosquito netting and the...everything. He made her feel completely normal in all of her craziness.

"Thought I should say that first."

"First?"

He gave her a solemn nod. "So that you know it before I say things like my tongue's never been inside a sweeter pussy."

Surprise and heat coursed through her. She was in love with this guy. This complicated, emotionally knotted guy who lived in a crazy-assed place where she couldn't imagine herself staying. And who made her laugh and made her feel all of those things he'd just told her he thought of her. No one had said those things to her, and for sure no one had made her feel them. Maybe she *could* imagine staying. Who would leave a setup like this?

"I will absolutely keep those things in mind," she said, stepping close and pulling his shirt up his torso. He lifted his arms so she could strip it over his head—and helped her since she couldn't possibly reach that high. "But if you're able to talk *about* my pussy like that, I'm not sure your tongue will be doing the job it's supposed to be doing down there."

His eyes darkened and flared with heat. He reached for her, cupping the back of her head and pulling her close. He lowered his face until he was staring directly into her eyes and she felt his hot breath on her lips.

"Not a bad point. So let me get these things said up front as well so that when my tongue's busy and my mouth's full, you still know them. Your pussy is the sweetest I've ever had my tongue inside, the sight of your tits bouncing while I pound inside you is the stuff I'm going to jack off to in the shower several mornings a week, the feel of your clit against my finger and tongue is something I'm never going to forget, and the sound of you saying my name as you come is going to be on a replay loop in my head as I go to sleep every night."

She stared up at him, breathing hard, her cheeks hot, but more turned on and stunned than she'd ever been. That had all been super dirty but also strangely romantic. "No pressure, huh?" she finally asked, trying to lighten the moment so she wouldn't rip off his clothes and climb him like a tree.

"No pressure," he agreed. "You're already the best I've ever had."

"The office was—"

"Not what I'm talking about."

Her heart melted and her lips parted to respond, but before she could, he'd whipped her dress off over her head, reached behind for the clasp on her bra, tossed the dress and bra over his shoulder, and tipped her back onto the bed through the V in the netting.

She landed on the mattress, turned on and in love and not caring that he could probably see both very clearly on her face.

Sawyer stripped off his jeans and boxers and stood before her, huge and hard, with a hungry but affectionate look on his face. He stroked his cock, almost absent-mindedly as he studied her, his hot gaze taking in everything from the top of her head to the nail polish on her toenails. Then he grasped one ankle and opened her legs. He knelt by the bed, took her ass in his hands, pulled her to the edge of the mattress, and dragged his tongue up her inner thigh.

Everything in her body went up in flames. Her scalp tingled, her nipples beaded, her palms got sweaty, her pussy clenched hard, and her toes curled.

He kissed his way to her mound, then opened her with his thumbs, sliding the pads up and down her outer lips, just studying her.

Juliet had never felt so hot and restless in her life. She

shifted against the sheets and reached for him. Probably to push him closer, though she wasn't entirely sure. She just needed to touch him somehow.

"Juliet," he said, not looking up.

"Yes?"

"I'm going to say this now, one time. Here are the ways you can move—you can lift your pussy closer to me, you can spread your legs wider, you can put your hands on your tits and play with your nipples, you can grab the sheets to hold on. Otherwise, you're going to lie there and take everything I'm about to give you."

She almost came right then and there.

Instead, she did...all of that. She grasped the sheet with one hand, lifted one to her aching right nipple, spread her legs and tilted her pelvis.

"That's my girl," he praised gruffly. Then he lowered his head and took her clit in his mouth.

He sucked hard, then licked, swirling his tongue over the sensitive bud. He sucked again, and Juliet felt her orgasm already winding tight in her core. He moved to thrust his tongue deep, tasting her with a satisfied groan that made her bones turn to liquid. Then he slid a thick, long finger deep, as his mouth returned to her clit.

He ate at her, finger fucking her, then using his tongue, then using two fingers, changing it up constantly, winding her tighter and tighter, until finally the dam burst and she came hard with a cry, her entire body trying to pull him deep.

He moved up her body, kissing over her belly, up her rib cage, sucking a nipple hard while rolling the other between thumb and finger, then tugging with just enough pressure to keep the ripples of her orgasm going. He dragged his whisker-roughened jaw up her neck sending goose bumps trickling down her body, then finally put his mouth against hers as he settled his huge cock between her legs. His kissed her slowly, stroking her tongue with his, making her taste herself, his hands gliding over her body, his calloused palms igniting her nerve endings and making her shift against him.

When she was wiggling against him again, her orgasm faded, but her body craving more already, he palmed her ass and rolled them both until she was on top of him.

Without a word, he handed her a condom.

Juliet sat back on his thighs, taking a moment to study him. He was just huge. She'd never been with a guy this big. Not just his cock, but everything. He was tall and broad, his muscles were thick and powerful, his hands were big, his fingers long. A little shiver of pleasure went over her thinking about those hands and fingers. She was *really* grateful for those. She took in the hard planes of his shoulders, chest, and abs. She ran her hand over his pecs, down the washboard bumps of his stomach, and then took his cock in hand. She stroked him a few times. He wrapped a hand around hers, making her squeeze tighter, and she stroked him like that a few times, too, relishing how his stomach and thighs tensed and how his jaw got tight.

God, she wanted to watch him lose it. She wanted him to come like this, losing his control, coming apart for her.

She lifted her hands to her breasts and toyed with her nipples. His gaze followed, his hand continuing to work his cock. She tugged and pinched, squeezing her thighs against his.

Then she slid a hand down her stomach to her mound.

"Where's the condom?" he asked, his voice rough.

"Not time for that yet." She rubbed the pad of her middle finger over her clit.

"No?" He watched her moving her finger.

She rotated her hips and saw him squeeze his cock tighter. "No."

"I'm not going to lie to you and tell you that I haven't imagined coming all over those gorgeous tits," he said.

Juliet squeezed her knees again. "I've never gotten myself off in front of someone before."

"Yeah, we're doing this," he told her immediately. "Play with that pretty pussy."

She did. She did what she typically did when she was alone and without her vibrator, but instead of thinking about the most recent dirty romance she'd read, she just watched Sawyer.

His dark eyes, his tense jaw, his huge hand wrapped around his throbbing cock, working it as he watched her. His hot gaze raked over her. He watched her pinching and tugging on her nipples, he watched her sliding two fingers deep and then circling her clit faster and faster and harder. Soon they were both breathing hard and Juliet felt the tightening of her pending climax.

"Sawyer," she said huskily. "I'm going to come."

He shifted, reaching for her and sliding a finger deep. With his huge middle finger filling her, thrusting into her, she came apart, calling his name, her knees clamping down on his thighs and her inner muscles clenching his finger.

The next moment, he shouted her name and came as well, hot white ribbons hitting her breasts and stomach.

He milked it until he was spent, then lay staring at her, his breathing ragged.

After a long moment, he gave a deep groan and reached for her, pulling her against his chest and rolling them, until they lay facing one another. Then he kissed her, hot and deep.

She'd never done anything like that and it felt like the most intimate moment she'd ever had.

And hot. He wasn't the only one who was going to be getting off to that memory.

When he pulled back, he held her face and stared at her. "Holy shit, woman."

She grinned. "Sorry. I know that wasn't the plan."

"Don't you ever fucking apologize for blowing my mind."

He grinned. "Of course, we do have a lot of things to still get to. Guess we're stayin' up late tonight."

She nodded, biting her bottom lip. "Yeah, we've only a few more days to get to everything."

Why had she said that? Did she want an invitation to spend the rest of her time in Autre here with him? Well, yeah, she did. But was she reminding him about her inevitable departure...or herself?

His grin disappeared and he swallowed hard. "Yeah." He stroked a hand up and down over her hip. "My list of dirty stuff is long." He paused. "You might just need to stay a little longer."

Stay a little longer.

She hadn't realized until that moment that *that* was the invitation she'd been hoping for.

"Yeah, maybe I will."

As she snuggled in next to him, she couldn't help one final thought—What if she stayed forever?

9

Iced tea wasn't cutting it. She needed more caffeine this morning. Desperately.

So desperately that she was walking across the grass toward the Boys of the Bayou office in only flip-flops rather than her work boots. Honestly, if she encountered a snake this morning, she wasn't sure she'd care.

Well, she'd care, but she wasn't sure she'd be able to work up even enough adrenaline to shriek.

She'd spent the past week with Sawyer finishing the dock, hanging out with his family, dancing to zydeco music, learning to eat crawfish—no, she did *not* suck the heads—

and making love all night long. Simply put, they hadn't been getting a lot of sleep. In the hottest, most delicious ways possible.

Then last night had been Chase's final night in Autre. They'd thrown him a huge party, complete with a live band and even more crawfish and beer. Along with moonshine. Lots of moonshine. Or—as Juliet had decided to refer to it—the vile potion of the Landry descendants. The party had gone on until nearly two a.m. Then everyone had gathered by Chase's rental car five hours later to send him off with hugs, advice, and invitations for him to come back anytime.

Juliet headed into the main office. It was either going to be coffee or soda, whichever she could get her hands on first, but she wasn't going to be able to handle the noise and crowd at Ellie's this morning.

Technically, it was nearing noon. Boys of the Bayou had shut down for the morning, clearly knowing how these parties went, and everyone had slept in. She still felt like she had cement in her head, and while the lunch crowd was smaller and quieter since a lot of people were working, Juliet didn't think she could handle anything spicier than toast for another few hours.

Sawyer had warned her about the potency of the moonshine she'd drunk last night.

Kennedy had, too.

Maddie had, too.

She hadn't listened.

She let herself in, instantly smelling the coffee, and sighed. Coffee it was. She honestly didn't care how she got the needed caffeine at this point and hey, the crazy Cajuns had been right about almost everything else so far. She should give their coffee a try. She glanced over to where Kennedy was slumped at the front counter. She lifted a hand, but Juliet wasn't sure if it was a wave or a don't-talk-to-me gesture.

Juliet headed for the coffeepot, filled a cup, and took a sip. She grimaced. That was nasty. But she was desperate. She doctored it with cream and sugar and tried again. Better. Doable.

Sighing, she turned and leaned against the counter, sipping slowly. She was hungover and tired, but she couldn't help but smile thinking about the party and Chase.

It sounded very much like he planned to spend at least part

of his Christmas break back here in the bayou, and Juliet had felt her heart kick thinking that maybe she'd join him.

He'd also been sent off with two huge bags. One was full of food and one was full of homemade creams and salves and potions for any and all ailments and situations—from stuck hinges to dirty bathtubs—that he might encounter as he headed off to medical school. It was almost as if they thought this was his first foray into the real world. Juliet smiled to herself at that. In many ways it was. It had only been two weeks, but she knew her little brother's perspective on the world at large had changed significantly. He was more grounded. More confident. More aware that he had a place in the world and a responsibility to fill that place to the best of his abilities.

Ellie had been the last one before Juliet to say goodbye to him. She'd taken his face in her hands, looked him directly in the eye and said, "I love you, boy. Don't be an asshole."

He'd nodded seriously and said, "I love you, too. I won't be."

"Call me when you get there."

"Promise."

"And I'll send you pie next Thursday."

"And I'll Facetime you when I get it and I'll eat while we talk."

"Then don't open it until seven and we'll Facetime in the bar. Then Cora and Leo and everyone can be there, too."

"Perfect."

Then they'd hugged.

Juliet had watched the exchange with wide eyes and a full heart. Chase hadn't needed to rebuild a dock or develop some blisters or repay a debt. He'd needed a grandmother.

He'd stepped in front of her next. "'Bye."

"'Bye." She'd smiled up at him. "I'm so proud of you."

He'd given her a soft smile she didn't remember seeing before. "Ditto."

"I'm going to miss you."

"Same."

"Be good," she'd told him with a little smile.

"I will. But you...don't be good, okay?"

"You don't think I should be good?"

"Let's put it this way—I know you like to be prepared because that makes you feel safe. But there are some things you can't prepare for." He looked around. "There's no way I could have prepared for all of this. But it was the best."

"So I should not worry about the stuff that's not already in my accordion file?" she'd asked, her chest feeling tight.

"Exactly. Because usually you have to fix it when things go off the rails. Here, there are a lot of people who will be there to help if that happens."

He was right. It hit her hard. There were people here who would help her with any plan that mattered to her. It didn't have to be their plan, it didn't even have to make sense to them. They'd have her back.

Sawyer would have her back. And he'd make her feel smart and beautiful and sassy and brave the whole time.

She'd pulled Chase into a hug and said, "Let me know when you get there."

"I will. And be sure you're over at Ellie's when I Facetime everyone later this week."

She grinned. It hadn't seemed that Chase thought it was strange that she was staying on without him. "Sounds good."

He'd gotten into the car and they'd all stood together, watching him drive off, like a big, happy family. Juliet wondered if her dad and older brothers even remembered that Chase was starting med school on Monday. Her mom would. Chase would call her tonight, too. But if their father didn't remember, Chase would be okay. He had a whole family full of people supporting him now.

She finished her cup, swallowed the ibuprofen she'd

brought with her, and fixed another cup. Ten minutes later, she was feeling a little better.

"This was bad timing," Kennedy said from behind her.

Juliet turned. "What was—"

Her question was interrupted by the door swinging open and two little kids came running into the office already talking.

Kennedy's entire demeanor changed in spite of her hangover. She lit up with a huge smile and slid off her stool. She rounded the counter and crouched to gather the little girl and boy into a hug.

"Hey, guys! Oh my gosh, you're here! I'm so excited!" She seemed completely sincere, too.

Juliet wasn't sure she'd seen Kennedy looking this friendly before. Then again, the kids were absolutely adorable and clearly ecstatic about being at the docks.

As the kids were greeting her and telling her about their baby sister and a trip to the aquarium, a big, good-looking guy stepped through the door.

Kennedy grinned up at him.

"Hey, Gabe, it's great to see you guys."

"Thrilled to be here," Gabe said. "It's been a while."

"Are Logan and Caleb with you?"

"Logan's girls had a dance competition this weekend and Caleb is working," Gabe said. "But they said to say hi and they definitely want a rain check."

Kennedy nodded. "Any time. You know that. I'm just so glad he texted you. I was shocked but—" She glanced in Juliet's direction. "There have been some changes around here."

The man followed her gaze and gave Juliet a smile. "Very glad to hear it." He stepped forward and extended a hand to Juliet. "Hi, you must be Juliet."

"I am." She took his hand, completely puzzled.

"I'm Gabe Trahan. I'm a friend of Sawyer's." He glanced at

Tori, who had slipped into the room from the other side of the building. "And Josh and Owen's."

"Josh used to work part-time for Gabe at his bar in New Orleans," Tori said. "Josh and Owen and Sawyer have spent a lot of time up at Trahan's with Gabe and his brother, Logan."

"We're very glad to be back down here with the gators in the wild, aren't we, Stella?" Gabe asked the little girl.

"Soooo glad!" Stella nodded her head so hard her dark curls bounced. "It's been *forever!*"

"It feels like it," Gabe agreed. He looked at Juliet again. "I've only got so many excuses for not building an alligator pond in my backyard."

"Someone wants you to build an alligator pond in your backyard?" Juliet asked.

He pointed to Stella, who was now peering into the tanks full of frogs and turtles that Maddie had put on shelves in the room to occupy the tourist kids while they were waiting for their swamp tours.

"Did you know that Stella and Sawyer were engaged?" the little boy asked her.

Juliet's eyes widened. "Is that right?"

"Because he's got the boats and the alligators," Stella said, turning back. "But he's old. And he hunts the alligators." She frowned. "When he works for me, I'm not going to let him do that though."

"You're going to have a swamp boat tour company?" Juliet asked her.

"I'm going to have *this* swamp boat tour company."

The girl had to be about nine, but she seemed determined and very sure of her career path. Juliet figured there was time for her to learn about conservation measures and other reasons that keeping animal populations under control was important.

"It's nice that you'll let the guys still work for you," Juliet said.

Stella shrugged. "They'll have to stop hunting and I think we need different hats."

Juliet grinned at Gabe and he lifted a shoulder. "Girl knows what she likes."

Juliet could respect that.

"So, *you* can marry him," Stella told her. "But he still has to do tours. He's the best tour guide."

You can marry him. She was nine. Those words should not have made Juliet feel like someone had sucked all of the oxygen out of the room. They meant nothing. Stella had been planning to marry him for his boats and the alligators after all. She didn't even know how truly amazing Sawyer was. In every freaking way. But it was just an innocent, little girl thing to say.

Still, Juliet struggled for that deep breath for a long moment.

"Sawyer is the best tour guide?" Kennedy asked. "I think Owen's pretty good."

Stella gave her an unimpressed look. "Owen drives fast and he messes around with Wilma and Betty, but he didn't even know that alligators can go twenty miles per hour in the water."

Clearly true knowledge about alligators was the most important thing. "Who are Wilma and Betty?" Juliet asked.

"The female alligators who are in love with Owen," Stella said with a little giggle.

"Alligators can be trained to recognize certain people by their voices and smells," the little boy piped up.

"The alligators *love* Owen?" Tori asked. "You're sure?"

"Yes. All girls love Owen," Stella said with a grin. "He's *super cute.*"

Tori laughed. "Well, I think Josh is cuter."

"Josh is cute, too," Stella agreed.

"I think I might have my hands full when she gets to be a teenager," Gabe muttered.

Juliet had the impression that his hands were already pretty full. She laughed.

Sawyer hadn't said anything about any of these people and Juliet wondered why. Obviously, they all knew each other and the Boys of the Bayou well. They'd apparently been here a lot. Stella was, unapologetically, a huge Sawyer fan. How had he not mentioned them?

"Well, I think also Josh is the best tour guide," Tori said. "He knows *everything* about alligators."

"Everything?" the little boy asked.

"That's Cooper, by the way," Kennedy said to Juliet. "He's our human encyclopedia. Just watch."

"Well," Tori said, putting a hand on one hip. "I am a veterinarian and I've taught him lots of stuff. I even pulled a fishing hook out of an alligator's foot about a week ago. The guys saw it and caught him, then held him down while I took it out."

Cooper and Stella stared at her.

"No way," Cooper said, clearly impressed.

"Way," Tori said with a nod. "The guy was *mad*, but I had to help him, right?"

"Do you have pictures?" Cooper asked her, looking fascinated and horrified at the same time.

"I do," Tori said. "Even a video."

Cooper's eyes got wide. "Did you know that there are American alligators and Chinese alligators and the Chinese alligators are endangered?"

Tori nodded. "Did you know they have two kinds of walk?"

Cooper nodded. "A high walk with their belly off the ground and a low walk where it touches! Did you know that an American alligator can weight up to *one thousand* pounds?"

Tori smiled. "That's *so big*. Did you know that the word alligator comes from the Spanish word el lagarto which means 'the lizard'?"

"Yes!" Cooper had inched closer to her throughout the conversation and he was looking at her with wonder.

So, Sawyer had a fan, but Tori obviously did now, too. Juliet grinned.

"Really happy that Sawyer invited us down," Gabe said. He'd moved closer to Juliet and was watching his kids as he spoke.

They were all talking to one another and Tori, peppering her with questions about other animals. She'd told them about the eagle she'd rescued—though she'd left out the fact that the bird was currently hanging out in Leo's trailer—and about the river otters. Juliet knew she was worried about Gus. He hadn't taken the bait in the cage yet, so he was still out, wild and free, and she was afraid he wouldn't come back. Or that he'd come back just in time to be caught by the wildlife woman.

"Sawyer invited you down?" Juliet asked Gabe. She was mildly surprised by the invitation portion of that. "You didn't just schedule a tour?"

"We've tried to schedule a couple," Gabe said. "But Sawyer hasn't been up to it."

Juliet frowned slightly. "Yeah, it's been rough for him."

"It has."

"But you guys came down regularly before?"

"Absolutely. I used the boat tour to win Stella and Addison over when I was first showing her how we could combine the parenting thing with the dating thing."

Juliet smiled. "And it worked?"

"Definitely. Stella is an adventurer at heart and the bayou won her over immediately."

"The bayou and Sawyer."

Gabe grinned. "And Sawyer. But it really was about the boats and gators."

Juliet shook her head. "It was the way he was clearly enjoying every bit of it, too, and how much he loved watching her discover it all. And the way he let her be curious and try things her way, but also let her know he was looking out for her. The way he made her feel safe and made her feel interesting and amazing and brave."

Gabe looked at her with surprise, but he slowly nodded. "Yeah. It was all of that, too."

Juliet swallowed. "Yeah."

"And now I know for certain why I finally got that text from him inviting us down here."

"Because of me?" she asked.

"Apparently you've made him feel safe and amazing and brave, too."

That hit her directly in the heart. God, she hoped she'd made him feel those things. She really wanted him to feel those things. And to think *she* might be helping him feel them...she got tingles thinking she was making him feel stuff he hadn't in a while. Could hearts get tingles? It seemed they could.

"We haven't seen him up in N'Awlins in a while, either. Glad to know that might change now, too. Missed having him around."

Juliet nodded. That didn't surprise her. Sawyer had really pulled back. That made her want to hug him. Then again, him walking into a room made her want to hug him.

Which he did just then.

"Hey, everybody!"

The kids squealed and Stella and Cooper beelined for him.

Juliet actually felt her heart flip over in her chest. He looked so good. He'd clearly *not* overdone on the moonshine. He looked great. Fully awake and ready to go. He was wearing khaki cargo pants and a black Boys of the Bayou shirt that clung to him. He had sunglasses on and a black cap set backward on his head.

She saw him take a deep breath, but she was sure that no one else would even notice—no one else was watching him as closely as she was—just before he took his sunglasses off, hooking them in the neckline of his shirt, and knelt and opened his arms.

A thought occurred to her just as Stella threw her arms around his neck.

"Oh my God, he hasn't seen the kids since Tommy's accident, has he?" she asked.

Gabe was watching his kids greet Sawyer, his eyes looking a little shiny. He shook his head. "Nope."

"So, they haven't seen his scar." Her gaze was back on the trio.

"No. I told them he'd been hurt though. They know about it. But they're both very...inquisitive."

"He's ready for that." Juliet was sure Sawyer had braced himself.

She watched Stella pull back and study Sawyer's face.

Sawyer just let her look.

Stella lifted her hand to Sawyer's scar, touching it gently. "Does it hurt?"

Sawyer shook his head, swallowing hard. Juliet held her breath.

"Not as much as it used to. It's getting better all the time."

"I'm glad it was just your face," Stella told him.

Juliet hugged her arms around her middle, watching the emotions cross Sawyer's face.

"Oh yeah?" Sawyer asked.

The little girl nodded. "Faces heal better than internal organs. Like hearts. Heart problems can be bad."

Juliet felt her breath catch in her throat.

Sawyer nodded. "Heart problems really can be."

"And livers," Stella added, immediately deflating the emotion around the idea of hearts being hurt. These kids were nine. They were talking about the actual organ. "You've only got one liver, so you can't just get rid of that like you can a kidney."

"You can get a liver transplant though," Cooper informed his sister, moving closer to Sawyer and Stella. "It's a long list though. So yeah, your face was probably better."

Juliet heard Gabe give a soft snort beside her and felt herself smiling.

"What about a spleen?" Stella asked Cooper. "You only have one but you can live without it, right?"

"Yes. But you'll get more infections," the boy said with a tone that indicated he was the authority on all things related to the spleen. "And you could actually live without *any* kidneys," he told Stella. Her eyes grew wider and he looked pleased. "You'd have to go on dialysis, but you could be alive."

"You could live with *no kidneys at all*?" Stella clarified.

"Yep."

"Wow."

"But," Cooper turned back to Sawyer. "Hurting your face was better than hurting your kidneys."

Sawyer nodded. "I think I completely agree." He looked from one kid to the other. "It doesn't look scary though?"

They both shook their heads. "You look badass," Cooper said.

"Coop," Gabe said with warning—while clearly trying not to laugh. "I don't think badass is appropriate for a nine-year-old."

"But he does," Cooper told his father. "And Uncle Logan says sometimes bad words are the only ones that really express feelings fully."

"I'm sure he does," Gabe said, clearly trying to cover a grin. "But Uncle Logan isn't right about everything."

"I'm going to tell him you said that," Cooper said, giving Gabe a mischievous grin.

Gabe sighed. "He already knows."

Juliet giggled.

Sawyer also grinned and it made Juliet's stomach flip. He

looked happy and completely at ease. Seeing the kids and talking about his scar had been okay. He was doing alright.

Seeing him happy and dealing with all of this with a smile, teasing and interacting with the kids with ease, made her feel a sense of happiness herself that she could only compare to how she felt when she saw Chase surrounded by the Landrys. Seeing someone she loved happy like that gave her a sense of deep satisfaction that was hard to explain.

And she definitely loved Sawyer Landry.

And she kind of wanted to tell him that suddenly.

"Can we go now?" Stella asked. "I haven't been out on the water in *forever*."

Sawyer grinned and stretched to his feet. He put a hand on her head. "We can definitely go now. I'm really sorry it's been so long."

Juliet heard the little catch in his voice, but no one else seemed to notice. The kids cheered and Gabe and Kennedy grinned. Tori led the kids out to the dock to get them onto the boats and Gabe followed them out.

Kennedy started after them but at the last minute turned back, crossed to Juliet, pulled her into a hug and whispered, "Thank you for making him smile again."

Juliet squeezed her. "It's the kids."

"You know it's not the kids." Kennedy let her go, gave her brother a smile, and headed out to the dock.

Through the window, Juliet saw Tori applying spray sunscreen. Kennedy joined them and started helping the kids with their hats and life jackets.

Juliet turned to Sawyer. "This is a big deal, isn't it?"

But instead of answering, he stepped close, cupped the back of her head, and pulled her up against his body. He kissed her, long and deep and sweet. Juliet wrapped her arms around his neck and kissed him back. She was going to take that as a yes. She was so happy for him.

It was long seconds before he lifted his head and let her settle back on her heels.

"It's a big deal," he confirmed. "And it's because of you."

Juliet blinked up at him. "What?"

He nodded. "I haven't been able to face these people, Juliet. I didn't know how to deal with their enthusiasm for something I hated. I didn't want to try to fake it with them like I do with strangers. But if you can get back on your bike after a stroke, I can get back on that bayou after Tommy."

Juliet took all of that in, her heart expanding as he said it. "Wow," she told him when he'd stopped. "That's...amazing."

"*You're* amazing. You live the life you want to live. Regardless of some physical weakness, some deeply engrained what-if scenarios, and a fear of water. I want to do that, too."

Juliet felt a strange combination of pride and love and trepidation.

This guy was putting her up on a pedestal that she wasn't so sure she deserved.

She loved that he admired her. She loved the way he looked at her as if she was amazing and as if he was...in love with her.

That was truly how he looked at her. Like he was falling for her. And wow, that did things to her she could hardly put into words.

But this was dangerous. He was falling for this idea of her that she wanted to be true but that she wasn't sure was entirely real.

She'd gotten back on the bike. But the bike wasn't where she'd had the stroke and almost drowned. She had *not* gotten over her fear of water.

"Sawyer, I'm not all that brave. Don't think that I don't ever worry or—"

"Woman, your worrying is one of the sexiest and sweetest things about you," he said with a grin that stopped her talking.

God, she loved when he smiled like that. He looked so damned happy.

"Will you go out on the tour with us?" he asked, running a hand down her arm and linking their fingers. "I would love to show you what the tours are like and have you get to know these people better. I'd also love to have you there in case I... start to overreact to something."

Oh, crap. He needed her support.

Out on the water.

The *water*.

Her gut clenched thinking about it. If she closed her eyes and let her mind go there, she could still feel the water pressing in on her, as if it was trying to push her down, as if it was sucking the air out of her lungs, as if she was wrapped in invisible rope, unable to move and fight. She could remember the moment when she realized that she wasn't strong enough to get out of it by herself. The fear, the helplessness, then the resignation. Then the relief when she felt her brother's arms around her.

Her heart raced and she felt light-headed at the *idea* of being out on the wild waters of the bayou, out of reach of solid land, nothing keeping her from going under but a lightweight boat propelled by a big fan at the back.

Then she looked up at the man in front of her.

Okay, nothing but the boat and Sawyer.

Sawyer would be there.

She looked up into his eyes and felt her head nodding. How could she say no? He was a pro. He'd done this a million times. The bayou wasn't that deep. She'd have a life jacket on. Stella wasn't afraid.

And Sawyer was asking her. Sawyer needed her.

He admired that she'd fought for her bike rides. And she had. She'd done that. She'd gotten on that bike in spite of the risks. That wasn't nothing.

She'd love to really feel that she deserved all of his admiration. She would earn the admiration of her bravery if she went out onto the bayou with him.

"Of course," she told him. Because what else could she really say?

The smile he gave her in response was everything she needed to see.

He gave her a big hug and then grabbed her hand, pulling her out to the dock where everyone was getting ready.

Juliet eyed the water and, ironically, felt her mouth go dry.

———

SAWYER BREATHED DEEP AS THE RUMBLE OF THE AIRBOAT HUMMED through his body, and he watched the front of the boat cutting through the water, the people bobbing on the padded metal benches of the boat. And not just any people. One of his best friends, some of his favorite kids in the world, and the woman that he was falling in love with.

He couldn't see her face, but Juliet sat right in the middle of the boat, her life jacket strapped tightly around the body that he was completely, officially addicted to, gripping the bench with both hands, her body stiff and tense.

Her being on the boat with him was a big deal. He got that. She was a little freaked out here. She was out on the water for him, because of him. She would have never gone out with anyone else and that meant the world to him.

But he was determined to show her that would be fine. He was determined to show *himself* that it would be fine.

Stella was, as usual, bouncing in her seat. Maybe more than usual. The little girl had been away from her beloved bayou for a while and it made sense that she was overly excited. At one point, he'd slowed considerably as he'd noted a big gator basking on the bank and wanted to be sure the kids saw it. He didn't point it out. For one, the airboat engine was too loud to talk over. For another, the kids were scanning the water and banks like hawks looking for mice. He knew Cooper spotted it when he pointed and Stella popped up and leaned close to the railing.

Juliet reached over and gently tugged Stella back into her seat by the strap on the back of her life jacket. Then she nodded as Stella looked at Juliet with a big grin and pointed at the alligator. She didn't have to hold onto Cooper. He was obediently sitting right next to Gabe in front of Juliet.

Sawyer grinned at the whole damned thing.

A few minutes later, he turned them into the area where Hank, the gator who loved *him* the way Wilma and Betty loved Owen—purely for the snacks they brought, of course— and killed the engine.

They all took their headsets off, and the kids were able to move around, standing and getting close to the railings on the sides of the boat.

Everyone moved, except for Juliet. Who stayed glued to her seat. With her headset on.

Sawyer didn't push. This was her first time out on the airboats. They were loud, they moved fast along the straightaways, and they drove right through the swamp grass into areas you couldn't get to any other way. The only way out of this part of the bayou was by boat—specifically airboat since a regular boat's motor would get almost instantly tangled in the grass and vegetation—or with a rope dropped from a helicopter.

They found Hank after a few minutes of floating and chatting. Sawyer tossed him a few pieces of chicken and he came close, delighting Stella and making Cooper look fascinated and sick at the same time. The way it always had been with these kids.

Sawyer kept casting looks in Juliet's direction. She met his gaze and gave him a wobbly smile a couple of times. For the most part she seemed...resigned. She wasn't delighted or thrilled. That was clear. Even Cooper seemed more interested in the whole thing than she was. But she wasn't hyperventilating. Or vomiting.

Maybe he shouldn't have brought her out here.

The thought floated through his mind.

She didn't *need* to be out here. He'd needed her. She made him feel better. But was that really fair if it made *her* feel anxious?

Sawyer frowned.

She was out on a fucking airboat, on water, far from solid ground, surrounded—whether they could see them or not—by alligators, snapping turtles, snakes, spiders, and more. Seeing her sitting there with her life jacket on, long sleeves to protect from sun and bugs, and the steel-toed boots that would actually *not* be great in the water, made him realize that she truly was facing her fears here today. For him.

"Juliet—" He started, stepping toward her.

Just then a huge drop of water hit the floor of the boat in front of him. Another hit him on the cheek. He looked up as a rumble of thunder rolled through the clouds overhead. It had been overcast all day, but that just meant it had been slightly cooler. That morning it had occurred to him that maybe they'd get a little shower at some point, but...he also hadn't looked at the weather forecast.

He'd been distracted. Chase's party last night and send-off that morning had thrown their usual Saturday routine off, and then he'd been preoccupied with the idea of seeing Gabe and the guys and kids again. *What if a storm rolled in while they were out today* wasn't something he'd prepared for. That was unusual. But he'd been excited about this group coming down, and his preparation had only gone as far as *get them here and hold your shit together.*

The raindrops started falling faster, and Gabe looked up as

another, louder, rumble of thunder sounded. Juliet didn't hear a thing since she still had her headset on, but she definitely noticed the rain falling. She looked up with a frown and pulled her headset off.

"It's raining, Daddy," Stella said, lunging for Gabe's hand, her expression worried.

Gabe nodded, drawing her close. "It is."

It was sprinkling, actually. But Sawyer didn't correct them. Darker clouds were rolling closer from the west and he knew it was going to be real rain real soon.

"Is this a hurricane?" Cooper asked, also moving close to Gabe and grabbing his father's belt.

"No, buddy, not a hurricane. Just some rain," Gabe said, in a calm, reassuring voice.

In spite of not looking at the forecast, a hurricane warning wasn't something Sawyer could have missed. Everyone in Autre would have been talking about it, as a storm like that affected everyone from the fishermen to the roughnecks. But a hard afternoon shower could make the bayou tours much less pleasant and even dangerous.

Dammit.

"But it could have lightning," Cooper said. "Lightning comes with thunderstorms and *lots* of people die from lightning while out boating."

"Okay," Gabe said quickly over the top of his son. "We don't need to talk about that right now."

But it was too late. Stella had heard him.

Gabe loved to talk about his kids, and Sawyer knew that Stella had a fear of storms. Sawyer hated the idea of Stella out on the boat on the bayou in one. His injury hadn't made her scared of the bayou but being caught in a storm out here really could.

But it was more than just Stella's fear of storms that had his heart pounding now. Cooper was right. Thunderstorms came with lightning and the people most often struck were those outside on the water.

"Okay, everyone back in their seats," Sawyer said, clapping his hands. "We're heading in."

The rain was picking up, making the bottom of the metal boat slippery, and he grabbed the backs of the benches as he made his way to his seat. He glanced at Juliet. She was still exactly where she'd started, still buckled tight into her life jacket, but now her face was white. He leaned in and kissed her on the cheek. She turned to look at him as if she'd been lost in thought.

"You okay?" he asked.

She read his lips and nodded.

He didn't really believe her. He shouldn't have brought her out here. Not only was she out on the water, no doubt realizing how far away from the safety of shore they really were, but now it was storming. Stella wasn't the only one he was worried about here.

But he wasn't sure how to fix it for Juliet. He wanted to pull her into his arms and tell her it would be okay. There were two things wrong with that, however. One, he had to drive the boat back to the dock. Two, he couldn't tell her that. She knew better than anyone that no matter how prepared you were, things could still go wrong. Knees still got scraped, bats still got caught in nets, splinters still got stuck in fingers. No, telling Juliet Dawson "it will all be okay" was never going to be an adequate approach.

He was just going to have to *show* her.

"You wanna help me drive, Stell?" Sawyer asked as he straightened. "We can go extra fast with two drivers." That wasn't true, but he was hoping he could get her thinking about something else.

This boat was one of their bigger ones and did have two seats, so he could put her back there with him and maybe distract her from the storm with a new view. Sometimes two of the guys would take it out together, one driving and one on the mic, talking to the tour through their headsets. He hadn't needed to do that today since all of these people had been out on the swamp tours before. Except for Juliet, of course, but he figured she didn't particularly want a play-by-play of what they were doing. She'd been concentrating on just holding on tight.

"Okay." Stella was looking a little nervous, but she managed a smile. Her tennis shoes also slipped on the wet floor, but she held on and made it to the shorter single seat that sat in front of Sawyer's at the back of the boat.

He got Stella strapped into the higher seat and was just turning back when he heard, "Cooper!"

He swung around to see Juliet come up out of her seat and lunge for the side of the boat.

Cooper was reaching over the side of the boat for something floating in the water. Juliet grabbed for the little boy, catching him by the back of the life jacket. Instinctively, Sawyer jumped over the seat in front of him and charged toward her.

He reached out just as she skidded on the wet deck, sliding forward.

He could admit he had visions of grabbing the back of her pants the way he had on the dock the first day, saving her just in the nick of time.

Unfortunately, he'd completely underestimated how much adrenaline was pumping and how slippery the deck really was. He slid and, rather than grabbing her and pulling her back, he crashed into her, sending Cooper over the edge, and Juliet and himself over the railing and into the bayou.

10

THEY LANDED WITH A SPLASH AND A SCREAM. SAWYER'S HEAD
dipped below the surface for a moment. The water wasn't cold
and Sawyer felt his feet brush the bottom almost immediately,
but his brain didn't care that the bayou was only about six feet
deep here. He could barely touch. It wasn't as if he could really
plant his feet firmly. Frankly, his instinct was to panic. He'd
been in this water thousands of times in his life. But not since
Tommy. He didn't think about all of the times it had been fine.
All he thought or felt was that this was dangerous, and that
Juliet and Cooper were in here. More specifically, that Juliet
and Cooper were in *danger*.

There were shouts from the boat and he could hear Cooper
crying for his dad. The rain was coming down harder now,
giving everything a gray haze, but he spotted Juliet and Cooper
right away. His heart hammered painfully against his chest, and
his mind raced as he realized they were too far away to reach.
Somehow Cooper had gotten further out from the boat than
Sawyer and Juliet and she'd had to swim to him. Probably
because Cooper was smaller and lighter than the two of them
and the force of Sawyer plowing into them had sent him flying.

Hell, it had probably sent Juliet out several feet, too. The woman who had almost drowned as a little girl.

"Daddy!" Cooper cried. "Daddy!"

"It's okay, Coop."

Sawyer heard Gabe trying to reassure his son. "It's okay, Sawyer's got you."

But Sawyer didn't fucking have him. Cooper was holding onto a woman who was too short to touch the bottom out here, who had only one good leg and arm to use to swim because the other side was weaker from her stroke. Not to mention that she had to be petrified right now. Oh, and there was a big old alligator swimming around out here.

Sure, Hank would likely get the hell away from all the splashing and screaming. Then again, Sawyer was one of the people in the water and he brought Hank chicken. It wouldn't be crazy to think that Hank might swim over for a closer look in the hopes of another snack.

Sawyer looked around, blood roaring in his ears. He didn't want to kill an alligator or lose a limb to one in front of a boatload of little kids, but he fucking would put himself between the animal and Juliet and Cooper if he had to. If he saw the thing. It wasn't as if alligators weren't masters at sneaking up on prey.

Dammit.

Sawyer tried to calm down. Hank wasn't going to be a problem and they were only a few feet from the boat. He knew those things were true. He dragged in a deep breath.

But then his eyes landed on a dark shape a few feet away. It was nearly black, and the odds were nearly a million to one that it was a log. A simple fallen tree. There were hundreds out here. Dark objects just under the surface of the water were very, very likely just logs.

But what if it's not?

The thought went through his mind unbidden. Tommy had

maybe seen the shark that attacked him that day. He'd maybe thought it was a log, too.

Sawyer's mouth went dry and he felt like he was going to be sick.

"What if there's a lightning strike?" Cooper called to Gabe. "I'm a sittin' duck!"

That was it. In a few powerful strokes, Sawyer was beside them. He grabbed Juliet's arm, but she pulled away.

"Dammit! Juliet!"

"I need my arm to stay above water!" she shouted at him. "Cooper will pull me down on this side!"

"Let me have him," Sawyer said, reaching for the boy.

But Cooper shook his head and squeezed Juliet's neck tighter. "I can't let go!"

"Let me pull you to the boat," Sawyer told her, reaching for her again.

"I'm not strong enough to hold him and paddle much longer."

Her voice was edged with panic and Sawyer reacted to it, fear and frustration surging through him. Sawyer wrapped a big arm around Juliet's waist, hugged her and Cooper to his side, and kicked off with everything in him. He got them to the boat and Gabe was immediately there, hauling Cooper onto the deck and then Juliet. Sawyer pulled himself up.

Adrenaline still pumping, Sawyer surged to his feet. Cooper was wrapped in Gabe's arms. Sawyer hauled Juliet to her feet and crushed her to his chest.

That's when the shaking started.

He wasn't sure if it was him or her, but his entire body was quaking within seconds. The life jacket was in the way of getting her up against him fully. He pulled back and started to unbuckle her.

But she knocked his hands away. "No!"

He looked into her face for the first time.

She was ghost white, her eyes were huge, and her breathing was too fast.

"Jul—"

"I'm not taking it off," she said firmly. She grabbed the end of one of the buckles and pulled it tighter in fact.

Right. She was still out on the boat. She'd just fallen in. Okay, she'd just been pushed in.

Sawyer dragged in a deep breath. He reached under the nearest seat and pulled out another life jacket. He wrapped it around her and the one she had on, tightened it, and then set her on the bench. He wrapped a blanket around her shoulders.

He'd been fine, having a great time in fact, when she'd been sitting stiffly and safely in the middle of the boat. The moment she'd moved, he'd freaked. That was a problem. The people in his life couldn't just sit still all the time. But clearly he wasn't over the overreacting after all.

She sat still, staring forward.

He glanced at Cooper and Gabe. The little boy was cuddled on his dad's lap with his sister right next to them, her hand on his back.

"Stell?" he asked, his voice gruff.

She looked over her shoulder.

He gestured toward Juliet. The little girl nodded and moved back a row to sit next to Juliet. She took Juliet's hand and Juliet let her.

It was sweet. And Sawyer hated it. He wanted to be the one comforting her.

But he had to drive the boat back.

He was also the one who'd pushed her into the bayou because he'd overreacted to her leaning over the side.

And he'd frozen up once in the water. He hadn't grabbed her immediately and gotten her back onto the boat. He'd panicked. He'd freaked out. And, with a weaker right side, she'd had to try to tread water while holding onto a scared little boy in the bayou that not only was she scared of, but that she had *every* reason to fear.

He'd lost Tommy because he hadn't been there.

But he could have lost Juliet today and he *had* been there. Right there.

Sawyer forced himself onto the seat at the back of the boat, started the engine, and turned them for the docks.

———

She had no idea how to feel.

Wet.

That was mostly how she felt at the moment. And *not* in a good way.

The ride back to the Boys of the Bayou dock seemed forty-seven hours long. The rumble of the airboat and the droning sound that cancelled everything else out put her in a bubble with her thoughts. She was vaguely aware that Sawyer had sat her on a bench, put her headphones on her, and wrapped her in a blanket. She felt Stella's hand in hers. She knew that Cooper was with his dad. She didn't have anyone to worry about. She knew that Cooper was physically okay. He'd been dunked under the water briefly, but she'd gotten to him quickly. But in the back of her mind she was concerned about his mental state. He was clearly a worrier. Something the two of them had in common. She'd seen him reaching for the hat that had blown off his head and she'd panicked. He'd been reaching too far and the deck of the boat had been slippery, so she'd grabbed the back of his vest...

And Sawyer had pushed them all into the bayou.

Sawyer. The guy who'd *caught* her the other day, who'd kept her *out* of the bayou day one, who understood how she felt about the water.

Juliet felt herself frowning.

She'd fallen in the damned bayou. Even with people right there around her. A couple of big, strong people. And with a life jacket on. She'd fallen into the bayou where there were snakes and alligators and sharks.

Because of Sawyer. Not that he'd meant to, of course. She didn't think that. But he'd clearly overreacted. And then...he'd frozen up.

Once she was in the water and struggling with Cooper, Sawyer had frozen up.

It had probably been for only a minute or so, but it had felt excruciatingly long. Juliet put her hand over her heart. It was racing now, remembering how it felt to hold onto Cooper with her strong arm and try to paddle with her weaker side. She'd known she couldn't keep it up for long. But she'd known that Sawyer was right there. That he'd come and get her. But he hadn't. Not right away. Not at first. Not before she was terrified.

Juliet forced herself to take a deep breath.

Okay, part of her terror was *her*. Her past near-drowning, the fact that she never swam, that she was afraid of water, that she'd panicked once she'd ended up immersed by surprise. Sawyer hadn't hesitated more than a few seconds, she was sure. But he wasn't without his demons around the water. They'd clearly established that. She just wasn't so sure they could both have water phobias. She couldn't help him with his if she was freaking out. And vice versa.

They pulled up to the dock seemingly eighty-four years later.

Gabe and his kids climbed out first. Sawyer waited until it was just the two of them.

For some reason, Juliet couldn't handle the idea of him helping her off the boat. She was jumpy and wet and cold, and the rain seemed to be an unrelenting mockery of her hatred for water.

She tried to scramble up the single step onto the dock, but

Sawyer was right there, his hand on her elbow, helping to lift her up. When she stepped up onto the platform she swung around.

"Stop, okay? Just stop. I don't need your help. Now."

Okay, she probably hadn't needed to add that *now* on the end.

He didn't seem surprised though. In fact, he looked miserable. "I'm so sorry."

"I just..." She took a deep breath and glanced around. Gabe and the kids had moved into the main office, out of the rain, and no one else was around. Juliet focused on the man in front of her. The man she'd fallen in love with. The man who lived a life that seemed like a horrible mismatch for her. "I don't belong here."

"I don't think that's true."

Her heart clenched in her chest. "Sawyer, I will *always* be a liability. That's what you have to understand. The bayou, all of this..." She pushed her wet hair back from her face. "This place is physically demanding, and I will always have a deficit in that department."

"You didn't fall in today because of your stroke, Juliet," he said, looking frustrated. "It was an accident, but I pushed you. It wasn't you."

"But it could *easily* be me," she said, feeling the fear still pumping through her veins, mixed with frustration over the truth of what she was saying. "If I was someone else, maybe I wouldn't have fallen in. Maybe I would have grabbed the railing. Maybe I would have grabbed Cooper faster and pulled him back so you wouldn't have lunged. Maybe you wouldn't have worried and lunged at all, if I was someone else. Maybe I fell in partly because I don't have good coordination." She held up a hand as he started to speak. "Or maybe it all would have happened exactly as it did, but I would have been able to get Cooper back to the boat on my own. *That* was on me. I needed your help for that when someone else wouldn't have. And that freaked you out. And me. And Cooper."

Sawyer shoved a hand through his wet hair. "I froze up, Juliet. I'll admit that. And I'm so fucking sorry. I had this bad reaction to the bayou and having someone else I love out there, in trouble, needing me..." He blew out a breath. "And I can't promise that won't happen again."

Juliet nodded, swallowing hard, forcing down the lump in her throat. "I know you're sorry. I know it was an accident." She took a breath. "But, I don't know if we're a good combination— you, me, and the bayou."

Sawyer shook his head. "God, please tell me that's not true. Please tell me we can work this out. I can do this, I promise. I can get my shit together and be there to help you when you need me. I swear it."

Juliet shook her head. If she started crying, no one would be able to tell if the drops on her face were tears or rain, but she had to hold it together until she was alone because she feared she was truly going to crumble.

Sawyer pulled himself up out of the boat. Juliet started to turn away, realizing that staying around long enough for him to get close had been a huge mistake.

But he caught her wrist and made her turn back. "Your mom learned," Sawyer said, leaning in. "She was scared. She probably froze up sometimes, too, but she learned, right?"

Juliet sniffed. "The thing is, Sawyer, eventually... I left." Her voice got softer. "She doesn't have to worry about the bike rides and what might happen because she's not there waiting for me to come home now."

Sawyer's jaw tightened. "I want to be waiting for you to come home."

"It will get old," she promised him. "You are a protector. You will worry. And I can't promise you it will get better. It won't. You worry about Tori and Josh and Maddie and Owen and

Kennedy. But they can fix things. They can do better next time."
She swallowed. "I can't."

"Jul—"

She pulled back from the hand he lifted to her face. "I need to go get dry and..." She looked down. She was muddy and dirty and confused. No, she couldn't *see* the confused, but it was definitely there. "I need to...go."

He paused, but finally nodded and released her.

"I—" She really had nothing more to say. So, she turned on her heel and headed up the ramp. She'd go to Cora's, she'd get in the shower, she'd clean the bayou off, and she'd...figure out what to do next.

"Thanks, Juliet."

The little voice stopped her at the top of the wooden walkway. She looked over to find Cooper Trahan standing under the eaves of the building with Gabe.

She gave him a smile. "Hey, sweetie. Are you okay?"

"I think so." Cooper looked down as if checking. "Stella thought that was—" He looked up at Gabe, then back to Juliet and whispered, "Badass."

Juliet felt herself smile in spite of everything.

"I think that maybe in this case, badass is appropriate," Gabe said with a low chuckle, setting his hand on his son's head. He looked up at Juliet. "Are *you* okay?"

"I'm..." She looked down at Cooper again. "Fine." She was. She was fine. She was who she'd always been. She'd done what she'd had to do. But she'd learned from the experience. After she'd skinned her knees, she'd started carrying the first aid kit. After she'd fallen in the bayou, she was going to...avoid the bayou from now on.

Gabe didn't look like he was buying the "fine" thing though. "Sawyer would have never let anything happen to you," he said.

She nodded. "The thing is, it happened to him, too, you know?"

"Did I scare you about the lightning?" Cooper asked. He looked sincerely worried. "I sometimes say stuff that scares Stella. And it's true. But I sometimes need to learn when to keep stuff to myself or say it at different times than I do."

Juliet didn't laugh but she kind of wanted to. That sounded like a talk that one or both of his parents had had with him in the past. "Well, the idea of being struck by lightning is a little scary," she said. "But I don't think that's a good reason to *not* say it. We should all know when things are dangerous so that we can make plans and be as safe as we can be."

Cooper's eyes got wide. "That's what I think, too!"

She smiled. "I knew we had a lot in common when we first met."

Cooper beamed at that. "And I'm going to have to work here at Boys of the Bayou, too," he said.

"Oh, I don't work here," Juliet said.

"You don't? You don't help Sawyer out?" Cooper asked.

"I..." Did she help Sawyer out? She liked to think she had, in some small way. "I do. But I'm his friend."

"Oh." Cooper nodded. "Well, I'm Stella's brother. But I'm going to work with her, too."

"You want to drive airboats?" Honestly, that didn't seem to fit the little boy.

"No," Cooper said adamantly. "But, I will," he said. "Someone has to look out for Stella."

That grabbed Juliet by the heart. "You would do that? Even though you don't like the bayou that much?" She'd figured that out by the way the little boy had stayed in the middle of the boat and had strapped his life jacket on first thing just like she had.

"Well, yeah," he said with a shrug. "Stella is excitable," he said, in a tone that indicated perhaps he'd also heard that from a grown-up or two. "I'm practical. I keep her safe and she makes sure I have fun. Everyone needs someone to balance them out."

Juliet felt the lump in her throat again. Everyone did need that. It had seemed that she and Sawyer could be that. Did she have anyone else to balance her? To be there for her when she was excitable? Or to calm when they were excitable? Chase, maybe. She smiled at Cooper. Brothers could be so awesome for their sisters.

And their brothers. Sawyer's brother and his cousin and sister were great for him, too.

But *she* wanted to be great for him.

"Do you want us to walk you up to the house?" Gabe asked.

She gave Cooper a smile because she really did want the little boy to know there was nothing for him to worry about. "No. I'm really okay. It was really great to meet you both." She stretched her hand out for Cooper to shake. "Stella is really lucky to have you."

He nodded. "Yeah. Both of my sisters are lucky. And the next one will be, too."

Juliet looked up at Gabe. He chuckled. "We aren't really telling people that we're having another baby yet, but yeah, the next one—brother or sister—will be lucky to have Coop, too."

Juliet laughed. "Congratulations."

"Thanks. And it was great to meet you, too." He paused. "It's great to have Sawyer back."

She gave him a smile and headed toward Cora's again.

Once she was under the shower and the rivulets of water on the tub floor were clear rather than muddy brown, Juliet braced a hand on the wall and decided to let herself cry.

She'd been scared. She'd needed help. And Sawyer hadn't come through.

She thought about that. She squeezed her eyes shut. She relived those moments in the water.

But after a few seconds, she lifted her head.

The tears weren't coming.

Because she didn't need to cry.

Sawyer *had* been there. Had he pushed her into the water and frozen up for a second or two? Yeah. But she'd had her life jacket on. Her arm and leg had worked for as long as she needed them to. Nothing bad had happened.

And, then, Sawyer *had* dealt with it. He'd been the one to swim to her and pull her and Cooper into the boat. It had taken him a few extra moments, but he'd battled his own fears—in seconds—had pulled himself together and hauled her butt out of the water before anything bad had happened.

Juliet turned her face up into the shower spray, letting the water course over her face.

She didn't love the bayou. She maybe never would. Or maybe, now that she'd fallen off this particular bike and skinned her knee, maybe she'd try it again.

After all, Cooper Trahan, even at age nine, recognized that sometimes you sucked it up and did stuff you didn't like because the people you loved needed you to.

Her eyes flew open and she almost choked on shower water as she gasped.

Coughing, she shut the shower off and reached for a towel. She dried her face and cleared her throat.

She was considering *staying*? Even after today?

Was that even an option? Would Sawyer want that? Did it make any sense at all?

She was a lawyer. There were plenty of people in New Orleans, if not in the towns and parishes around Autre, who could use a patient advocate, of course. It wasn't as if she wouldn't be able to find work.

And she loved the Landrys. All of them.

It was hotter than Hades down here. There were lots and lots of bugs and creepy crawlies, but there was also a big Cajun who seemed happy to hang mosquito netting and deal with things like bats. And, if she did end up bit, Ellie and Cora seemed to have a cream or salve for it, no matter what it was.

Yeah, maybe she could stay.

As long as she didn't have to go out onto the bayou very often. Or ever.

She honestly couldn't think of a good reason that she'd ever need to get on an airboat again. There were millions of people that lived their entire lives, happy and fulfilled, without ever getting on an airboat.

Sawyer was the only reason she'd ever considered it in the first place. But he had plenty of people willing to go out there with him. Hell, in a few years, Stella would be taking the business over and Sawyer would be lucky if she let *him* take the boats out.

Juliet grinned. And damn, it felt good.

She could live *beside* the bayou on the dry land. A loud clap of thunder rattled the house and she rolled her eyes. Okay, *solid* ground, if not always dry.

Juliet wiped the steam from the mirror and ran her fingers through her hair. She needed to go find him and drying her hair at this point would not only take more time than she wanted to give, it would also likely be pointless. The rain was still coming down hard and she didn't have time to search for an umbrella that would probably just blow away anyway.

Her phone rang as she was rummaging in her suitcase for clothes.

She grabbed for it, hoping it was Sawyer. But it was Tori.

"Hi, Tori, what—"

"Is Sawyer with you?" the other woman interrupted her greeting.

"Um, no. I'm not sure where he is."

"Dammit." Tori sounded upset.

"Is everything okay?"

"No. Crap. Dammit. I've been calling him but he's not answering. He's probably down trying to secure stuff with the guys but I was hoping I'd catch him. None of them are answering."

Juliet hit the button to put the call on speaker and started getting dressed. "What's going on? How can I help?"

"It's Gus," Tori said. "It's maybe nothing, but I'm at the clinic with a dog that was hit by a car because of the rain, and it just occurred to me that Gus might be in the cage."

"The cage down on the bank?" Juliet asked, pulling her hair up into a ponytail.

"Yes. I mean, he hasn't gotten in it yet and maybe he's not, but if he is and the water is rising..." She trailed off.

Juliet's stomach flipped. The cage had been set up so that Gus would go inside for the treat Tori had left and then close behind him. It was hidden and anchored securely on the bank so he'd think it was just part of the vegetation that was there. If the water rose because of the rain and he couldn't get out to float and swim with the water, he could...

"I'll go check it," Juliet said.

"Oh, no. You don't have to. Can you just find Josh or Sawyer maybe?" Tori asked.

"It's fine. It's way faster for me to go directly over there. If I see them, I'll ask for help but if I don't, I'm not going to leave Gus down there."

There was a long pause, then Tori sniffed. "Okay. Yes. Thank you. If he's there...you'll have to get in, Juliet. You'll have to pull the cage out and get him up and out of there."

Juliet nodded, then realizing Tori couldn't see her, said, "I know. I'll handle it."

"Okay." Again Tori paused. "I know this is a big deal."

"It's not," Juliet told her firmly. "This is just what needs to be done."

"Okay. Please call me when you get there and let me know if you need to get in or not. Be careful."

"I will."

Juliet pocketed her phone, slipped her shoes on, and headed for the docks. She wasn't going to think about the rising waters, the pouring rain, or anything else. She was going to focus on Gus and the fact that he might need help.

But she almost wilted with relief when she saw Sawyer striding up the hill toward the house.

"Juliet!"

"Come on!" she said, hurrying past him and making sure she was out of arm's reach. She knew he'd try to stop her and want to talk about what had happened and they didn't have time right now.

"What's going on?"

"I need your help."

That was all it took to get him to turn and fall into step beside her. If she hadn't loved him before, that would have done it.

"Where are we going?"

"To the dock. We have to check on the cage for Gus," she said, hitting the wood and hurrying around the corner. "If he's in there, he could be in trouble."

"Fuck."

Juliet headed for the railing where Sawyer had found her that first morning. She was sure he realized it, too, especially as she got down on her stomach to peer over the edge. The bank where Gus lived and played for the tourists was right below where she'd nearly fallen that first day. The cage was right about where she'd dropped her phone.

"Oh, crap," she said quietly.

Sure enough, there was a frantic river otter inside the cage below the dock.

"Fuck."

She looked over at Sawyer who was lying beside her.

"We have to get him."

Sawyer nodded.

"You have to lower me down there."

He didn't seem surprised by her suggestion. But he shook his head. "No way."

"Yes. It's the fastest way, Sawyer."

"But what if—"

She covered his mouth with her hand quickly. "We don't have time for that. Yes, there are things that could go wrong. But if they do, we'll deal with them."

His gaze burned into hers for a moment, but finally he nodded.

She moved her hand and leaned in to kiss him quickly. "I love you, Sawyer."

He cupped the back of her head and pulled her in for a longer kiss. "I love you, too," he said, when he let her go. "And I'm the one going down there."

Juliet got to her feet. "Don't be stupid. You're too heavy for me to pull back up and the dock is too high for you to pull yourself up. You can lower me down and pull me back up easily."

He got to his feet, too. "You've had a big day already."

"Yeah."

"You up for more?"

"Doesn't matter. This has to happen."

He shook his head, but it was as if in wonder rather than to negate what she'd said. "You think you don't belong here? You dig deep when you need to and you don't let a little dirty water set you back. That's the bayou way."

Juliet gave him a smile. "Well, then, I guess I was wrong."

Emotion flickered in his eyes. "I'm not letting you go."

"I really hope you mean when you're lowering me over the side of this dock *and* forever after."

He chuckled. "I mean all of it."

"Okay. Then let's do this."

It wasn't graceful and Juliet definitely needed another

shower afterward, but they managed to rescue Gus and get him up to Tori.

The second shower was a lot more fun than the first, though, because it was in Sawyer's shower. With Sawyer. He was a very good...soaper.

After the longest shower she'd ever taken in her life—and the most satisfying—she sat wrapped in a towel on his bathroom counter. Sawyer knelt in front of her and applied ointment and a bandage to the knee she'd scraped on the edge of the dock when he'd pulled her back up. He leaned in and pressed a kiss to the bandage, then looked up.

"I'm moving to Alexandria."

Juliet blinked down at him. "What?"

He nodded and stretched to his feet. "The bayou is... complicated. For both of us. I just want to be with you." He braced his hands on the counter on either side of her hips. "I want you to feel safe and I want you to be happy."

Juliet lifted her hands to his face. "But I want to be badass," she said. "And Cooper Trahan helped me see that. When I went out on those bike rides, that wasn't really brave. I was never really scared of the bikes. Or of falling. I was scared of scaring my mother and scared of being left out of things. Getting on the bike wasn't brave. The water, on the other hand, *that* I was afraid of and I've never faced that. But now I know that I still don't like it and never will, but I can handle it if I have to." She took a deep breath. "I also don't really want to get bitten by a bat or a snake or a black widow. But if I do, there's a big, sexy man who will apply his grandmother's best friend's cream and then kiss it all better." She scooted to the edge of the counter and let her towel fall, wrapping her arms around his neck. "And I'll tell you, there's a little part of me that was wondering about how to fake a good snake bite once in a while just for that reason."

He pulled in a ragged breath and ran his hands down her

sides, his gaze never leaving hers. "Okay, how about the Grand Canyon?"

Juliet felt her eyes widen. "What about it?"

"We should go."

"Sawyer, I—" Wow, she really wanted to go to the Grand Canyon. With him.

"That's something we can both do. No sharks. No life jackets required."

"I can't climb up and down the Grand Canyon," she said softly.

"I think you can do more than you think you can. And I'll carry you up and down however far I need to."

Her heart melted. He would. She knew that. Her eyes filled with tears and she nodded. "Yeah, let's go. I'll research a few things."

He grinned. "I know you will." He scooped his hands under her butt and lifted her, naked, off the counter, the towel drifting to the floor. He carried her into the bedroom and laid her down under the mosquito netting. "Now, did you say that you might have a snake bite that needs some attention?"

"I'm clear of snake bites," she told him.

"Oh."

She pulled him down beside her. "But I was reading up about Lyme disease. I was wondering if you know anything about checking someone for ticks?"

His grin was fast and huge and definitely wolfish. "'Course I do. I'm a bayou boy, Ms. Dawson."

"That's great news. You know me...take every precaution, be totally prepared."

He leaned in putting his mouth against hers. "I promise that you will never have an inch of your body that is not thoroughly examined on a daily basis."

"I feel safer already," Juliet said, her voice breathless as his big hands started their inspection.

EPILOGUE

Two days later

"They know we're watching them, right?" Tori asked.

"Oh, they for sure know," Maddie agreed with a grin.

"What a bunch of idiots," Kennedy muttered.

Juliet was gathered with the three women at the window of the Boys of the Bayou office watching Josh, Owen, Sawyer, Mitch, and Bennett Baxter put the dock together.

The three sections were finished and the pilings had been put in yesterday.

Watching the big machinery rumble in and pound the thick metal stakes into the floor of the bayou had been fascinating. It was very much like a deck off the back of a house, but the poles holding everything up had to be driven through the mud and into the solid ground underneath the water. They also had to be constructed to withstand being constantly submerged. They had to be tall enough to stand up out of the water, of course, and solid enough to support the dock and several hundred pounds of weight from the human beings on top of it, not to mention the storms that blew into this part of the country.

Juliet couldn't help but feel a little thrill at watching the structure she'd built actually being put together out there. It was just as she'd imagined it. Not to mention the thrill of watching Sawyer lifting and pounding and flexing and yeah, being wet.

The guys had to wade into the bayou to the pilings and then lift the sections of the dock into place, nailing and screwing to secure them.

Sawyer was making her like water *a lot* more. But she was *not* skinny-dipping.

"Oh my God, what the hell is he doing?" Kennedy asked, breaking into Juliet's thoughts.

The girls all leaned closer to the window.

"Um, he's taking his shirt off," Maddie told her with a smirk.

Juliet pulled her eyes away from Sawyer and realized that Bennett had just stripped his shirt off like the other guys had.

"Why?" Kennedy asked crossly. Though her gaze was definitely glued on Bennett.

"So his shirt doesn't get wet?" Tori said, teasingly, looking at Kennedy.

Juliet glanced over, too.

"Oh," Maddie said, staring out the window.

Tori and Juliet spun to look. Bennett had just shucked out of his jeans as well, leaving him in only navy-blue boxers.

Kennedy's nose nearly hit the glass.

"They're going to let him get in the water?" Kennedy asked. "What the hell? That guy doesn't know how to put a dock together."

"You mean, the ivy school educated attorney with a master's degree in conservation and biodiversity can't figure out that you put the flat wooden parts on top of the poles and then screw them into place?" Tori asked, this time not looking away from the scene outside.

"The guy lifts briefcases for a living, not tools and docks and... stuff," Kennedy's voice trailed off as Bennett hoisted one of the dock sections up overhead and waded into the water. "Oh...um...wow."

"Same," Tori said in agreement.

"Damn," was Maddie's assessment.

Juliet had been watching the guys, too, and felt the same way. Wow. Same. Damn. That all covered it.

The girls watched without speaking as the guys put the pieces of the dock together. At one point, they pulled stools up and settled in as if it was a sporting event. Kennedy literally grabbed popcorn from behind the counter after a little while and passed out cups to each girl. Maddie handed diet sodas around. They made small comments here and there, but for the most part they all seemed quite content just watching the whole scene.

When the guys were done, they all emerged from the water like a small team of water warriors. Their shorts were soaked and clinging to their bodies, their torsos were glistening in the sun, their hair was slicked back, and they strode up the bank with huge, satisfied grins, clearly proud of themselves and feeling the testosterone flowing.

It was like candy to the girls. They all got off their stools, got rid of their snacks, and watched their men stride across the side yard.

At least Juliet assumed they were all coming toward the building. She really hadn't looked away from Sawyer in about forty solid minutes.

"Bennett looks damned good, too," Maddie said.

"With mud all over his ass and blood dripping down his arm?" Kennedy asked crossly, moving away from the window, scraping one of the stools across the floor behind her. "Sure.

Super hot." Then her voice dropped to a mutter, "Dumbass city boy. They never should have let him out there with them." She moved behind the counter and pulled out the first aid kit, setting it on top with a thud.

"Mud and blood?" Maddie asked, looking out the window again.

"Well, your eyes were clearly on Owen," Kennedy said. "Baxter fell three times, including slipping coming up the bank. Right in the mud. At some point he must have tried to put a nail through his hand or something because there's blood everywhere."

Maddie frowned and leaned closer to the window. Juliet did, too. She definitely hadn't seen Bennett fall and couldn't see any blood from here.

"He's laughing right now. Seems fine," Tori commented.

"That's because he thinks this is all a big game," Kennedy said, pulling gauze and ointment and cotton pads from the first aid box. "He thinks coming down here and jacking around in the dirt and water is so fun. Just because he was a stuck-up snob growing up and did stupid shit like playing tennis and golf and now thinks he's going to be all manly and tough by messing around on the bayou with real men. He doesn't realize that he could get hurt out there. Or hurt someone else. The man needs to stick to file folders and briefcases. Stuff where he can't make an ass of himself."

Juliet felt her eyes go round. Kennedy cared about people, of course, but she also figured most of the people she hung around knew what they were doing. She was definitely not the type to fuss about others. She was the type to figure that falling down was a great way to learn about walking carefully on the slippery banks of the bayou. But right then she sounded a lot like her big brother. Juliet looked over at Maddie and Tori. They were both fighting smiles as well.

"Maybe he makes an ass of himself in his big fancy office

building and conference rooms, too," Kennedy continued, still setting first aid supplies out. As in, every single thing that was inside that box. Including an Ace wrap and a neck brace. She almost seemed to be talking to herself. "Who knows? Maybe he is just an idiot who doesn't know what the fuck he's doing ever. Maybe he's always gotten by on his good looks and charm and money and doesn't actually have one damned brain in his head."

"Anyone I know?"

They all pivoted toward the door that led from the main deck on the north side of the building into the office.

Bennett stood in the doorway. His eyes on Kennedy. Grinning.

He'd pulled his jeans back on, but left them unbuttoned, and hadn't added his shirt yet.

Juliet was all about Sawyer, but as a heterosexual red-blooded woman, she had to admit that Bennett Baxter looked pretty damned good underneath those suits and ties he allegedly wore all the time.

"You," Kennedy told him, propping a hand on her hip and not looking a bit abashed at having been caught ranting about him. "You must not have one damned brain in your head. I'm surprised you didn't tear a rotator cuff or fucking drown out there."

"All I heard was that you think I'm good-looking and charming."

"You should stick with legal briefs and whatever else you do all day."

He came further into the office and headed straight for her. Juliet suddenly had a feeling that he'd completely forgotten that she, Maddie, and Tori were even there.

"You thinking about my briefs, Kennedy?" he asked, stopping in front of her.

Kennedy reached for his hand and pulled him close, then

twisted his hand so it was palm up and began cleaning the blood away. "I'm thinking about how I'm never gonna be able to walk on that dock out there without worrying about it collapsing because they let a city boy lawyer help build it. Did you even play with Legos growing up, or was it all just Monopoly?"

Bennett chuckled, letting her clean his hand. "I did really like Monopoly."

As the blood disappeared, it was easy to see that the wound was really a cut up near his elbow and not nearly as bad as it had looked.

"I'll get you some Legos for your birthday," Kennedy said, bending over his arm and applying ointment, then a bandage. "Maybe that will satisfy this manly craving of yours to play at building stuff and will keep everyone else safe."

"My manly cravings aren't going to be satisfied by multicolored plastic, Kennedy," Bennett said in a low voice.

Even Juliet felt a little shiver of awareness at his tone. She glanced at the other two. Yeah, they'd noticed, too. Tori's eyes were wide, and Maddie was looking wildly entertained.

Kennedy looked up at Bennett as she pressed the bandage onto his cut—apparently very firmly judging by the little wince he gave—and said, "Funny, my cravings are handled just fine by colored plastic. Maybe you need to get the kind that vibrates."

Bennett gave her a slow smile. "I sincerely doubt there's anything or anyone that fully handles you, Kennedy."

That was a very accurate statement from what Juliet had witnessed about the youngest Landry so far.

Kennedy nodded. "You should remember that."

Bennett shrugged. "I love a challenge."

"Do ya? I saw you go under out there," Kennedy said, letting go of his arm and inclining her head toward the window.

"Yeah, a little deep in a couple spots."

She nodded. "You think you quickly got in over your head

out there? Keep thinking of me as some challenging game that you like to mess with when you're bored."

Bennett didn't even blink. "And you keep thinking that you can intimidate me by pointing out that things down here get *hot, wet,* and *dirty*. In spite of my suits and *briefs*, those are three of my favorite things." Then he reached up and lifted her chin with one finger, closing her mouth. "Don't forget to send me those files I need by the end of tomorrow." He turned and headed out of the office.

Juliet, Tori, and Maddie all watched him go, then swung to look at Kennedy.

"I hate him so much," she whispered.

That was so clearly not true it was laughable. Which was probably why Maddie and Tori laughed.

Juliet just grinned. She hoped Bennett came back to the bayou soon.

She had a feeling Kennedy did, too.

And *that* was what she hated.

———

Thank you for reading Beauty and the Bayou! I hope you loved Sawyer and Juliet's story!

And don't miss Kennedy and Bennett's book, **Crazy Rich Cajuns!**

A sexy, small town, opposites attract rom com!

He wears suits and ties. He'll one day inherit a fortune. He has a law degree. He shines his shoes, for God's sake. What is she doing attracted to a guy like him? But she is. She *so* is.

She drives air boats on the bayou, drinks and cusses, and gives city boys in suits a hard time just for fun. Why can't he get her out of his mind? But he can't. He definitely can't.

A weekend trip to Savannah for a fancy-schmancy party with his highfalutin family is the surefire way to prove that they have nothing in common but intense chemistry. And to maybe scratch this I've-never-wanted-anyone-like-I-want-you itch once or twice. Or five times.

But it takes only about twenty-four hours for the bayou girl and the city boy to figure out that they don't really know much at all--about each other, or about themselves. And figuring all of this out is going to be downright crazy.

———

You can find it and all of Erin's books at
www.ErinNicholas.com

ABOUT THE AUTHOR

Erin Nicholas is the New York Times and USA Today best-selling author of over thirty sexy contemporary romances. Her stories have been described as toe-curling, enchanting, steamy and fun. She loves to write about reluctant heroes, imperfect heroines and happily ever afters. She lives in the Midwest with her husband who only wants to read the sex scenes in her books, her kids who will never read the sex scenes in her books, and family and friends who say they're shocked by the sex scenes in her books (yeah, right!).

Find her and all her books at
www.ErinNicholas.com

And find her on Facebook, Goodreads, BookBub, and
Instagram!

MORE FROM ERIN

If you loved Beauty and the Bayou, don't miss the rest of
The Boys of the Bayou

My Best Friend's Mardi Gras Wedding

Sweet Home Louisiana

Beauty and the Bayou

Crazy Rich Cajuns

———

And there's more Louisiana fun in the
The Boys of the Big Easy

Easy Going (prequel novella)

Going Down Easy

Taking It Easy

Nice and Easy

Eggnog Makes Her Easy (Christmas novella)

———

If you're looking for more sexy, small town rom com fun, check
out the
Billionaires in Blue Jeans series!

Diamonds and Dirt Roads

High Heels and Haystacks

Cashmere and Camo

———

And much more at

ErinNicholas.com

CPSIA information can be obtained
at www.ICGtesting.com
Printed in the USA
BVHW081056180221
600496BV00003B/331